VIP TREATMENT

"No," he said, still laughing, "we'll have to give these friends some VIP treatment. We'll take them to the International ourselves."

The American felt his spine icing over. For he understood the meaning of VIP treatment in Uganda: VIP treatment was death after torture.

"Come, gentlemen, please let us make haste," Wakholi grinned. "You are VIPs in Uganda today."

Wakholi nodded in a direction between Kruger and Yazov, where two guards waited . . .

BLOODBATH

William Wingate

BANTAM BOOKS
TORONTO · NEW YORK · LONDON

For Wendy

This low-priced Bantam Book
has been completely reset in a type face
designed for easy reading, and was printed
from new plates. It contains the complete
text of the original hard-cover edition.
NOT ONE WORD HAS BEEN OMITTED.

BLOODBATH
*A Bantam Book / published by arrangement with
St. Martin's Press, Inc.*

PRINTING HISTORY
St. Martin's edition published January 1980
Bantam edition / May 1981

ISBN: 0-553-14707-2

PRINTED IN THE UNITED STATES OF AMERICA

0 9 8 7 6 5 4 3 2 1

1

"How would you feel if the United States assassinated Obama Okan?" Michael Tarrant tried to imagine the scene in the Oval Office of the White House when the Director of Central Intelligence put the question to the president.

The director was in Washington with the president, the secretaries of state and defence, and the chairman of the Working Group on Terrorism. Mike Tarrant was sitting at a wooden table in a closely guarded complex of the CIA's basement under that agency's headquarters in Langley, Virginia. The complex was called the Pit by the CIA, and although the nine-foot diameter round table could seat fifteen executives, Tarrant sat alone. Tarrant worried about the president's reaction because he had prepared for the director much of the groundwork and justification which motivated the proposed "executive action." Since he wanted to know at the very first possible moment when the Oval Office conference was over, Tarrant was glad to be in the Pit. From there he could satisfy his desire to know almost anything.

On the Pit's north wall, facing Tarrant, were five different screens upon which IBM computers could print out tens of millions of items: what the weather was like in Entebbe; the names of KGB agents in the Soviet embassy in Kabul; the day's flight times for Heathrow airport, London; the whereabouts of the CIA's logistic group which was closest to Kampala; the current estimate of the Communist Chinese wheat or rice production; latitude by longitude, the positions in the oceans of Russia's nuclear submarines.

Selected titbits from thousands of top secret messages that the agency received from all over the world, every twenty-four hours, were constantly keeping the computers up to date. Data also streamed into Langley from long-

1

range cameras, sensitive radio receivers, and satellite-surveillance systems. After processing, such data was stored in the IBM memory banks. If this flow of information were not enough, the computers could dig into a card-file index of over seventy million documents.

Behind Tarrant, on the south wall, eight digital clocks told the time in Peking, Moscow, Tokyo, Bonn, Paris, London, Washington and Los Angeles. A pressing of plastic buttons, and the clocks would tell the time in Kampala, La Paz, Leningrad—or anywhere else of any importance.

Why should the United States go after the dictator of a tiny, unimportant, landlocked country in central Africa, the president would want to know. Was Okan really a menace sufficient for the might of the US to be organized to remove him?

In the autumn of 1960, two CIA men had tried to assassinate the Congolese nationalist leader, Patrice Lumumba; the CIA was implicated in the shooting of Rafael Trujillo, the Dominican Republic dictator who was killed in May 1961; so it did not matter that Okan was not the ruler of a strategically important land. What did matter was secret word that Okan was ready to use Entebbe airport as a haven for terrorists who were planning spectacular, concurrent assaults on airlines and world leaders.

It would surely weigh with the president that among the hostages were likely to be many American citizens. While the first Entebbe raid had been a resounding success, any direct assault on the airfield would this time almost certainly be a total disaster. Unless Okan had learned nothing from the Entebbe rescue, the skyjacked jetliners would be surrounded by tanks and armoured cars, and obstacles would foul the runways. The extrication of hostages would be virtually impossible without great loss of life. On the other hand, in a long, Aesopian memorandum which Tarrant himself had compiled, he had stated something else that was obvious: "Once the US yields to blackmail, there will be no end to it."

The Pit was a windowless room, and Tarrant gazed unseeingly at the wisps of tobacco smoke rising into the air from his cigarette, drifting slowly upwards to disappear into an air-conditioning outlet. The cigarette itself, a Lucky Strike, sat on Tarrant's lips, its grey-white ash ever

2

lengthening, sagging, dropping at last on to the lapel of his stylish, charcoal-grey suit. Tarrant dragged the tips of his fingers across the lapel to clean off the powdery residue and the fingertips left behind grey streaks.

Five drooping Lucky Strikes later, he reached for one of the nine phones which rested on the heavy mahogany table. With a push on the button of the red phone Tarrant could speak directly to the president in the White House. Instead, he depressed a button on the blue phone and asked, "Where is the president of the United States?"

A few moments later, an IBM computer printed on one of the screens, "US PRESIDENT MEETING OVAL OFFICE WITH SECRETARY FOR COMMERCE."

So the meeting with the DCI was over.

Tarrant pressed the blue button again, asking: "Where is the DCI?" "DCI RETURNING IN BELL HELICOPTER TO OPERATIONS ROOM CIA LANGLEY," the computer printed.

Soon enough, Tarrant would know whether the operation to assassinate Okan—a project code-named Brimstone—was to be scrapped or taken further. Although he knew it was much too early for even the computers to have been programmed, Tarrant was unable to resist a final word through the blue mouthpiece, "Give me the status of Brimstone."

"BRIMSTONE IS ONGOING," the computer answered on the screen.

It had been "ongoing" for three weeks, so that did not add much to what Tarrant already knew. Now he knew, though, that the president had not straightaway negated Brimstone. . . .

When the summons to the DCI's office came, it did so with a buzz on the yellow phone. Tarrant reached across the table, cradled the receiver, listened, and after identifying himself, said, "I'll be right along, sir."

The strange thing about the Pit was the lack of any direct access to the DCI's quarters. Once he stepped out of the lift, Tarrant found himself crossing the area outside the CIA's main entrance. The November sun had dropped to the horizon and radiated a grey, weak light.

As he walked by the bronze statue of Nathan Hale, with its hands tied behind its back, Tarrant felt a pang of annoyance, as he always did: Nathan Hale, the first American spy, had concealed his message in his shoe, where the British had easily found it after his capture. He had arrived too late on Manhattan Island to spy on the British order of battle. Thus Hale had been a hopeless, failed intelligence agent, and it irked Tarrant that the CIA had erected a likeness of him immediately outside the main entrance to the main building.

Tarrant walked into the foyer, past thirty-one stars chiselled into a wall which represented CIA officers killed in action. He nodded at the security officer at the guard post and strode towards another lift.

After another walk down a long, bright, wide corridor which had potted plants spaced at regular intervals, Tarrant reached the anteroom to the DCI's office. He rapped lightly on the door of the DCI's room, opened it and went in.

"Hi, Mike. Thanks for getting across so quickly." The director was sitting behind a large desk upon which rested several trays of documents and papers, much of the paperwork being gummed with bright orange MOST URGENT stickers.

"Good afternoon, sir." Tarrant eased himself into a leather-covered chair. "How did the meeting go?"

"To wrap it up, in general, the president thinks that a good covert operation can possibly solve the problem at this early stage. He knows that most major league countries have to operate somewhere out on the edges. Brimstone is still alive."

"Poor bastard. He had no option."

"That's where you're wrong, Mike." The director smiled a tired, wry smile. "He wants the option of cancelling Brimstone anytime, if *we* decide to go through with it."

This was not lost on Tarrant. "You mean any authority is written in disappearing ink?"

"There's no authority, period. But there's no prohibition either. Whatever happens, if anybody ever investigates this thing, nobody is going to establish any guilt or innocence at the white House. . . ."

"And what about us? The CIA?" Tarrant wanted to know.

4

"As always, we'll be acting in the belief that, at all times, our actions were sanctioned by high authority."

"You mean the buck kept right on moving after it got to the president's office?"

"Went right around his chair. Perpetual motion." They both laughed at the same time, knowing what the other man was thinking. If anything about Brimstone ever came out, nobody would be able to pin any definite responsibility on the CIA or on the White House.

After six months, thousands of pages of evidence, and scores of witnesses, a recent investigation by a Senate Intelligence Committee of CIA assassination plots had dug up no certain conclusions. Among the charges scrutinized were alleged CIA plots to kill Lumumba, Trujillo, Fidel Castro, South Viet Nam's Ngo Dinh Diem, and Haiti's Duvalier—the latter being a vicious dictator in Okan's mould.

All that the committee could say was that the United States "was implicated in several assassination plots." Nowhere could it prove that any US president had authorized an assassination; any CIA involvement was always undertaken under "the highest authority."

"How did the White House do it this time?" Tarrant asked.

"Well, basically the president was talking about a two-track operation. Track one is a diplomatic and economic track. Here we'll work with State. By the way, Fackman came out strongly for some kind of action against Okan."

"He did?" Joseph Fackman was the US Secretary of State.

"Yes, he did. Spoke in that polished way about the Soviet's growing influence in east and central Africa. On balance, he was more for taking out Okan than against it. On the terror aspect, he described Okan as a walking time bomb. He joked about his own fears for himself."

"Anybody go against it?"

"Chairman of the Joint Chiefs was anti. Very. He saw a big potential for international 'opprobrium,' if the whole thing went badly wrong. He was worried about US bases in other parts of the world."

"And his job." Tarrant laughed. "It may have occurred to him that all of us are lame ducks, except him." What

Tarrant referred to was the fact that, having lost the November election, the president, his cabinet and other major appointees, would be out of office in January.

"Okay, so Track one is diplomatic and economic. What's Track two?" he asked the director.

"Well, now, the president didn't quite say exactly." And they both laughed again.

"You mean Track two was a euphemism for Brimstone?"

"Well, not exactly that either. Whatever it was, Track two was another way, all by itself. If Track one doesn't work—and I pointed out time was short for diplomatic and economic pressure to work—then Track two will have to succeed. As the president remarked, 'Track two, I leave to you.' "

"Nice."

"Very."

"I think Track two is the only way," Tarrant said.

"Yes. It'll probably come down to Track two in the end."

"There is going to be a civil war. A lot of people could be killed. The president know that?"

"Yes, I suppose he does. He'd like us to do it without bloodshed, though." And yet again the two men laughed.

"So we've got no authority but . . ."

". . . we'd better damn do it," the director finished. "Also, the president wanted to know in what kind of shape the agency was these days."

Tarrant took the DCI to mean that the president had referred to the aftermath of more than a year's hostile scrutiny of the CIA by House and Senate committees. While the congressional probing had gone badly for the CIA at first, the investigations had later become partisan and opportunistic, so much so that they had boomeranged.

"I guess you replied that we were back on top," Tarrant said.

"That I did. Told him not to lose any sleep about our image with Middle America. Nobody was campaigning against strong intelligence anymore. College recruitment was up, along with the quality of recruit. I told him that I hated to say it about Congress, but I reckoned we'd won too much."

6

"I'll bet you did."

"It all ended with the president saying, 'I'm not cancelling Brimstone. You handle it from the CIA's end.' He didn't say yes, and he didn't say no. But it sounded more like yes than no."

The tall figure of the director rose from behind his desk. With a tug of the cord, he opened blue, damask curtains over the south window. The very last of the late November light hardly made any impression at all under the bright, fluorescent ceiling lamps.

"If we move along Track two, Mike, we'll want Okan taken out quickly. And cleanly," the director said soberly.

"We're working on it, sir."

"You still want to use that Bulgarian defector, that Yazov feller?"

"He's the best I can think of."

"I suppose so." The director knew that Yazov was about the best they had. Two years earlier, he had killed fifteen men of the Bulgarian MGB in that country's secret service headquarters on Brzina Street, Sofia and blown up the building. He had also killed a number of the CIA's own men in different parts of the world.

"I suppose so," the director repeated.

"That's if he'll do it," Tarrant responded.

The DCI quickly turned from the window saying, "You having trouble, Mike?"

"He wants out. Reckons he's earned it as a double, or treble, agent. He wants retirement. Maybe we'll handle him, perhaps not."

"Have you anybody in reserve, if you can't handle him?"

"Yes, sir, we have. We've shortlisted a half dozen who could do it. But none of them is in Yazov's class."

"Track two needs the best man, Mike."

"I'm well aware of it, sir."

"Good." The DCI held out his hand, and when Tarrant took it he could feel the callouses. The director was always shaking hands, the hands of politicians, members of the administration, of the intelligence establishment.

On his way to the door, Tarrant asked, "What was it that most impressed the president, sir?"

"Apart from our own intelligence, he liked the stuff

from Israel best. You have to remember that Tel Aviv was right about the Refusal Front's plot to use a SAM 7 on an El Al flight out of Nairobi. They had also got it straight on a try for Hussein's life at Rabat in 1974, and on a raft of other things. No doubt, Mossad has men infiltrated high up in the Front."

"The president wasn't worried about our lack of detail?"

"Not particularly. It's understandable that we only have outlines. He asked about timing, though. I told him we had about four to six weeks before anything big happened. That's still right?"

"Four weeks."

"And there's still nothing to show we're getting our facts wrong? I mean, you'll still bet everything that Okan is going for broke?"

"I never said I'd bet everything, sir. I said I'd bet a lot. A whole lot."

"But not everything?" The director grinned sardonically.

"A whole lot," Tarrant repeated evenly.

Mike Tarrant need not have worried, because he could have bet it all.

In a way, it would have reassured him to know that, even as he and the director spoke, deep in southern Libya men and a few women were firing their Hungarian AMDs and launching grenade attacks in night-time training through rough mock-ups of narrow hotel corridors, doorways, and the bigger spaces of a conference room. "Obey orders, all the time," a woman's voice barked through a bullhorn. "Do nothing more than is ordered. Do nothing less. Do exactly as I say, when I say. Anyone who cannot do this has no place in Commando Marighella."

There was a Commando Meinhof, a Commando Badawi, and a Commando Marighella.

To complete their training, other young men and women were in the embattled city of Beirut, weathering fire, returning fire.

Still other groups in Iraq, Yemen and Algeria were in bed, or sitting up to perfect simple cryptography, the Morse code, map reading, navigation. Or they were committing to memory air maps, aircraft timing, the details of the complicated, instrument-laden flight-decks in Boeing 707 and 747 jetliners from huge, blown-up photographs.

"You must always know your bearings, what course to give your captain. You must always be sure he is flying where you want," the woman with the bullhorn had instructed them.

For weeks, the trainee terrorists had familiarized themselves with the Hungarian AMD and Czech Model 61 machine pistols. Soon those who had done best in their lessons would be selected. After all the testing, nineteen in twenty would be eliminated, but there would be more than enough men and women for the tasks planned.

Tarrant need not have hedged his bet, for the threats were real enough. Had he known the full gravity of it all, the details of preparations already underway across the Atlantic, he might have given up on Ivan Yazov and looked elsewhere for a Brimstone assassin. The reason was that unless Tarrant quickly got Brimstone off the ground, he would run out of time.

2

The man whom Tarrant wanted to kill Obama Okan had defected to the United States in Paris, two years previously. Although nobody was absolutely certain, he was believed to have Bulgarian origins, and his name was Ivan Yazov, but whether that had always been so was not known for certain either. Yazov was reckoned to be in his late thirties or early forties.

It was not strictly correct to classify Ivan Yazov as a defector, because for some years he had been employed as a double agent by the CIA, which had greatly valued Yazov's position as a full colonel of the Bulgarian MGB. In fact, the matter of Yazov's precise loyalties had not ended with his doubling as a CIA agent; it transpired that he was also working for the Russian KGB, hence his so-called "defection" in Paris.

Nobody knew with any great confidence where Ivan Yazov's allegiances rested at any time. He was, and remained, a mystery, and this despite all his debriefings, long sessions of questioning, psychiatric examinations and polygraphings.

The investigations had started as soon as Yazov arrived from Paris in an air force jet. With no distractions save for a bottle of iced Stolovaya vodka, which was obtained through Sojuzplodimport of Moscow, the Bulgarian had spent eight to twelve hours a day with his interlocutors and cross-examiners in the wearing initial sessions. Within a week of Yazov's Paris defection, the CIA had minutely gone over his entire career as a spy. Then the polygraphing had started.

In the two years since his defection, Yazov had been repeatedly polygraphed, because it was the CIA's policy to carry out such tests, especially in the cases of defectors from Communist spy agencies.

Now, a day after Tarrant's meeting with the DCI, Ivan Yazov sat on a black leather easy chair in a small room used by the CIA's Office of Security. He was not alone. A fresh-looking young man sat behind Yazov, and he was asking questions. Once again, the man who had worked variously for and against Bulgarian MGB, Russian KGB, and American CIA, was undergoing testing with the so-called lie-detector.

Punctuating the silences between the questions and answers were the familiar, barely audible scratchings of three pens on slowly moving graph paper. Each pen was electronically connected to a cuff, tube and electrode into which Yazov had been hooked. In this way, each pen monitored changes in his pulse and blood pressure, his breathing rhythm, and the rate at which his hand sweated. As Yazov responded to the interrogation, so the pens traced graphs, recording small changes in his physiology.

In theory, a well-trained interpreter of such polygraphs could tell whether the man in the easy chair was answering truthfully or lying.

Yazov sat quietly, looking ahead at a blank, white wall. The interlocutor's questions, each of which was asked in a flat monotone, droned. To every question, the Bulgarian was required simply to reply either "yes" or "no."

10

"Have you ever been a Communist?"

"Yes."

"Do you still support communism?"

"No."

"Are you still working for any Communist intelligence agency?"

"No."

It persistently nagged the CIA that Yazov might possibly be an especially dangerous Communist agent who remained part of a complex plot to dupe the United States.

"Would you ever again work for any Communist spy agency?"

"No."

"Were you ever instructed to infiltrate the CIA?"

"No."

Above all, the CIA wanted to guard against a "defector" who might have been a Communist spy all along.

"Have you ever lied in any interrogation or debriefing?"

"No, not consciously."

"Just say 'yes' or 'no,' no more. Don't add anything. Please don't elaborate," the young man said, a note of irritation creeping into his voice when he added, "I bet you must know all this by now."

Ivan Yazov's mind drifted over all the months of debriefings and polygraphs. Yes, he knew. They had wanted almost anything and everything, even frivolous gossip about the other Communist agents: tidbits about their sex lives, salary scales, drinking habits, styles of dress, their preferences for food and delicacies. Everything.

"Have you ever practised as a homosexual?"

The Bulgarian felt his hand slip with sweat over the spring-loaded electrode.

"No," he answered.

The initial debriefings had taken place at Brushy Hill, Maryland, a 250-acre estate about twenty miles from Washington. Under heavy guard at all times, the Bulgarian had been housed in one of the rooms of an old stone mansion. When at last he had been allowed walks within the grounds, he had seen the high fences, guards at the gates, and fierce Alsatian dog patrols along the estate's perimeter.

11

It was just the place for the quiet, undisturbed debriefing of spies and defectors.

"Did you sign your statement willingly?" This question referred to sheets of paper which lay on the desk alongside Yazov. Every time the Bulgarian underwent a lie-detector test, the CIA required him to sign the papers, thereby consenting to a polygraph and agreeing not to hold the agency answerable for invading his privacy.

"No."

On average, during the sixteen months that had lapsed since Yazov's defection in Paris, he had been polygraphed at least twice a month. In the last four of those sixteen months, though, the Bulgarian had been tested only three times. In a way, this was progress. It underlined the defector's changing status: Yazov was being prepared for resettlement in the United States. Satisfied that it had extracted from the Bulgarian all of the useful information that was possible, the CIA had to make a place for him in America. Yazov would be slotted in somewhere in the United States where he could live free of reprisal by the KGB. So a CIA resettlement team had taken over from the interrogators, to work with the defector on a new identity which would allow Yazov to re-emerge into the mainstream of day-to-day living.

"You have killed people?"

"Yes."

"You have killed more than five people?"

"Yes."

It was a familiar scenario, and the electrodes in his hands felt more slippery than ever.

The months of preparation had started with a visit from a famous plastic surgeon who had come to Brushy Hill to study Yazov's features. A few weeks later the surgeon had operated, giving Yazov a new face, volunteering to the CIA his expert opinion that the Bulgarian had previously undergone plastic surgery.

Even as Yazov recovered in a CIA-approved hospital, a member of the resettlement team had arrived, bringing with him a white folder upon which was neatly stencilled the legend "Hardacre." Skimming the more than fifty quarto-sized pages inside the folder, Yazov found details of the life of a fictitious person named John Hardacre.

12

This was to be his new identity: someone orphaned when young, a man who had spent much of his working life on the drill rigs of the Persian Gulf and the North Sea. It was vital to learn every detail, and within a few months the Bulgarian knew a great deal about the practical, daily business of working on oil rigs. In the final weeks before his pending resettlement, the man called John Hardacre had even served two short stints on exploratory Exxon and British Petroleum rigs, in the burning heat off Saudi Arabia and on the stormy seas south-west of Norway.

"More than fifteen people. Have you killed more than fifteen?"

"Yes."

The stints on operational rigs had been a big success, for none of the Bulgarian's fellow roustabouts—men alongside whom he had dragged 300-lb. sections of pipe and stacked 100-lb. sacks of chemical mud—had thought that John Hardacre was anyone other than an old hand.

Where would the CIA resettle him? They needed an area where it would be difficult for the KGB to reach him. Having consulted with Yazov, the CIA had decided on Spencer, Iowa. The little town in the Mid-West had a number of advantages, including that of being the place to which Harvey Tyler had retired.

Harvey Tyler had once worked for the CIA as a guard and dog-handler at Langley. He was in his sixties, not a young man, but just the kind of employee whom the CIA tapped when it needed help in resettling defectors. Understandably, if it were at all possible, the agency liked to have one of its own to keep a look-out and to warn against unwanted developments. The CIA wanted to know quickly about any psychological depressions that afflicted defectors who were settling into their new lives. Depressed defectors could become dangerous, obviously. Knowing the defector's true identity, a Harvey Tyler was among the few people who could lend a sympathetic ear. He could also take up where the polygraph left off, and keep a limited check on the possibility that the defector was a Communist spy all along. In brief, a Harvey Tyler was indispensable to a well-run CIA resettlement programme.

"You have killed more than twenty people?"

13

Yazov did not think that the CIA knew more than about eighteen, so he denied the question.

"You like killing people?"

"No."

"If you had to, you could do it again?"

"Yes."

"You have always answered all the questions in previous tests truthfully?"

"No." The Bulgarian recalled some clear untruths, lies of which he was certain the CIA had knowledge. It was stupid to persist in claiming that he had always told the truth, and because that was so he admitted his lapses.

"You could kill for the United States, on a legitimate assignment?"

"No, not again. No more killing."

"Please say only 'yes' or 'no.' Don't elaborate. We may have to redo the whole testing procedure." The annoyance was back in the young man's tone.

"I'm sorry."

"You should be. You really should."

If it was possible, the CIA liked to re-employ defectors. Yazov knew of the policy. The agency sometimes gave them jobs as translators, analysts, even interrogators. Almost since his defection, the CIA had been sounding out the Bulgarian about his own speciality, which was killing people.

"Do you have a conscience about your killings?"

"Yes." Of course that was not true. He had no real remorse or guilt. The last few killings he could recall; most of the others were vague shadows in his mind. Sometimes he remembered a name or a place, a face maybe, the kind of weapon. But most of the details were gone. That was why he had been so good at it: the killing had meant so little.

"Do you enjoy taking life?"

"No."

"Have you answered all the questions truthfully?"

"Yes."

Behind both the Bulgarian and his tester, Yazov heard a faint rustle of paper as the interviewer gathered in the long polygraph printout. The sound of a click signalled that the polygraph was no longer operational, a fact which

14

was confirmed by the silence of the pens. Yazov heard the paper crackle as the polygrapher pulled in the chart, reviewing parts of the record.

"What were you thinking about when I asked you whether you enjoyed taking life?" the young man asked.

"Nothing in particular."

There was another silence, broken only by the reviewer rustling paper between his fingers. Then he said, "You know something, we're going to have to do this all over again."

"That's okay."

"It may be okay by you, but by me, negative. I'd like to go home. So just do me a favour, and this time no elaborations. Save it for a memo, if you have to. All I want is a plain 'yes' or a plain 'no.' Got it?"

"Yes."

"I'm sure you have. Okay, let's go."

"Ready."

"Your name is Ivan Yazov?"

"Yes."

"You were born in Sofia, Bulgaria?"

"Yes."

"You are forty-one years old?"

"Yes."

"You have no surviving father, mother, brother, sister?"

"Yes."

Yazov flexed the muscles in his neck to ease the strain there, then he raised his head to count the number of tiles in the white ceiling. They were watching him, he supposed. If they were professionals, which they were, even as he sat in the chair they would have him under observation. He wondered from behind which tile they were spying. Unless the picture was going to be slightly off line, it would be the tile straight ahead, six down from the ceiling.

Yazov's surmise was correct, and the way the CIA did it was simple enough. They had hidden a thin bundle of optic fibres in one of the tiny black holes in an acoustic tile in front of the black leather chair. After travelling over a hundred yards, changing direction a couple of times and stepping up two floors, light carried in the optical fibres transmitted Yazov's image to a screen in Tarrant's office,

15

where Tarrant and an executive named Arnie Kruger were watching.

In order that they could more easily hear the interrogation, Tarrant had switched the system on his three phones. Now, instead of bleeping sounds, lights blinked in the faces of the phones to signal an incoming call. Although two of the faces were flickering with light, Tarrant made no move to get up. Instead he remained seated at a leather-topped desk, watching the TV console.

"I think you were having a little difficulty with the number of kills," Tarrant heard the polygraph expert say as he tapped the polygraph chart with the point of a lead pencil. "If you have more trouble, try and remember what you were thinking, when we go over it later."

"Okay, I'll try," Yazov replied.

"Have you ever stolen government property, in Bulgaria or Russia?" the polygraph expert restarted the test.

"Yes."

"Have you ever stolen such property, excluding pens, pencils, or stationery?"

"No."

Both CIA executives had watched closely, and with interest, the testing which was proceeding two floors below where they sat. Before he spoke, a weary smile flitted across Tarrant's mouth, then he said, "The sonofabitch, we're not even sure how many kills he's made. He may be beating the box."

His concentration broken, Arnie Kruger turned away from the screen to look at Tarrant. "Looks that way, Mr. Tarrant."

"Polygraphing Americans is no problem. Same culture, same general background. But testing east Europeans is something else. They're too emotional."

"So I once read, sir." Kruger tapped a flip-top box of cigarettes on the table's edge, then went on, "But this feller doesn't seem emotional. In fact, the opposite."

"I suppose that's right too, Arnie. He may be beating the polygraph for some other reason. But you've put your finger on something else. We could use him. The best killers need to be about as excited with their work as a guy washing dishes."

True, Kruger conceded to himself. Tarrant was proba-

16

bly correct. When the polygraphing had started, there appeared to be nothing remarkable about the man sitting in the leather easy chair. Kruger did not react to anything before the question on Yazov's homosexual experiences. All that the Bulgarian had said was a simple "no," but something indefinable existed in his demeanour that had struck Kruger. From that time he had watched the TV console even more closely, sensing danger in the easy, relaxed way Yazov answered vicious, probing questions. The man under interrogation had seemed vaguely bored, uncaring. But even in this slack, careless indolence there was the hint of a flashing blade, a flat and hard hand. Yazov's easiness was that of a man drawn taut, hands sweating.

Arnie Kruger had also felt other faint stirrings . . . inside himself. What he was unsure of was whether he feared the other man more than he was attracted to him. Both emotions were there, mixing inside.

"We've got something coming up. We need this sonofabitch." Tarrant again broke into his thoughts.

"If you need an assassin, I'm impressed. He's got a wonderful track record. Wonderful."

"He could give us the quick, clean kill we want, Arnie. Killing requires a certain art, and the man's an artist."

"Instead, he wants to live quietly in Spencer, Iowa?" Kruger prompted.

"So he says. I'm not sure. Not exactly sure about anything with this guy. My intuition tells me to push him in front of a runaway truck. . . ."

"And save the Russians a lot of trouble. And the US taxpayer the expense of resettling him."

"Save you a lot of bother, too, Arnie," Tarrant smiled knowingly. "A lot of emotional stress. I've seen the way you've been watching him. Now I don't want you falling in love . . . again."

"I'm just a handler, sir. I love the CIA."

"The best handler in the handling business, Arnie. That's why you're here."

He probably was the best in the business, Arnie Kruger thought. Tarrant had been right to assign him to watch over Yazov's resettlement. He, Kruger, had the qualifications, no doubt about it: a psychiatrist, a sometime practising Roman Catholic priest, he was also a master spy. Kruger reckoned that being a homosexual, one of the few known gays in CIA service, was a help too.

As a handler, Kruger was brilliant at making friends, being understanding, helping out. Always he manipulated his relationships to benefit the CIA, and when the end came and an agent was no longer needed, Arnie Kruger was expert at that severing too. . . .

"I'm not exactly sure about what we'll do with him, Arnie. I'd like to turn him around, get him with us for this upcoming thing. But time's against it. Maybe you'll be able to turn him around for something else, later. This kind of guy we'll always need, sometime."

"How soon do you need him?"

"Four, five weeks."

"Too little time."

"No doubt. We'll just think of him as an asset, unless I can get through to him on the direct approach basis later today. But what's also important is to stop any redefection if he starts getting lonely. I don't know. This guy's a puzzle. We can't keep him under wraps forever, but we can't risk him being with the other side, either. . . ."

"I get the picture."

"The picture is . . . uncertain. I hope that's what you're getting. CIA's feelings are ambivalent. We don't want him alive particularly unless we can use him. And we don't want him dead."

"Sure, not if you want another defector ever again."

"The trouble with defectors is that they outlive their usefulness. . . ."

". . . and they get expensive, cranky, ornery, or even dangerous. But as they say, sir, you wouldn't do without them, now would you?"

"Like I have said, Arnie, if everyone would believe it was a simple, runaway truck, I'd use it next week. Right now, I've got to use you."

"The picture is dirty, but clear."

Tarrant stood up from his desk to stretch himself. "It's finishing," he said, making Kruger turn to watch the TV console.

And so it was, for through the speakers Kruger heard the slightly metallic voice of the polygraph expert, a voice

18

which insisted that Yazov was having difficulty with some of his answers. "No, you've got the truth. All of it," Yazov persisted.

With a slight show of annoyance, the interrogator undid the pressure cuff, replaced the electrodes in two slots cut into the desk behind Yazov, and untied the thin rubber pipe around the Bulgarian's chest.

"Thanks for the test." Yazov got up from the easy chair.

"Sure." As Yazov moved to the door, Kruger watched the polygrapher flop into the easy chair, holding the charts.

"He'll be here soon," Tarrant said, and motioned Arnie Kruger to sit at a conference table which stood in another well-defined area of the spacious office. Tarrant used his desk area to do his paperwork. He conducted meetings at the conference table, provided that more than two people were present.

A short while later there was a soft rap on the door and Tarrant himself opened it, "Come in, come in. I don't know what I ought to call you, John Hardacre or Ivan Yazov," Tarrant smiled, wringing the Bulgarian's hand.

"Maybe you should call him Crystal. That's what it says here." A smile rose around the edges of Arnie Kruger's blue eyes as he said it. Crystal was the defector's CIA code name.

"I'd like you to meet Arnie Kruger, your case officer during resettlement," Tarrant said. Yazov found himself in the grip of a friendly right hand.

"Yep, that's me. Your guardian angel."

"Nice to meet you, Mr. Kruger," Yazov smiled back.

"Butterfly, that's me. You call me Butterfly, or Arnie— but never Mr. Kruger. Doesn't sound right."

"Butterfly? That's okay. Then it's nice to meet you, Butterfly."

"The pleasure's all mine. I've read a lot about you." Admiration crept into Kruger's tone.

"Not bad things, I hope."

"Oh, so . . . so. You know. Depends. In Moscow right now it won't read half as good as here in Langley."

Yazov laughed politely, albeit without real feeling, and

19

Kruger felt slightly uneasy, a little threatened. In some strange way, Kruger felt the menace of the man.

"Well, this calls for a small celebration." Tarrant saved them all from a few uncomfortable moments. Some well-informed secretary had placed three glass tumblers and a pitcher of ice cubes on the table—together with a half-litre bottle of Stolovaya vodka, with the green and gold, black and white label. After pouring them all stiff drinks, he proposed a toast: "To John Hardacre, Ivan Yazov, Crystal—dammit, whoever you want—a big thank-you from CIA."

"I'll drink to that." Kruger raised his tumbler, exclaiming "*Nasdravja!*" the Bulgarian for "Good health!"

"*Nasdravja!*" Yazov reciprocated, then downed his cold, pure vodka in a single, jerking motion.

"And if anyone thinks I'm going to chew the glass, they're wrong." Kruger wiped his mouth with the back of his hand.

"You speak Bulgarian very well," Yazov said of Kruger's toast, joking with a trace of goodwill.

"Not really. That's all I know."

"In Bulgaria, that's enough."

They all laughed, and to Kruger it seemed that Yazov was not feigning his amusement. If the humour was a little heavy, nonetheless Kruger considered that he had made a start.

Clearly, the little unstrained moment had not escaped the attention of Tarrant either. To him, Yazov's obvious ease was the opening he needed. "What a pity, what a damned pity," Tarrant said as lightly as he was able to say it. All the while Tarrant shook his head.

"How do you mean, Mr. Tarrant?" Yazov made the required response.

"I mean, damn you, here's the world's greatest. And he's going off into retirement."

"The world's greatest?" Yazov was suddenly much cooler.

"The world's greatest . . . artist," Tarrant managed to say, and though his mouth was twisted in a smile, his eyes gave him away.

"I am an artist?" Yazov asked.

20

"Of course you are. An artist. Not a killer. A killer is a squalid little man who gets a big kick out of killing. Pulling the trigger makes him ten feet tall. He's a sordid, grubby little sonofabitch."

"And I? I am a fine person. I am fine and pure?" Was there a mocking strain to his voice?

"You're all right," Tarrant responded awkwardly. "Don't sell yourself short, Crystal. Nothing wrong with you. . . ."

"You want me to do some killing?"

"I want you to do some good. Good for all of us, especially the United States."

"You want me to do some good works?" This time there was no mistaking the irony in his voice.

"You know, in some ways we in the secret services are like monks," Tarrant sounded a little unsettled, a bit unhappy. "It's a life of discipline and sacrifice, for a higher good. Almost like serving in a medieval order for the good of others. . . ."

"I see. Yes, I think so. You want me to give somebody some good works?"

"If that's how you want to put it."

"Why me?"

"Like I said, you're tops. You have four things necessary. No emotional hang-up, that's vital. It means when you're under pressure to act quickly, there's no excitement to get your hand shaking. You're not a choker. Then again you're a natural with weapons of any kind. You're just naturally part of that pistol or rifle. An extension of it."

"Go on."

"Killing for you is a nothing. Pulling a trigger is simple, anyone can do it, provided the gun is aimed anywhere except at somebody's head. If you don't count moments of agony or great fury, then very few people indeed can pull the trigger on somebody they don't even know. Have never met. You can."

"I'm a good angel of death?" The irony was still present.

"Angel, or messenger of death. That sounds a lot better, yes."

Arnie Kruger's hand clutched tightly around the empty

glass tumbler. He would hardly have believed it possible of an assistant to the DCI. The whole thing was being approached so ham-handedly.

"And what else?" Yazov wanted to know.

"Experience, of course. You've plenty of that," Tarrant replied promptly. "So now you know it all. How about it?"

"I really don't think so, Mr. Tarrant," Yazov replied slowly and evenly.

Unless he had imagined it, and he might have done so because Kruger fully expected it to happen, the CIA man thought he saw Tarrant's eyes register momentary anger. Therefore Arnie Kruger chipped in brightly, "Well, we've lost us a good man, Mr. Tarrant, but not a friend. If Crystal ever changes his mind, I'm sure we'll be the very first to know. That right?"

"Quite so, Butterfly."

"There is nothing that we can offer to change your mind?" Incredibly, Tarrant had pressed again. The DCI assistant was undoubtedly still a Pig, Kruger thought to himself, a hardliner who did not take no for an answer, a survivor of the Bay of Pigs.

"Of course, Mr. Tarrant, if he wants the job, Crystal will let you know right away." Kruger rescued the situation again, smiling warmly at Yazov. "Now let's make him happy. It's his constitutional right as an American citizen. 'We hold these truths to be self-evident,'" Kruger recited from the Declaration of Independence, "'that all men are created equal, that they are endowed by their Creator with certain inalienable rights, that among these are life, liberty and the pursuit of happiness.'"

"Thank you, Butterfly. I needed that kind of protection. You carry on, and I will be all right, I am sure," Yazov said.

"Damn right you will, Colonel. Now let's go and do a little of that pursuing."

Kruger chuckled lightly, marvelling at Yazov's neat American accent, noting too that the Bulgarian's syntax was too formal.

"Well, the recruitment pitch is over," Tarrant spoke again. "Let's get down to other business. Crystal, I want you to know that Butterfly here is your panic button. At any time, day or night, you can contact Butterfly by using

22

an unlisted number. The panic button is manned around the clock. And don't be shy: Butterfly gets paid for it."

"If I have to, Mr. Tarrant, I'll call. Don't worry."

"In the event of anything suspicious happening—strangers start snooping about, suddenly a girl gets interested, you find you're being followed—you call Butterfly. And you tell Harvey Tyler, too."

The Bulgarian nodded again, satisfied.

"A couple of things you need reminding of. Your Social Security card number has never actually been issued, nor has your Army Service number. There is no official record of your birth certificate, and one of your addresses is a vacant lot in Philadelphia. Nobody has ever heard of you at John Bartram High School. So what I'm saying is don't rely on those cards and details when you get into any kind of scrape with outside authorities. Call Butterfly instead."

"I understand, sir."

"Good. Now to repeat, the CIA has appreciated your full co-operation. You'll find we look after our own. Be happy in Spencer, but take it easy until you settle in. Tyler's a good, reliable man."

Tarrant held out his hand to the Bulgarian, who took it.

"And from me a special thanks," Tarrant went on. "If you ever want your old job back, hit that button as fast as you can."

"You've really got to be something, Crystal. These guys never give up." As he said it, Arnie Kruger shook his head sadly.

"That they don't." Yazov was still pumping Tarrant's hand. "Anyway, thank you, too, sir."

"Good luck, kid. Now Arnie here will go into some details with you. He'll buy you a steak, some dry French wine."

"I'll meet you at the elevators." Kruger ushered him to the door, where a security guard waited.

"And turn *that* in at the foyer guard post," Tarrant pointed at the laminated plastic badge which was pinned to the lapel of the Bulgarian's suit. Printed on the badge was Yazov's picture, and surrounding the badge's edges were little boxes filled with red letters which allowed access to the CIA's main building.

23

"I will, sir."

Yazov left the room, falling into step with a guard who took him to a turnstile that barred entry to and egress from the CIA's executive suites. The man accompanying Yazov flashed a pass to the armed guard who sat inside a bullet-proof glass cage. The turnstile clicked open.

In Tarrant's office the mood of strained bonhomie had passed with Yazov's leaving, being replaced by more honest, if also more sombre, deliberations. "You think it'll work out?" Tarrant asked. "Now that you've met the guy, what's your view?"

"Who chose Spencer?"

"He did. We gave him half-a-dozen places to choose from."

"Spencer? Are you kidding? From the pictures I've seen, they've boards covering some of the store windows, and weeds pushing through cracks in the back streets. Anything strategic around there?" Kruger asked suspiciously.

"A Minuteman missile base not too far away, but that's all. Can you make him out at all?"

"Not yet."

"Whatever happens, my feeling is that his could be one of your toughest handlings, Arnie."

"Could be," Kruger half murmured, recalling the sensual feelings, and the fear the man had stirred within him.

"I hate to give that sonofabitch anything, Arnie. Even Spencer. If I could, and it didn't matter to the overall defector programme, I'd hire a runaway truck. Especially since he's no use to us."

"Give it a little time, Mr. Tarrant. Ten years of agent handling has taught me this: to start with, if possible, leave them smiling. Know what I mean?"

"You think he could still be working for the Russians?"

"Who knows, Mr. Tarrant? Only the Russians would know that."

Had Tarrant known for certain that Ivan Yazov was not working for the KGB, or any other Communist spy service, which was a fact, he would have felt much happier. As it happened the KGB had its own plans for the defector, and these plans were well advanced.

* * *

24

Thanks to Arnie Kruger's influence, Yazov managed to buy himself a second-hand, late model VW 1600, even though it was past closing time for the dealer. The purchase went smoothly, with Kruger doing all the talking. And Yazov was quite satisfied, because the VW 1600 was the best small car he could think of: it cruised fast enough, was reliable in all kinds of weather and on all sorts of terrain. Yazov was also influenced by the fact that he had used VWs previously on missions for the Bulgarian MGB. It was a standard practice for the MGB to hire VWs for work outside Bulgaria, and, MGB agents were even taught enough about a Volkswagen's mechanics to make minor repairs.

Once all the paperwork involved in the sale was completed, Yazov and Kruger drove off the car lot to the Shoreham hotel on Calvert Street, where the Bulgarian was newly booked. The two men had dinner in the Shoreham's elegant Blue Room, and the CIA agent gave Yazov more details. "That panic number. It's wired to ring simultaneously at an all-day, all-night monitor in Langley, as well as in my office and apartment."

As for advice, Kruger told him, "Look out for everything. Check everybody out with Harvey Tyler—he knows Spencer like the back of his hand. And be careful about dames. Any good-looking dame could be a plant. Face it, you're always going to be alone."

After dinner was over, Kruger insisted on "doing a couple of nightclubs, seeing a little night life."

At the Foxy's Burrow, on M Street in Georgetown— Kruger called it "The Strip"—a chorus line of girls were can-canning in short skirts and without panties, and Yazov was a little disconcerted at how closely Arnie Kruger watched his reactions. When the act finished, Kruger promptly suggested taking in a safe, clean massage parlour "for a little relaxing action." Yazov declined.

The very early morning hours found them in a gay club between Twenty-eighth Street and Key Bridge, since Arnie Kruger wanted to show the defector "just how wide open Washington is." Kruger moved into an empty cubicle and ordered two drinks, a person of indeterminate sex taking the order.

"Crazy place, isn't it? What do you think of it?" he asked Yazov.

"Interesting."

"Any places like this in Sofia?"

"A few."

The seat in the cubicle was a little too small, and Yazov was aware of Kruger's thigh pressing against his. Maybe it was the drink, too, but the CIA agent was becoming slightly mushy and sentimental. "You've got to admit it," he went on at one stage, "I don't know where they get guys like Tarrant. He's about as subtle as a broken wind. You know what I mean, someone breaking wind."

"I understand."

"Still, what you've got to know is that he's okay. Just listen to his prose, but not the poetry. If you get my meaning."

"Now I don't understand."

"Ah, well. Not important, old buddy." Kruger leaned into the other man. "But what you've got to do in this game is not to trust anybody. Me included. Don't trust completely. I'm for the CIA. Always remember that with me. CIA comes first. If you make a bad mistake, and I have to do it, I'll strap a bomb to the sump of your VW myself."

"Why not use the magnetic kind of bomb casing?" Yazov failed at being funny.

"Any kind, Crystal. As long as it works. C'mon, let's go. You've got a long trip coming up."

Even though the cost was high, Kruger had made the cabbie wait. "Here's another tip," he had told Yazov when he instructed the cabbie the first time, outside the Foxy's Burrow. "Don't take a cab if you can walk. And once you've got a cab, stick with it. It's a good device in spy stories—and real life—for the opposition to operate a cab for kidnappings."

In the taxicab, Arnie Kruger sat in the back seat and snuggled into Yazov's shoulder, seeming half asleep. Afterwards, when the cab got to the Shoreham, Kruger stirred enough to say good-bye, his mouth breaking into a warm, lopsided grin, "So long, Crystal. Tomorrow is the start of the rest of your life."

"So long, Butterfly. And thanks."

"And remember, when in doubt, hit that panic button. Like the man said, that's why I'm paid."

"I'll remember."

Yazov watched the taxi's red tail lights disappear around a bend and then walked to the Shoreham's entrance.

In spite of the long hours he had kept with Kruger, Ivan Yazov was up early the next morning. He couldn't sleep and because he saw no merit in simply lying awake on his bed in the room, the Bulgarian checked out shortly after five.

His first task was thoroughly to inspect the VW. Before opening the left-hand door, Yazov spent the best part of ten minutes in checking the cautionary monitors he had prepared: still in place, across the edges of both doors, were two hairs; another hair teetered delicately at a strategic point along the rear engine's bonnet. Using a small flashlight, Yazov examined the engine. The last of the external checks was of the VW's underside, when Yazov dipped his head under the line of the car's body. Nonetheless, skin still crept over the back of the defector's head as he twisted the key into the Volkswagen's left-hand door lock. His skin tingled, too, when he gently swung the door open. Turning the starter was also disagreeable to him. The way the engine broke into life, first time, came as a welcome relief.

Still not sure of his safety, Yazov leaned a small leather bag of his toiletries against the accelerator, and promptly took cover behind the nearest column in the underground parking garage. His purpose was to escape the blast of a bomb which may have been too well hidden, the sensitive, mercury-based rocking detonator of which was likely to be triggered by the rough idling of the cold VW engine.

When nothing happened for five minutes, Yazov thought the Volkswagen was safe enough. After stowing away all his luggage, he reversed out of the parking bay, dropped a few coins into the slot of an automatic gate, and drove the Beetle up two ramps, into the street and the early morning darkness. Yazov was on his way to the town of Spencer and Interstate Highway 70.

He had still not bested his fears, for it was not impossi-

27

ble that a bomb wired to the VW could be of the more insensitive kind, something which would detonate with the jar of a wheel taking a pothole at speed. Therefore the Bulgarian only relaxed finally after the Volkswagen thumped solidly over a corrugation, which happened despite his careful lookout.

It worried the defector that his time alone had only started, and he was already sweating. He could feel the damp under his shirt. In retrospect, the stay at Brushy Hill had been a rest cure, a time free of anxiety over his personal safety. Later, while working on the rigs, he had experienced the first twinges of fear. Yazov had found himself checking safety chains and ropes. During the times he had worked along the deck's edges, he had taken care to know where everybody was, what anyone close by was doing.

Were his nerves crippled? Yazov was concerned to know, as he steered the Volkswagen out of central Washington. Or was he being extra cautious, and showing good common sense? He had good reason to worry, because he knew well enough that the KGB did not forget, nor did it forgive.

Undoubtedly he was marked high on the KGB's reprisal list.

So far, Yazov had not used any kind of tranquillizer or sleeping pill, and his drinking habits remained moderate. How long would that last, he wondered. What he needed to do was to take a firm grip on himself, and the sooner he succeeded in doing so, the better. Obviously, he could not take up hours every day with bomb checks. Commonsense precautions, yes, but he would have to beat back his wilder fears. He could use a little stoicism, for he knew better than most that not much could be done against a skilled, determined assassin who held a rifle mounted with a telescopic sight.

It was a 1200-mile run from Washington, DC to Spencer, and Yazov was content to drive the journey in easy, lazy stretches, over four days. As he motored along, he wanted to see and experience something of the United States. So he stopped frequently that first day, and by the time he got to Friendsville, which is on the Youghiogheny River, he had only journeyed about 120 miles. Here he stayed the night, in a little motel which provided lock-up garages.

He sat near a crackling log fire in the lounge until late. Afterwards, in the cabin, he lay on his bed in the dark, listening to the night.

The next day he got clear across Ohio State. Yazov would have chosen to stop earlier, but owing to the lack of motels with suitable lock-up garages, he had driven past Speedway, Pittsboro, Jamestown and Crawfordsville. There were no lock-ups at Hillsboro either. Nonetheless that was where Yazov stopped the second night—spending a bad, wakeful time of it. Outside his cosy room he could hear strong, November winds blowing, and Yazov was quite sure that all his markers on the VW would be swept away. Of course, they were gone when he examined the car in the morning—nothing like the three hairs would have remained in place in the strong gusts—but as Yazov turned the key in the door's lock, he felt the cold on the back of his neck.

Shortly after crossing the Illinois River, and north of Peoria, he anxiously noticed a black Ford. The Ford hung behind him, a good 200 yards to the back of the VW, and it stayed like that, even though 60 to 70 miles an hour on Interstate 74 was too slow for the car. The Ford's speed, or lack of it, was the reason why Yazov felt growing anxiety. The big car had not turned into Bloomington, nor had it stopped at Peoria.

Sitting behind the wheel of his Volkswagen, Yazov tried to rationalize away his fears. The probabilities—the overwhelming probabilities—were that the Ford was innocently tooling along Interstate 74, its driver quite happy to drive at a moderate speed. . . .

What Yazov could not dismiss was a possibility—small though it may be—that the Ford was trailing him.

In the end, the Bulgarian decided to put his fears to the test.

Coming up ahead was the turn-off to a place called Kickapoo, and Yazov resolved to leave the main highway. So as not to alert the Ford's occupants, he took his foot off the accelerator, allowing the VW to slow down under its own weight. Yazov also kept his foot clear of the foot-brake.

Now the Ford began to gain rapidly. The bigger car loomed larger in the VW's rear-view mirror. Yazov's impression was of two men in the front with hats pulled down.

Yazov's heart fluttered against his ribcage. He was unarmed, and if the Ford's driver wanted, he could overtake easily. It was a mistake not to have bought a faster car. Also, he had been grossly stupid not to have insisted that the CIA provide a weapon for his protection.

With great effort, he clung to the steering. Slowly the VW edged towards the slipway, a hundred yards down the highway. For a moment the big, black car drew level with Yazov. The Bulgarian and the passenger shot one another glances. The passenger had a pale, white face, a hat pulled right down to dark, bushy eyebrows. Then the Ford surged by.

Yazov drove on to Kickapoo anyway. The plastic steering wheel was slippery with perspiration. Down his back, Yazov felt drops of sweat trickle. Afterwards, he sat drinking coffee at a roadhouse outside the tiny hamlet. What the incident had rammed home to him was his helplessness, unless he armed himself. He had sat in the VW, squeezing the wheel, feeling scared and useless. From that time he was determined to procure a gun so that he could shoot back, if he had to.

The night prior to his drive into Spencer, Yazov chose a motel room close by a tributary of the Iowa River, a place which was a few miles from Homestead. Most of that night too he lay awake, staring ceilingwards, in the dark. He had his hands behind his back, and in the early morning he turned to watch the dawn slowly light up the drawn, cream curtains of the room's picture window.

Before driving into Spencer, the Bulgarian motored through the surrounding areas. Much of the countryside was familiar by now: farmlands and prairie; grey hamlets, tall grain elevators etched against grey, November skies; white-washed farmhouses standing in the long, pancake distances between towns. Breaking up the monotony outside Spencer was a string of small lakes and a wooded area.

Yazov had been shown slides, newspaper cuttings, even a movie of the town, so he knew what to expect when he

30

rolled his Volkswagen down Grand Avenue. There were showrooms crammed with new tractors, corn driers, combines and other farm implements. Tarrant had liked the town because the inhabitants were white, mostly Protestant, Republican—and because it was quiet enough for the townsfolk to leave their homes unlocked. "You'll find the pressure's off in Spencer, the folks are friendly, all twelve thousand of them. The skies are blue and bright," Tarrant had told him.

Harvey Tyler owned a vintage general store on Grand Avenue, and in the late afternoon Yazov stopped right outside, finding it no trouble to park.

The defector climbed out of the front seat and stretched the muscles below his neck and between the shoulderblades. That was not enough, so he gave them a painful squeeze with his hands, and rubbed them with his fingertips, too. Then he walked on to the boardwalk outside Tyler's store, making the boards squeak as they flexed under his feet.

Inside the general store it was gloomy. Ancient and inadequate light fittings hung from an old, patterned tin ceiling, which was painted a faded white. Yazov saw heavy wooden shelves, neatly stacked with groceries. His gaze shifted to the delicatessen section, where a sign over cucumbers pickling in a large glass crock, read: "GERMAN POPSICLES (HARVEY'S DILL) 40 CENTS OR THREE FOR $1.20."

Then he took in a medium-built man who stood behind an old-fashioned cash register. Harvey Tyler. He was in his late sixties, he wore a white baseball cap, gold-rimmed spectacles, and, over his left ear, a lead pencil.

Harvey Tyler turned away from the customer he was serving to greet the Bulgarian with a lean, outstretched hand, and a yellow-toothed smile. "You must be John Hardacre," he pumped Yazov's hand. "Here's a big welcome to Spencer." Next he turned back to a middle-aged woman who was loaded with a large packet of groceries, saying, "Mrs. Adams. Mary. I'd like you to meet John Hardacre."

A limp, pink hand was thrust to the side of the packet, and Mrs. Adams's head bobbed clear of her purchases.

31

"Pleased to meet you, Mr. Hardacre. Old Harv told us about getting a little help."

"Nice to meet you, too, ma'am," Yazov replied.

"Well, I hope you'll like Spencer. It's a quiet place, but a good place to set down your roots, you'll find."

"Mr. Tyler wrote a glowing report, ma'am."

"I'm sure he did, old Harv does well out of Spencer. We all pay cash on the barrelhead here."

The former CIA dog-handler coughed, nodded sheepishly, and said, "Now, if you'll excuse me and Mrs. Adams. . . ."

For a while, the only sounds were those of the jangling cash register. Once his eyes were accustomed to the gloom, Yazov ran them over the well-stocked general store, quickly bringing them to rest on what he sought. His eyes alighted on a large glass case, which stood in a corner of the store. Through the glass he thought he saw the dull gleam of gun metal, and he was right.

Yazov set the floorboards creaking again as he ambled casually over to the stock of weapons. A twist on the key of the lock, and the door swung open under its own weight. Gently, Yazov removed off its pegs a 12-bore Remington shotgun. It had twin barrels.

When Mrs. Adams had completed her buying, she popped her head around the bulky package once again, and when she saw Yazov with the shotgun in his hands, she hesitated. Then she smiled uncertainly and said, " 'Bye, Mr. Hardacre. I'll be making more of your acquaintance, I'm sure."

If Yazov heard, he said nothing. Mrs. Adams glanced at Harvey Tyler, shrugged, and struggled out of the general store, with Tyler lending a helping hand. The storekeeper returned, making the floorboards creak as he walked to the corner where Yazov was studying another shotgun.

"Expecting any trouble, son?" Harvey Tyler cleaned his hands on a well-used, heavy blue apron.

"Not that I know of. But something like this could come in useful."

"Have you got any authorization from Washington? To pack a gun, I mean."

"They didn't tell me to go out and buy anything. But nobody said I couldn't either."

32

"Well, I'm not sure. . . ." Something in the way Yazov handled the gun disconcerted Harvey Tyler. It was a little obscene, or repellent, and gave him the kind of feeling he got when he saw a human kiss a pet dog. He watched Yazov gently break open the breech of a shotgun, play his fingers lightly over the barrel, weigh and balance the weapon, turn it over, move the barrel against a dully shining light and examine its precision rifling. Tyler did not like the manner in which Yazov almost seemed to stroke and fondle the inanimate weapon, with deadly familiarity.

"All we need is Striker," Tyler said at last.

He was referring to the dog, which had lain in a shadowy pool between the lamps. Tyler snapped his fingers, and instantly the dog was up. Another snap. The dog loped towards Tyler, its ears pricking. It was a dark brown Alsatian, black patches on dark brown, and as it loped along the dog's jaws fell open to expose a moist, pink tongue and sharp, white teeth. Harvey Tyler ran his hand gently through the hair under a silver chain which hung around the big dog's neck.

"He looks a nice dog," Yazov said.

"He is. Real nice. But he'll take your arm off, if I want."

Yazov nodded and smiled.

"I fixed a place for you upstairs." Tyler changed the subject, at the same time jerking his thumb to the rear of the dimly lit store. "Used to be my sister's kid's place. Make yourself comfortable."

"Thank you, Mr. Tyler."

"No use in you calling me that. Everyone else calls me Harv or Harvey." The old man fondled his dog. "Nothing much doing here. I'm kind of surprised, in a way, that you picked the place. Fun for me and the boys is to settle down to five-card stud every Wednesday and Saturday. You're welcome."

"Thanks, Harvey."

"If you like some home-cooked mashed potatoes, spare rib and watermelon pickles, after the store's closed we'll take a run to Stub's Range Kitchen on Highway 71, a mile out of Spencer."

"I've seen the place. Right now I could use a hot bath."

"You've got it. Upstairs, on the right. Fresh towels."

"I'll need some heavy-duty bolts or chains, too."

"Mister, this is a quiet town," Harvey Tyler was suddenly regretting his deal with the CIA. "I hope you and Spencer will get along fine. I'd hate any real trouble."

"The fact is, Harv, I would hate trouble, too. We're about as far from Moscow as I can get. . . ."

3

By the time Yazov got to sleep in a room upstairs, over the general store, he had fitted the door with a strong steel bolt and chain. A shotgun was stowed under his bed. If, in a way, Tarrant would have been reassured to know that President Okan was deep in a massive plot against the United States, so Yazov might have been mollified to know that his precautions were well taken.

In fact the defector's safeguards were probably inadequate, for in a building on Dzerzhinsky Square, in Moscow, plans for Yazov's assassination were far advanced.

The square is in the middle of Moscow, and gusts of strong, cold winds blew there that November. As often as not, the giant statue of Felix Dzerzhinsky was covered in snow which obscured its details from the view of people in the nine-storey building housing the vast organization he had helped found. While the universal judgement of history is that Nathan Hale was a bumbler, the verdict on Dzerzhinsky, outside the Communist bloc at any rate, is that this Pole was a curious mixture of sadism, idealism and fanaticism, and a success.

While the highway sign on George Washington Memorial Parkway in suburban Langley, Virginia, reads "CIA," no sign or flag indicates that the building to the rear of Dzerzhinsky's statue is the headquarters of the Soviet KGB.

On the fifth floor of the squat KGB building, at the corner closest to its founder's memorial, is the office of General Vladimir Ardalion Shebrikov. In that cold November, Shebrikov headed Department V of the KGB, a part of the Russian secret police and spy service within whose jurisdiction defectors and other traitors fell.

Shebrikov was at work, and he conferred with a deputy who sat in an overstuffed armchair. As Shebrikov juggled the inevitable bottle of vodka and crystal glasses, the KGB officer gave him a first-hand briefing. When he spoke it was against a background of softly sung Russian folk songs, which were piped into Shebrikov's office to mask the conversation and prevent any possible monitoring of the vibrations which the sounds of their discussions made on the narrow, rectangular windows behind the general.

At last, Shebrikov's assistant finished briefing the boss of Department V on Colonel Ivan Yazov's resettlement in Spencer, Iowa. The report which contained such details had reached the KGB headquarters the previous day, and had been immediately deciphered.

"They love to resettle them in the Mid-West, comrade, don't they? Deep in the bosom, as far from Dzerzhinsky Square as they can make it. Safe and secure," General Shebrikov observed.

"Or in Canada, the central states. Of course, that does make logistics more difficult, comrade general."

"Quite so. I'll come to that later, the logistics. Whatever they are, we won't be stopped by them. To overlook the Bulgarian traitor's duplicity and defection was always impossible. Out of the question."

"Of course, comrade general."

Shebrikov went on to test the details. "The whole affair will start and end within seventy-two hours of our men arriving in New York?" He made it sound like a question.

"Yes, comrade general. Two men will take the easy route: entry to Sweden through Finland, then to Paris, and from France to New York. The Technical Division's faked identifications will cover our men for at least seventy-two hours."

"The time, approximately, the FBI would take to check through Interpol and the issuing country?"

"Yes, comrade general. Our Technical Division has issued passports and other documents from the usual stocks of excellently forged blanks. All the cover we've given our men are falsely stated identities, occupations, addresses,

35

reasons for entry into the United States, marital status."

"If anybody is arrested, comrade, and checks are made. . . ." General Shebrikov sounded anxious.

"Any deeper cover is a waste, comrade general. These men will be in and out within seventy-two hours. They will enter Finland on one document, pass into Sweden on a second, pick up a third passport in Stockholm, and the forged US documents they will obtain in Paris."

"Very well, I approve." Shebrikov's deputy had described the routine, multiple-passport tactic which was much used by Communist spies and Arab hijackers. A well-tried and tested way of flitting through countries, the tactic allowed agents to assume and drop several false identities and to shake off hostile security services, which almost inevitably lagged a passport or two behind.

"What I don't like," Shebrikov continued, "is the risk. Our men are not familiar with the United States. Going in, hitting and running. . . ."

"No other way, I'm afraid, comrade general, unless we postpone. . . ."

"No, I want no delays. I have discussed the business with higher authority, and this is a priority mission. We'll have to assume reasonable risks."

"If for political and deterrent reasons we have to deal with Yazov directly, comrade general, we are at some risk."

General Shebrikov got up and opened the curtains covering the narrow, rectangular window. Outside, it was snowing in the square. The pate and shoulders of Dzerzhinsky's statue were covered in white. Speaking from the window, Shebrikov said, "A defector of Colonel Yazov's class must be destroyed by us directly. Potential traitors must know we will reach for their throats from straight out of this building, from this office. . . ."

"*Da*, comrade general."

"What we have to do is keep the risk acceptable, comrade. Obviously, our men are well trained . . . ?" Shebrikov trailed off.

"Our best men, comrade general. Experienced. Of course, you know we used them very successfully in Afghanistan."

Shebrikov nodded. His deputy was talking about a

quick and clinical assassination of an anti-Russian editor, a killing that had taken place in Kabul. The dead man had in life exposed KGB operations in the Middle East and had also repeatedly written hostile editorials. In fact, Moscow's information had been that he was in the CIA's pay.

Two Department V agents had flown to Nepal, then Kabul. At Kabul airport they had hired a car from a rental firm, and after driving to the victim's home, they had moved in and shot the newspaperman as he soaked in a hot bath. The killers reached New Delhi on the next flight out of Kabul. The men who did the killing were Semyon Vladimir Yegerov and Leonid Bevz.

"I approve of your choice of men," General Shebrikov stood sideways to the window as he spoke. "What I don't approve of are the logistics." With that he drew the curtains closed again, walked back to his desk, and enquired, "Where exactly is Spencer, comrade?"

With a rustle of heavy paper, the Department V officer unfolded a metre-square map of the north-central United States. Laying the map on Shebrikov's desk, he smoothed it out and pointed to where he had drawn an irregular circle in red. "Here, a small town close to the north-west corner of Iowa State."

"Exactly. And how far from New York?" Shebrikov wanted to know.

The other man extracted another map from his briefcase, this being a map of the whole of the United States. Already, a route had been plotted in heavy red ink from New York City, through New Jersey, Pennsylvania, Indiana and Illinois to Spencer in Iowa. "With my dividers, I have made it about nineteen hundred kilometres, say two thousand kilometres. Twenty hours, hard, fast driving."

"Exactly. Too far, too long. It never occurred to you to use our Chicago *residentura*, comrade? How far—by road—from Chicago to Spencer?"

While he used his dividers on the route between Chicago and Spencer, the deputy said, "Our Chicago *residentura* is badly undermanned, comrade general. We can use two, perhaps three men, including the resident himself. I thought that . . ."

"The distance, please. What is it, comrade?" Shebrikov spoke impatiently.

37

"I estimate it to be six hundred to seven hundred kilometres."

"Very well. Six to eight hours' easier driving. Do it that way, through Chicago. There's not much to be done. Not so much that two men can't handle transport and supply from Chicago."

"Very well, comrade general."

"Otherwise, your planning is approved. I'll drink to your success in advance."

The Department V officer stopped in the middle of refolding his maps, a task that was giving him a little difficulty because the folds were bending the wrong way. What he did not like was how General Shebrikov seemed to end these discussions by making the mission "his." Nevertheless, the KGB general's subordinate knew his place, reached for a crystal glass filled with iced vodka and said, "I'll drink to that, comrade general."

Celebrating slightly in advance made him feel uncomfortable, but the clear, colourless liquid, which he drank in a single, jerking movement, warmed him as well as ever.

He was not to know that Department V had unwittingly added its shove to a complex train of events that was on the move across Russia, the United States, Europe, the Middle East—and Africa.

4

In early December, Obama Okan was doubly safe from Yazov. Not only had the CIA failed to procure the Bulgarian assassin's services, but, thanks to the intervention of the KGB, Yazov was himself marked for killing. Of course, none of this was known to Okan, though he lived by the assumption that his many enemies were constantly plotting his death anyway.

Okan was under constant guard. Even as he sat in a sunken bath of hot water, tinted green with bath salts, the shadow of a Russian-made Kalashnikov AK-47 fell across him. It was carried by a guard in Arab headdress, a sentry who faced discreetly away from the president of Uganda. Beyond the marbled bathroom, in the vast bedroom of Command Post, there were two other Palestinians. They sat on wooden benches in different corners of the presidential suite, their AKs resting against their shoulders.

On the flat roof above the bathroom, more guards stood watch. Here two men lay prone behind a Russian-made light machine gun mounted on a bipod. Once in a while a pair of night binoculars changed hands, as the men shared the chore of scanning beyond a roll of barbed wire.

Still more troops were dispersed in the grounds of Command Post, including an elite company of paratroopers, all armed with AK-47s; parked in the front and back driveways of the redoubt, which overlooked Lake Victoria, were jeeps carrying recoilless guns.

Obama Okan was well guarded, but a prisoner of his own security forces. He hardly dared move about openly, as several attempts had already been made on his life. The latest had occurred but ten days previously.

Had he not been tipped off by the Russian embassy, he might have attended a police passing-out parade where a bomb had fragmented the podium, killing several high officials.

The big, custom-made bath easily contained Okan's barrel-like, 300-lb. frame, and the Ugandan president lay in the water, brooding. Ahead of him, his midriff was a mound of black flesh, protruding from the light green froth like a tiny island. For more than an hour, arms loosely folded on his chest, Okan had re-examined his anxieties in the place where he did all his serious thinking.

Part of his difficulties was a Russian estimate that more than half his 40,000-strong army was against him. It was true that 10,000 of the most discontented troops were already more or less permanently confined to barracks. The bulk of his army, loyal or disloyal, had not been paid for several months. What money he could spare he gave to his Palestinian, South Sudanese and Kakwa loyalists, the latter being men of Okan's tribe.

The ordinary Ugandan's lot was manifestly wretched, Okan admitted to himself, with shortages of everything for everybody, save his closest followers. Except for coffee exports, which earned what little foreign currency he could lay his hands on, the country's economy was almost non-existent.

There was also the matter of his personal prestige: the Israeli rescue at Entebbe had been a profound humiliation. While the hijacking to Entebbe airport of an Air France jetliner had started as a master stroke, allowing him brief glory, the aftermath had been a complete disaster. He had even prohibited Ugandans from talking or writing about it, on pain of death.

Accordingly, Okan had welcomed the Refusal Front's proposal, which came to this: allow the Front to use Uganda as a sanctuary, a haven for the Front's agents after a spectacular assault on the West's airlines and politicians. "Terrorism is great, massive drama," Hassan Jabril, the Front's leader, had put it, "and Uganda will be its theatre."

Not that he had needed much incitement. Like the KGB in the context of Yazov, provided the risks were acceptable, Okan was in wholehearted, enthusiastic agreement with the plot. In the nights after the Entebbe raid that July he had lain awake, fearing for his life, but also contemplating a soothing vengeance. Both Okan and the Front burned for a retaliatory stroke on a grand scale.

Nor was he troubled by the massive scope of it: the hijacking of El Al and US jetliners, as well as the kidnapping of American and other leaders. Rather the contrary: the very sweep and size of the operation would ensure unprecedented "theatre," ransom demands, and a mighty retribution.

What worried Okan was not the vast dimension of the attacks but the manner of them. He wanted no mistakes. The risks had to be acceptable. He and the Front were preparing to blackmail the most powerful nation on earth, as well as the resourceful Israelis. Both nations had adopted consistently hardline attitudes to terrorism. Should the operation backfire, Okan was certain he would not survive.

He had already met twice in secret with Jabril. Both had agreed on the El Al hijacking. The other missions had been a trade-off: Jabril insisted on striking against the US, Israel's most important patron; Okan had been adamant

40

on an operation against the Rhodesian and South African regimes.

How the hostages and aircraft would be secured in Uganda had also been worked out by the two men. Okan would roll his Russian-made armour on to the runways, the captives would be broken into groups and separated; some hostages would be kept under guard at Entebbe, others would be taken to Kampala and Jinja.

With all these safeguards taken, no power, however great, would be able to stop a bloodbath, if it ever came to it.

Thus far the discussions had gone well, but then came disagreement. It had arisen over who ought to be commander-in-chief of the field operations.

Okan agreed that Jabril's selection for this post was ruthless and clever, commanded respect, had worked hard and had also co-ordinated most efficiently the training of separate assault groups.

But it alarmed Okan that she was a woman.

He pretended to appreciate all Jabril's arguments about her excellent qualities, her complete devotion to Jabril and his cause, as well as the known fact that women hijackers were often fiercer and braver than their male counterparts.

It was just that Okan was wholly convinced of the necessity to appoint a man to the field command.

Jabril was adamant about his own choice.

So far, neither man had given any sign of backing down.

It was especially over this issue, and how to resolve it, that Okan brooded in the bath. Somehow he could not bring himself to believe that a mere woman could successfully carry off the spectacular undertaking.

A rap on the door intruded upon his thoughts, and he turned to find Colonel Oyok, his security chief, with a message in his hand. "Excellency, an urgent, secret cable from the president of Libya."

The disturbance caused Okan some immediate annoyance. For months past it had become the Libyan president's irritating habit to bombard the Ugandan with urgent, secret messages, and to keep him on the phone for long stretches while Okan listened to advice on how best to govern Uganda. But whatever his resentments, Libya's billion-dollar oil revenues had kept Uganda afloat, and its president had rushed to Entebbe twenty Russian Mig jet fighters to replace those destroyed in the Israeli raid.

"Very well, what is it?" Okan asked curtly.

Colonel Oyok raised his eyes meaningfully at the Arab guard, a warning gesture which conveyed to Okan that the matter was secret.

Okan rose unsteadily to his feet in the bath, sending the hot, greenish water over the marble rim and onto the floor tiles. The Palestinian guard unslung his AK-47 and helped towel down the dictator.

Dressed in a white bathrobe, Okan led the way out of the bathroom, through his bedroom, and into an adjoining office, where a man was working at a desk.

"Well, my friend?"

Colonel Oyok stood mute and embarrassed, holding the deciphered telex with a limp hand. It required a few moments before Okan remembered that Oyok was as illiterate as he was.

"Of course, colonel, let our loyal secretary read the message," Okan solved the problem.

Colonel Oyok handed the document to the other man who adjusted his spectacles and read out loud,

"To president, Uganda. Arrange to meet Maaten es Sarra ten hundred hours. December three. Latitude north twenty-one degrees fourteen minutes. Longitude east twenty-one degrees forty minutes. From president, Libya. Message ends."

"Is that all?" Okan asked.

"That is all, excellency. The message ends."

"Give it to me, my friend." Okan took the document and pretended to study it. As he looked at the decoded telex the three tribal scars, which caused the Kakwas to be nicknamed "One-Elevens," stood out sharply on his forehead. "Ah, yes. That is all. The message ends," he spoke at last. "What do you make of it? I mean, what is the president saying?"

"I believe the president of Libya is calling for a meeting, on December third, excellency. Ten in the morning. The place is called Maaten es something." The private secretary paused, slightly uncertain. "You have it in the

42

message, excellency. And the president of Libya has given you the precise location by the latitude and longitude."

"Exactly, my friend. That is what I thought, too. Do any of you know this . . . this Maaten place?"

Both Oyok and the other man shook their heads.

"Very well, then we must definitely find it on a map. Please see to it."

"Immediately, excellency," the secretary bowed his head, then retreated out of the office.

Okan's three vertical scars stood out more sharply than ever—in smouldering anger. It was typical of the Libyan president to summon him without warning or consultation. Yet there was not much he could do about it, if he wished to retain the Libyan's goodwill. Had it not been for the Libyan president's money and active support, Okan knew that he would probably have been ousted months ago.

Okan could well imagine what the meeting was going to be about. Time was short, and the deadlock over the choice of field commander had to be broken. He did not need telling that the president of Libya had set himself up as a mediator.

A little later the private secretary returned with a large map of northern Africa. After laying it out on Okan's desk, he said, "The meeting place is roughly here. Deep in southeast Libya. Let me use the ruler, and I will have it exactly."

The secretary jiggled the ruler over the map, and exclaimed, "Ah, here we have it, excellency. It is marked, too. Maaten es Sarra."

5

The cause of the stalemate between Okan and Jabril was Gabriella Garst. When Okan received the telex from the president of Libya, Gabriella Garst was in the abandoned schoolhouse of El Hawra, a small coastal town on the Gulf of Aden in South Yemen.

As was by no means unusual for her in the hectic, preceding weeks—and in the more slowly paced months before—Garst was taking a personal hand in the training of her groups.

This particular group was called Commando Meinhof, named after the young woman who had been found hanged in her prison cell in Germany. She was a heroine to all the young men and women sitting on rough, wooden benches in the tumbledown schoolroom. Garst had dubbed the group Commando Meinhof so that the dead woman might be honoured—and for the sake of propaganda.

Ten young men and women of mixed nationalities sat before the crudely made wooden desks, facing Garst. She was a slim young woman, and she was pacing the area in front of the commando. As she walked, she tucked the fingers of her hands into the inside waistband of her faded, blue Levis.

Was she beautiful, or merely pretty? Nobody could tell, for a black nylon stocking was drawn over her head, distorting her features.

Gabriella Garst was concluding her lecture with some advice concerning a few essentials of hostage holding. "Never relax. Not for a second, not even if you are in overwhelming control."

Her feet were slightly apart when she stopped her walking, and she spoke without any notes. "Be careful of how you word your demands. Your every word, your every phrase will be studied minutely by the enemy authorities and their lackey psychologists."

She started to move again, saying, "Do not worry about what other members of Commando Meinhof are busy doing. You do your own job. Make certain of your own task."

After another pause, the lecture continued, "Try always to gain the sympathy of your hostages. Yes, their sympathy. You don't want trouble. And they need to know that if they are patient, and well behaved, it will all end soon and well."

She had repeated the same lecture to other groups, in places as far away from Yemen as a Spartan guerrilla camp in the Iraqi mountains, a pleasant compound set in flowering gardens near Algiers, and at the isolated Kufra

Oasis, far in the Libyan Sahara. Always it had startled her to find out on these inspections and training sessions how quickly intelligent, motivated young people learned.

"Always hold out hope. Hope that freedom is close at hand. Never provoke hysteria."

They had all learned well. In Yemen, in Iraq, in Algeria and Libya. In order to test some of their training, Hassan Jabril had insisted that Garst's squads be taken through live immigration and customs barriers in Greece, Italy, France, West Germany and Great Britain. In such circumstances the trainees had felt what it was like to pass through check points, using false papers. And Garst had no doubt they had gone through with their emotions controlled, not too talkative, not too polite. "You must seem ordinary when you move past passport controls. You must know the precise details of your false papers." Her admonitions had certainly rung in their ears. Not a single trainee had been caught.

And every aspect of training had been equally thorough: how to check in to hotels and fill in the forms, how to rent a car, how to use different kinds of pay phones, even how much to tip taxi drivers, hotel porters, waiters, cleaning women.

Now she was almost finished with her final lecture to Commando Meinhof. It was a vital point, something which she had kept for last. Garst stood still, hands on her hips. "Above all," she said, "deal quickly and very decisively with any hostage who attacks you or undermines your authority. At all times, you must have total control. I thank you for your close attention, but remember Commando Meinhof has a vital mission."

The final lecture was over, and Garst's class broke into polite, restrained clapping.

All the commandos would have vital tasks. To Commando Meinhof fell the business of hijacking an Inter-Continental Airways 747 either from Latakia airport, Athens, or from Rome's Fiumicino. In order that it might carry out that purpose as expertly as possible, Commando Meinhof had rehearsed time and again the proposed takeover, using crude mock-ups of parts of Boeing interiors. The mission would be an essential part of the three-pronged outrage planned by the Front, but it was probably

45

less dangerous than the El Al hijacking, or the kidnapping of the US Secretary of State.

Garst waited until the last of the clapping died down before going on to say, "Now I must ask you to be patient. Commando Meinhof is ready to strike. What remains for me to do is to select the final assault team."

There was a brief buzz of excitement.

"As you know, the team will be made up of a squad of only four." Garst paused. "Six of you will be left behind. Whoever you are—the team has not yet been finally chosen, and each of you is being considered—do not be disappointed. If you are not selected for this mission, I can promise that you will be needed later."

Again, a burst of brief applause erupted from the benches, pleasing Gabriella Garst, making her mouth twist under the nylon when she smiled. "Those left behind will be held as reserves. Do not worry. The Front will need you all, sooner rather than later. I thank you again."

The lecture and the meeting were over. Garst walked over to the rickety classroom door, motioning to a young woman member of the group. The girl who followed Garst out of the schoolhouse was a former kindergarten teacher, and she had already taken part in several bank robberies, bombings and kidnappings. Together with three other dangerous prisoners, after managing to overwhelm their female guards one midnight, she had escaped over a prison wall, using a knotted bedsheet.

This was the girl Garst wanted to lead Commando Meinhof. Garst wondered what Okan would say if he knew how many women were involved in the combined operations.

Garst and the other girl spoke for a short time, in muted tones. They embraced briefly, then the girl went back into the schoolhouse. The door closed behind her scraping the dark mud floor. Garst strode in the opposite direction, on to an unpaved street, and climbed into the front seat of a battered jeep.

It was a short ride in the jeep to an open flat area outside the town, where a Russian-built Kamov 25 helicopter waited to take her back to Aden. The slim girl boarded the Kamov and settled herself in one of the folding seats by the middle window, on the port side. Next she gave the pilot a sign with her left thumb up, and the helicopter's two engines broke into life.

The Kamov rose suddenly into the sky, and Garst felt the thrill brought on by the quick, upward bound. Only after the rapid ascent to 2,000 metres had been completed did she drag off her black stocking mask, and instantly cover her eyes and upper face with large sunglasses. Her long blonde hair she tucked under a floppy white tennis hat.

Had either of the two crew members aboard the Kamov turned at a critical moment, he would have enjoyed the striking beauty of Jabril's mistress.

Far below the helicopter, a straggling caravan of camel-mounted desert tribesmen broke into a canter, hooves trailing small puffs of dust in the desert. Even if Garst's eyes seemed lazily to follow the caravan across the desert's sandy face, her mind was preoccupied with thoughts of the upcoming Front operations.

Supposing the deadlock between Okan and Jabril was satisfactorily broken, she would soon see action. The plans were made, training was all but completed. It had all been stimulating. Yet nothing she had done in the months that had gone before, or the more exciting previous few weeks, would compare with the exhilaration of the actual attacks.

The reprisals would eclipse the multiple hijackings of September 1970, when TWA, Swissair and BOAC airliners had been seized and later dynamited in the desert outside Amman, Jordan. Garst was sure of it. Only the massacre of Israeli Olympic athletes by Black September in Munich would rival Jabril's latest sensation.

"Terrorism is theatre, and you will be the star," Jabril had promised. Once again, the world would be shocked into reminding itself that the Palestinians lived, and that their cause had not passed out of existence. The Front would collect a vast ransom, and Jabril's prestige would be restored where it mattered to him. Whatever the Palestine Liberation Organization's recent reverses in Lebanon, the world would be reminded that the Front could sting mercilessly.

"Naturally, it will also be a fitting revenge for Entebbe, Gigi." Jabril had used her pet name when he had first out-

47

lined the scheme six weeks after the Israeli rescue in Uganda. Then they had made love.

With Hassan Jabril she had felt alive every moment of the time she had been with him. Now he controlled her mind, her will, all her feelings, completely. Garst felt emotion engulf her chest, shortening her breathing.

If anything bedevilled the abandonment of herself to Jabril's will, it was the well-established fact that Hassan Jabril had used every woman he had ever besotted. Used, manipulated, exploited. However much she tried, Garst could not quite purge herself completely of all suspicions that she might possibly be only another obsessed chattel.

Nor was there any comfort in knowing that at least three ex-mistresses of his were serving long prison sentences in West Germany, Norway and France. Still another of his women had died horribly when a grenade had fragmented in her specially constructed brassière while she sipped champagne in the upper deck of a Boeing 747 she was about to hijack. It was on that very night that Garst and Jabril had first made love.

Nonetheless, as soon as Garst glimpsed the bungalow overlooking the docks of Aden, she knew what she wanted.

The stubby helicopter slowly dropped to the bungalow, with its three-metre-high walls, rolls of barbed wire, and a swimming pool set in a small garden. From the flat roof, painted silver, two of Jabril's bodyguards waved their AK-47s in welcome. When the whirling of the Kamov's roars got close enough, the draft made their flowing white robes flap.

Using a strong rope ladder, Gabriella Garst clambered to the roof. The Kamov hovered until she was safely down, whereupon it banked steeply and clattered away.

What she wanted, Garst got . . . as she mounted the steps of the swimming pool, on her way out of the water.

Right after embracing Jabril in his large work room to the back of the bungalow, Garst had taken off her Levis and shirt and made for the pool, hurrying through the opened, sliding doors and across the patio.

At the pool's edge, she unhooked her soft white brassière and pulled down a pair of white nylon panties, stretching the elastic as she dragged them down her thighs to her ankles. Garst lifted her right leg out of the dainty garment, then used her left foot to flick it away.

She removed her sunglasses and placed them at the pool's side. Next she doffed her white bonnet and shook free her blonde hair, making her ripe, shapely buttocks quiver. Just for a moment she leaned naked over the pool's edge, round, tanned, her breasts pendulating slightly.

Then she launched her sweaty body in a graceful dive for the cool, sparkling swimming-pool water.

Jabril flung himself after her.

There was a short, playful chase through the water. The Arab splashed water across her face with the flat of his hand. Then they swam together, leisurely, on their backs, the girl trailing her hand over Jabril's crotch. When he in turn moved his hand up between her legs, Garst broke away and swam furiously for the stainless-steel steps at the shallow end of the pool.

She was halfway up the steps before Jabril got to her. When he did, he clamped his hands over the handrail to block her escape. Thereafter, in a feat of some agility he had her impaled, and Garst had to grip the tubular rail hard.

Afterwards, they sat talking in the big room which fronted on the pool and was Jabril's office.

Garst reported on her latest visit to El Hawra, and Jabril nodded approvingly. "Teamwork, patience, endless attention to detail, Gigi," he repeated his touchstones again, "and a gambler's boldness to take calculated chances. You have learned better than any other."

"Am I different from all others, then?" Gabriella Garst asked teasingly.

"Better, wilder, more passionate than all others, Gigi. Does that satisfy you?"

"And what else?" the girl smiled.

"Cleverer, more loyal, deadlier, lovelier, more enchanting . . ." Jabril went on flattering her.

They sat in a room that had once been the playroom of the British colonial administrator's children. Because he was something of an ironist, Jabril had not removed from

49

the wall a tattered Noddy poster. Alongside this poster, in counterpoint, was taped another banner: it pictured a heavily armed Fatah warrior and the legend, *My Path, My Blood, My Name, My Home, My Address . . . Palestine.*

Elsewhere, the converted playroom's walls were covered with charts and maps. What would have especially interested the CIA, Israel's Mossad, MI6 or the French SDECE—and every other Western spy service—was a giant-sized Hammond International Map of the World. It used Mercator's projection, a favourite projection of navigators, since straight lines on it represented a constant bearing. The big Hammond map stretched from one end to the other of a long wall, and Jabril also liked the manner in which the map was divided into time zones.

He had extracted from the Worldwide Edition of the Official Airline Guide information concerning the then current schedules and routes of target airlines, and he had himself marked such routes on the map, using pens of different colours. Multi-coloured drawing pins, as well as flagged markers, littered Europe, the Middle East, and Africa. When it was not in use, Jabril was careful always to draw a thick, black curtain across the map.

He had just finished telling the girl of a proposed meeting at Maaten es Sarra between himself, Garst, the president of Libya and Okan. Now he got up from a collapsible canvas seat—a chair commonly used in the field headquarters of Russian regiments—and stuck a green pin into a part of the Hammond map which depicted south-east Libya.

"The president of Libya wants us to meet there. Maaten es Sarra. Precisely at 21° 14' north, 21° 40' east."

"What do you think of it?"

"What do I think of it? My dearest Gigi, I called for it. This is merely the president's approval." The Arab waved a piece of paper on which he had written details of the meeting place, saying, "Of course, the president has chosen the place, but the idea of the meeting is mine."

"To break the deadlock?"

"To get the operation going, yes. We've waited long enough. Now it is urgent. Now we must get general approval for your command."

"You think that'll happen?"

50

"But of course, my dear. What else do you think can possibly happen?" Jabril smiled from where he stood at the Hammond map. "The president's confidence in you has grown steadily, as we planned. He has been most impressed with your planning, training, liaison work. . . ."

"I suppose I should be flattered," Garst laughed lightly. "The president is not normally a campaigner for women's rights."

"Well, dearest, he is now probably more than half in love with you," Jabril still smiled. "I would gamble a lot on that."

"You flatter me . . . much too much."

"Never enough, moon of my delight."

Garst shifted to seat herself more comfortably, and asked, "What will Okan have to say?"

"The usual. But we'll out-think, outnumber . . . and outwit him. He has no real option but to go along with whatever the president decides. And the president will decide what we want. Okan's bankruptcy makes him a hostage himself . . . to the president. Besides, time is running short for Okan, too. There are even more reports about than usual concerning a major assassination attempt. . . ."

"Yet another," Garst appeared to discount what Jabril had said.

"No, dearest Gigi. This could have big power backing. Very big power backing."

"Perhaps Okan will be more impressed than me."

"I don't know what he will think or do. The trouble with our Ugandan friend is that he is rash. . . ."

"And vain, headline-grabbing, cunning. A big poseur, ruthless . . ."

"No need for you to go on, beloved light," Jabril chuckled. "What you are saying is that he is our perfect tool."

"Of course, so he is," Garst continued. "And I am *your* devoted slave, foolishly obsessed with you. Madly in love."

"You are my light . . . my love," Jabril said evenly. "But now we have some work to do."

From a wooden bookcase behind an antique desk, he pulled out the Koran. After wetting his left thumb with his tongue, he flicked over pages until he got to that part of

51

the book which served as the agreed cipher between the Front and the president. While Jabril called out the code, Garst sat at a transceiver of the kind employed by regimental headquarters of the Red Army. She tapped out in coded Morse Jabril's promise to be at Maaten es Sarra on the appointed day.

Once that message was completed, Garst continued to tap out a few scraps of intelligence which had been received by the Front, items from the signals that had streamed from the Front's network over the Middle East, Africa and Europe. These coded reports had been picked up by the efficient aerial strung on the bungalow's roof.

Among the items transmitted by the girl was something probably known to the Libyan president: US Secretary of State Joseph Fackman would soon be on his travels to southern Africa.

Finally, Garst also signalled that she herself would be leaving for Tripoli almost immediately, to check on the Front's preparations in Athens en route, and also to satisfy herself about explosives being developed by Libya's Special Intelligence Service for use in the El Al hijack. After ending the transmission with a request that Commando Marighella be airlifted from Kufra Oasis to a safe house in the Tripoli suburb of Gargoura, Garst signed off.

Like Jabril, Garst revelled in codes and secret missions, so the whole exercise of tapping pips and squeaks through the ether had been another pleasure for her. Though she would never admit it, at the keyboard she felt she was a woman apart, a mover of fates and destinies.

"You have a heavy few days ahead of you, my dearest." Jabril knelt before her, rested his head gently on her thighs, stroking her lazily, almost absently, with his thumb. Under the Arab's practised hand, the girl gradually felt herself tingling.

At last, she needed more than Jabril was giving, so she rose from the canvas chair, unzipped her Levis, worked her panties loose, and settled down again, her thighs slightly splayed.

"The president has converted Okan to Islam. He'll convert him to you, too, you'll see."

Having said that, Jabril dropped his strikingly hooked nose between Garst's legs and flicked out his tongue.

52

The following day when Gabriella Garst was at Latakia international airport, the Russians Bevz and Yegerov left for Finland to start their journey to Chicago and their mission to murder Yazov. At the same time, the Bulgarian was still asleep in the room above Harvey Tyler's general store in Spencer, Iowa.

By now Yazov had neatly sawn off the barrel of the Franchi shotgun which he kept by his bed.

In Washington, Michael Tarrant was also asleep, but sleeping fitfully: he worried about Operation Brimstone, and he was unhappy about the men shortlisted for the attempt on Okan's life. The CIA's channels for ferrying the necessary arms into Kampala had also broken down temporarily, with the arrest and killing of a key courier in the Ugandan border town of Tororo.

Garst was at Latakia to make her final decision as to whether the Inter-Continental Airways 747 would be hijacked out of Athens or Rome. Both airports were strategically located, with Athens being marginally better in this respect. Latakia was still in Europe, but closer than Fiumicino to the Middle East, and the Greek airport served as a major access to the Orient and Australasia. And it was part of the plan to bring Commando Meinhof to Latakia or Fiumicino on a Singapore Airways flight from Hong Kong or Singapore.

What had also weighed with Garst and Jabril was the fact that in the past the Greek regimes had dealt relatively mildly with hijackers and other armed attackers.

So far, Garst was satisfied that security had only slightly improved at Latakia, in spite of a recent visit to the airport by inspectors of the International Air Transport Association.

The Greeks had installed glass screens and were using X-ray machines as well as metal detectors. But the authorities still did not adequately check the hand luggage of arriving transit passengers. As she walked through a checkpoint in the cream-coloured marble departure hall, her own bag was only cursorily inspected.

Garst had also seen that it was quite possible for visitors to reach the international transit lounge through the airport's restaurant kitchen, which did not appear to have any security control. And although she was not able to satisfy herself personally about another matter, she knew of reports that security checks were especially lax after midnight, and that floodlighting on the main tarmac was wanting.

Owing to the Front's plans for Latakia, what impressed her most were the poor controls imposed on airport staff, who meandered about at will. It would be simple for unauthorized persons to walk on to the tarmac from the airport's basement parking if they wanted to do so.

Naturally, this pleased Garst. Even if Commando Meinhof was not going to smuggle arms on to the ICA 747 through any of the checkpoints, the relatively relaxed stance on security at Latakia boded well for the actual means to be used. This means came in the form of a Front agent who had already infiltrated the airport's work force.

When Garst walked from the marbled terminal building into a sunny December's day and on to the airport bus, she was personally able to check that the agent was in place at the wheel of the blue bus.

In profile, he looked very much like the man whose small, four-inch-square photograph she had memorized. After he had turned to check on the passengers who were filling the bus, Garst was quite sure. And he looked ordinary enough, this man, the Front's agent, now working his third day shift.

He pressed a button, bringing the bus's engine to life. Meantime, as he shifted a gear, Garst had decided: it would be Athens, and not Rome. Making the decision, the girl experienced another fresh, exciting surge in her chest.

Later, on board the flight to Rome, she peered out of the window to see a runway heavily scarred with tire marks. She also saw an armoured car on patrol, something that must have only recently been decided upon at Latakia, since neither she nor Jabril had known of it previously.

Had she been able to, now that the Latakia choice had been made, the girl would have flown directly on to Tripoli. Instead, because she did not want to call any attention to herself, even by changing her booking, she flew to Rome. There she also studied the security layout and methods, though more out of an academic interest.

Once the Alitalia jetliner was high over the Tyrrhenian sea, its shadow skimming over paler patches in the deep, blue water as it headed almost due south to Tripoli, Garst found herself going through another, periodic bout of worry and uncertainty. The hollow feelings in the pit of her stomach were nothing new to her and had often alternated with the exhilaration which had brimmed through her chest during the previous weeks.

Later, west of Naples, she tried hard to concentrate on a small boat as it made a long, slow and curving turn in the blue water. The fishing smack trailed a white wake. Whatever concentration she managed to muster was broken by the Alitalia air hostess, who had trundled the coffee trolley to the rear of the jetliner, where Garst sat in a window seat. *"Caffè, signorina?"* the trim, attractive hostess had to repeat. "Thank you, yes," Garst replied, snapping the folding plastic table into place as she said it.

With her finger crooked through a white plastic cup, Garst was back with her thoughts, anxieties and plans.

The Front had plotted well, there was no gainsaying it. Commandos Marighella, Meinhof and Badawi were reaching their peaks of readiness. There was no shortage of money or materials. And the friendlier Arab governments were co-operating well, though no Arab state save Libya knew the details of the massive attacks. Weapons were even now being shipped across frontiers in Arab diplomatic bags, and another instance of Arab assistance was that she herself travelled on two Algerian passports, issued in the names of Leila Kamal and Julietta Bella.

What worried Garst was whether she had decided correctly in choosing to lead Commando Marighella. Theoretically, Commando Marighella would carry out the most complicated assault: the kidnappings of the US Secretary of State and others in Johannesburg, South Africa, and their subsequent removal to Jan Smuts airport, where the hostages would be forced aboard an aircraft to take them to Entebbe. Including herself, Commando Marighella comprised two squads of four, making it the largest assault group.

Should she not have elected to lead Commando Badawi? Badawi, named after the squalid, ramshackle Palestinian refugee camp outside Tripoli, Lebanon, would have the most difficult single assault: Badawi would hijack an El Al 707 out of Kastrup international airport, Copenhagen.

On account of the very stringent security measures the Israeli airline adopted, the Front had previously considered an attack on El Al to be too risky. Garst and Jabril had come up with a feasible scheme only after days of debate and discussion. But the plan called for the bravest, best squad leader. . . .

Were it not that the Marighella operation was split into several, perilous stages of ticklish negotiating, Garst would have led Commando Badawi. It was she who had christened Commando Badawi—Badawi being her birthplace—and Garst was tied closest emotionally to the El Al hijack . . . but the kidnapping of the US Secretary of State would be the most vital job. Once the most powerful nation in the West was held to ransom, everything would be on a grander scale: the sensation, publicity, demands, everything connected with the operation would be that much bigger.

So by the time she had finished her coffee, Garst was once again reassured that her decision to lead Marighella was tactically correct.

She wondered about the president of Libya. Would he overrule Okan and back Jabril, once and for all? If he did so, would he use enough tact not to outrage the capricious, stubborn Ugandan? It was too late to find an alternative haven to Entebbe, supposing such existed. Only Okan was sufficiently unstable and reckless to take on the US—and the condemnation of the world.

She wondered, too, whether Hassan Jabril truly loved her. He possessed her, mind and body. She took great risks, mostly out of her madness for him. All of this did not matter, provided he loved her in return. But Jabril's flowery, easy flattery made her uneasy.

Without warning, a jolt shuddered through the jetliner and told Garst that the landing gear was being lowered.

She watched arid land rush up to meet the aircraft. A dull roar swelled in the beautiful girl's ears. With her hand she brushed into place a strand of hair from the black wig she wore. The hair had strayed on to her forehead under

56

the jet of air which washed downward over her fresh, tanned face.

The Alitalia jetliner touched down on Tripoli airport's main runway with a hard bump. The roar in Garst's ears increased as the engines reversed their thrust. Later, the aircraft rolled towards the low, whitish airport buildings.

Forty-five minutes after that—once Garst was safe in Tripoli's Gourgoria suburb, being warmly welcomed back by members of Commando Marighella—a light-skinned Arab girl boarded Aeroflot flight 421 to Lagos, Nigeria. She was dressed in clothing which matched the white scarf, white blouse and light blue skirt worn by Garst. She also used a passport in the name of Leila Kamal. If anybody ever tried to make anything of the Alitalia and Aeroflot passenger lists, he would find that a certain Kamal had travelled from Rome to Lagos, after having waited briefly in transit at Tripoli. What made the switch-over as simple as all the others which had gone before was Garst's colouring: she could have passed as a national of any of the states which bordered on the southern shores of the Mediterranean.

6

On the day of the meeting at Maaten es Sarra, Bevz and Yegerov were in Paris, getting ready to board a flight to Chicago. Both Russians were finding Charles de Gaulle airport a little confusing, and they strained to stay alert for the airport announcements in French. Already Bevz had an annoying collection of useless small change in his pockets—Finnish markkaa, Swedish kronor and French francs.

Nobody could be blamed for not seeing any connection between Yazov, who was feeling low and out of sorts in Spencer, the Russians and the meeting at Maaten es Sarra. The place itself was as remote from Paris as it was from Spencer: no scheduled airline flies to Maaten es Sarra,

57

which lies deep in the extreme south-east of Libya, beyond the Rebiana Sand sea, close by Libya's borders with Chad, Sudan and Egypt. It is a tiny, scruffy way station, its attraction being drinkable water found sixty metres below the Saharan sand. Bedouin tribesmen occasionally visit Maaten es Sarra, as they wander along the unmarked track from Kufra Oasis. Libyan Army engineers have built a short, all-weather airstrip just south of where the track ends.

To this airstrip had come Obama Okan, who flew 1600 miles in an Israeli-made Westwind jet. The president, so Uganda Radio claimed, would be paying a surprise visit to Ugandan army units which were stationed along the northern border with Sudan, near Moyo, close by the Albert Nile. Instead, the jet had taken a hazardous, four-hour flight, skimming unannounced along the wild and lonely borders of Zaire, Sudan, Central African Republic and Chad.

Hassan Jabril got to Maaten es Sarra by a different route. He filed a false flight plan for his Lear executive jet. It permitted him to fly south over the Gulf of Aden, hug the coastline, move over the Straits of Bab El Mandeb, fly over northern Ethiopia, and then cross the Sudan north of Khartoum on to the false destination of Abu Simbel, on Lake Nasser in south Egypt. Jabril's aircraft disappeared off Khartoum radar a little east of the Nile's third cataract. It crossed into the vast nothingness of north-west Sudan, heading for Maaten es Sarra.

Okan arrived only six minutes ahead of Jabril. After landing, both small planes were parked off the runway, under tents supplied by the Libyan army.

Even in this tiny, desolate place, four heavily armed young men stood guard. Two of these guards lounged against the Lear, in the tent's shadow: Okan's guards sat in the Westwind, in the open doorway of the aircraft which had come as a gift from Israel, in happier times. Tiny rivulets of sweat drained over all their eyes. They could hear disjointed scraps of the hot exchanges between Arab and African from where they panted in the heat.

Okan and Jabril stood behind a long wooden table which was strewn with maps. Also on the table were gourds of tepid water, and both of them upended a gourd frequently, pouring water into tumblers from which they continually sipped.

Jabril had started confidently enough, reviewing all the proposed missions for Okan, giving the Ugandan new, impressive details. By taking the president into his confidence more deeply than ever, Jabril hoped to gain Okan's own trust.

Next, the Front's mastermind recalled for Okan all the successes of a ten-year career devoted to international hijackings, kidnappings, embassy raids, and other attacks. The purpose of this was to inspire still more confidence in Jabril as an experienced, practised organizer.

Having impressed Okan with his mastery, past and present, Jabril spoke bluntly of all the benefits that the Ugandan could expect. "Excellency, a ransom of $100,000,000 is not impossible."

Okan grunted, shook his head in slight disbelief.

"Believe it, excellency," Jabril nodded his head persuasively. "You can believe it. We got fifty million each for the release of the Saudi Arabian and Iranian oil ministers." Here Jabril underscored a spectacular Front success, that of kidnapping Arab oil ministers from OPEC headquarters in Vienna in 1975.

"And you will remember that the OPEC affair happened in December too," Jabril went on a little mysteriously, as if the month of the year was a good omen. Thus the Arab even attempted to play on Okan's superstitions.

"Of the one hundred million, excellency, I have agreed with the president of Libya that you will keep eighty million. Eighty million dollars," Jabril paused to let the extent of it sink in on Okan.

Thereafter, the Arab stressed that time was running out. Joseph Fackman, US Secretary of State, would very soon leave for Africa to help solve the racial conflict in Rhodesia. "He leaves this week, starting in Zambia, visiting Botswana, then Tanzania, before flying to Johannesburg. Disrupt the peace moves, and you prove that Uganda can fight the racist whites everywhere. That there can be no peace without Uganda, just as there can be no settlement with Israel without PLO. Uganda is with us in Palestine, we are with Uganda in Zimbabwe, Namibia, Azania." Jabril gave the Third World names for Rhodesia, South-West Africa and South Africa.

"I don't want the woman. She can go with one of the commandos, yes. But we must have men leading the assaults. And a man in overall command." The African spoke simply, levelly, anticipating Jabril's next submission.

After all Jabril's carefully argued groundwork, the Ugandan had annoyingly forestalled him and foredoomed his argument that Okan ought to accept the experienced mastermind's carefully considered appointment of Garst, especially as Okan would benefit generously, thanks to Jabril.

So Jabril tried another way, saying, "Garst is an excellent, intelligent, totally reliable lieutenant. Through her, I direct everything." Jabril paused to smile, then said, "With her I have a closeness. She has a loyalty. Men with their own ambitions may not serve as loyally as she will."

"Come, let us reason together." Okan was unconvinced. "What key men have you got? Definitely, there must be a few. . . ."

"I'm telling you, excellency, the president of Libya will be most disappointed in your attitude. He has the fullest confidence in Garst," Hassan Jabril could not resist saying.

Okan experienced a fleeting uncertainty. He could deal with Jabril. The president of Libya was another matter.

"And the president of Libya has been most generous to you in the past," Jabril was close to jibing when he said it. "I know he has invested many tens of millions in his great friendship with you."

Okan glared across the table at the Front leader. Had it not been for the high-pitched whine of a Libyan Air Force transport jet, the two men might have smashed an uneasy alliance and damaged their joint cause irreparably.

The interruption was timely, and instead of snapping at each other, the Arab and the African walked over to the edge of the tent's roof and watched a speck in the blue skies as it grew into a Fokker Friendship airliner. Painted on the aircraft's wings were rondel-and-palm tree insignia. After a slow circle of Maaten es Sarra, the Friendship landed on the blistering, concrete runway.

The Libyan leader was dressed in drab army fatigues.

By the time he got to the tent under which Okan and Jabril sheltered, he was sweating profusely. Garst walked alongside him, struggling ankle-deep through the hot sand.

"Jambo, my friend," the Libyan simultaneously startled and disheartened Okan with the traditional Swahili greeting. Obviously, the president was going out of his way to be charming.

"My great and wonderful friend," the Libyan continued in broken Swahili, "let us make sure your long, danger-filled journey does not go without reward." Okan found his right hand in the Libyan's, being pumped energetically.

The president of Libya only nodded cursorily to Jabril. However, the Ugandan noticed Garst and Jabril exchange a long, deep, exploratory stare.

Okan was hot and tired, regretful again of having to come to this tiny watering place in the middle of nowhere. He could handle them all, singly, even the Libyan. But when they were all together. . . .

"We must hurry, excellency," the Libyan spoke through an interpreter. "This very morning we intercepted news of Fackman's departure for Africa."

He took from his pocket a telex which he waved about. "Let us talk about our worries. Let Arabia talk to Africa. I already feel we are at destiny's crossroads, here at this humble meeting place of Maaten es Sarra."

Okan felt a trap spring shut.

"I have every confidence that the woman will bring great glory to us. She has every quality we desire. Now what are Africa's worries about her?"

The Ugandan's spirits sank still lower. Could he really tell them all about his seer, who, after poking through the entrails of a freshly killed white cock—a chicken from one of Okan's own runs to the rear of Command Post—had warned against . . . ?

7

At Maaten es Sarra, Obama Okan's opposition to Gabriella Garst was finally broken. The multiple operations would proceed under her overall command in the field, with the agreement of all.

In the days which immediately followed, the Front had much to do. Within twelve hours of the last jet's steep ascent off the desert landing strip by the Rebiana Sand sea in the Sahara, cables hummed between cities of east and west Europe, Africa, the Middle East and North America. The messages, all in code, were for the Front's agents in place, everywhere.

Typical of the cables moving to and fro across continents and seas was one despatched from the post office nearest the Gare St. Lazare, in Paris. It was sent off by a young man who had walked into the post office after taking a short stroll into Rue Tronchet from the Hotel Ambassador along Boulevard Haussmann. The cable read:

SHIPMENT ARRIVING ONE WEEK. PAYMENT WANTED IN FRANCS. CASH AGAINST DELIVERY.

Upon being teleprinted in Johannesburg, the telegram was promptly given to a black messenger in a faded khaki uniform who cycled from the main Jeppe Street post office building to the Yellow Panther boutique, which was only three street blocks away in Rissik Street. There he handed the cable to its addressee, a quiet, ordinary-looking shop assistant. She was, of course, part of the Front's increasingly sophisticated network.

Having signed for the telegram, the girl tore open the cellophane pane of the reddish envelope. As she read the contents, she froze briefly with excitement. What the cable told her was that men—Front men, no doubt—were coming for the contents of a strong steel trunk which she kept padlocked in the luggage bay of her wardrobe in the room where she lived in a tall building of cosmopolitan Hillbrow, a Johannesburg suburb.

Only recently had the last of the arms arrived—in bits and pieces—for stowing in the trunk. There was no denying that her mission had been perilous. Had anything gone wrong at any time she could have been arrested by the South African Security Police. Every shipment had carried a risk, with parts coming in over the months in the false bottoms of suitcases as unaccompanied hold baggage. Still other pieces had been imported under the cargo manifest of a fictitious company. Thanks to the vast goods traffic through the seaports of Cape Town and Durban, the chances of routine discovery were much against the authorities.

By the middle of November, the steel box brimmed with grenades, pistols, AMD assault rifles and ammunition.

The girl at the Yellow Panther regained her calm and disposed of the cable down the toilet in the boutique's ladies' room. She then gave some thought to booking her airline ticket out of South Africa. Her work was done.

Meantime, the black post-office messenger had returned to the Jeppe Street building. He was wheeling his cycle into a rear doorway at the same time as a blond young man filled in his own telegram at the cable counter. His cable was addressed to Herr Karl Stammler, who was staying at the Penta Hotel in Munich, West Germany. This cable read:

48, 59 OR 70 AVAILABLE DECEMBER. MOTHER IS WELL.

This meant that the US Consulate in Johannesburg wanted a booking for a cocktail party at the Carlton Hotel's Top-of-the-Carlton cocktail bar, on 21, 22 or 23 December. It was to be a celebration at which Secretary of State Fackman wished to honour local and national leaders of all races.

The cable writer had access to this information because he was employed by the Carlton, the largest, most luxurious hotel in the Southern Hemisphere. It was yet another proof of Hassan Jabril's foresight to gamble that if Fackman ever visited Johannesburg, the Carlton would be a venue for either his stay or an official function.

In his turn, the cable writer would receive instructions to examine, once more, all entrances and exits to the Top-of-the-Carlton. If the young man had any more news of security arrangements, he should pass these on. He was well placed to provide excellent information, for the Front's Carlton agent was employed in the catering department.

In fact, when he crossed the small square in front of the Carlton Hotel after returning from Jeppe Street, a manager of the hotel caught sight of him. No sooner had he emerged through the entrance's all-weather swing doors, than the manager said, "You're a little late, Kurt. We're getting to depend on you a lot over here."

"I suppose I stay a little too much at the language class," Kurt smiled.

There was no getting away from it, Kurt was a hard-working self-improver, and the manager wondered whether he approved of it or not.

"I see. Well, I have to say you try hard. Not too many newcomers bother to learn Afrikaans," the manager said. "Now I'd like you to look over the Top-of-the-Carlton. Catering arrangements are going to be switched because of the high-level American cocktail do. We'll close some entrances for security reasons, and we'll cut down on staff, too."

For the next three hours, Kurt worked hard on planning changes to catering arrangements at the Top-of-the-Carlton.

Meanwhile, across the road, at Kine Centre, the US Consulate's day-to-day work was disrupted, as hectic plans and preparations were made for Fackman's visit. An advance unit of the US Secret Service had already arrived, and the unit's first request was for a list of local subversives and virulent anti-Americans.

Fackman himself was setting out for Paris, from where he would fly to Lusaka, Zambia. It was Commando Marighella's mission to kidnap the US Secretary of State, and its members were already making their way to Johannesburg, travelling singly or in pairs.

The El Al 707 to be hijacked in Copenhagen was still

on the ground at Lod airport, Israel, where it was undergoing repairs. The commando which would attack it, Badawi, was assembling in Denmark.

Using perfectly forged passports, two members of Commando Meinhof arrived in Singapore. The couple behaved like any ordinary, honeymooning pair. The girl stood in water up to her thighs in the sparkling blue pool of the Shangri-La Hotel, sucking a cocktail through a plastic straw stuck in a freshly cut coconut. Her "husband" waved tiredly at her from the pool's side, then he walked down a wide, shady pavement, stopping with hands in his pockets to watch a game of tennis.

Far away, outside New York City, the pilot of the ill-fated Athens ICA Boeing 747 had worries on his mind far removed from hijacking. He had just been thrown out of his untidy flat by his wife, now a faded beauty queen, and she had told him not to come back. The ICA captain was in a sombre mood while he drove under heavy grey skies to John F. Kennedy airport.

In the bungalow overlooking Aden, the man under whose direction most of these comings, goings, frontier crossings and gatherings were proceeding, stood behind a pretty Arab girl. She was seated on the canvas chair, behind the Russian-made transceiver. Dressed in tight-fitting Levis, her pale blue shirt-ends knotted over her navel, she tapped a constant stream of Morse at half-hour intervals from the thick pile of coded messages which lay in front of her.

Jabril's orders were to use the transmitter only every half hour, on the half hour. He explained that he did not want to attract attention by heavily increasing traffic in radio messages. She might have to stay the whole night to get everything done.

And as Jabril stood behind her, his hands cupped over her breasts, which he gently kneaded, she was not going to argue.

Continents away from the bungalow in Aden, an aircraft was landing at O'Hare International airport. It was Air France Flight 031. Aboard the Boeing 747 were the Russians Bevz and Yegerov. Because of the faulty headphones, Bevz had not enjoyed the in-flight movie. And he resented the manner in which Yegerov could fall asleep,

65

whatever the time or circumstances—or the cramped seating.

The Boeing 747 made a bad, heavy landing, though a consolation was the way it shook Yegerov out of his slumbers.

8

As they had come to kill Yazov that very night, it was curious that both of these Russians were calm, almost nonchalant. Vladimir Yegerov had drunk a great deal of French wine and had fallen asleep, more or less mid-Atlantic, after saying with a burp, "Comrade, wake me up in Chicago." Leonid Bevz had hardly slept at all. He cursed the headphones and the fact that he was seated too close to the in-flight screen. He developed severe back and neck pains because of the cramped seating arrangements, and he was ill tempered, but not particularly worried about the killing in hand. After all, he and Yegerov were professionals. And it was not part of the job to get excited. Excitement got in the way.

Professionals are not concerned much with the whys and the wherefores, but both Bevz and Yegerov understood the KGB's policy on the Yazov business: the Bulgarian was, in the Russian idiom, a pig. The KGB had to destroy pigs, and thereby make it so risky to defect that all but the foolhardy would be deterred. It went without saying that the killing must not be linked to Moscow, so Bevz and Yegerov had better not be caught.

The two Russians cleared customs and immigration. Then Bevz waited in the vast arrival lounge at O'Hare while Yegerov walked to the men's toilet.

Fortunately, Yegerov found the second last cubicle at the north wall was free. He even urinated into the bowl. But promptly after zipping his fly, Yegerov hooked his right hand around the back of the toilet bowl. Under his gently searching fingertips, he found what he sought, a

66

rough obstruction: a car key was taped to the underside of the bowl.

Minutes later the two KGB men, carrying overnight bags and luggage bought in Paris, walked down to the underground car park.

They strode quickly to row K, their steps echoing dully in the narrow spaces between parked cars. It reassured them both to note how accurate the map which they had memorized in Moscow was.

Still more reassuring was the Oldsmobile Tornado which they found parked in row K, by the most southerly concrete column. All was going well, and though the key was still sticky with adhesive it made no difference to the car's lock. The right-hand door swung open under Bevz's hand.

All this time the Russians had walked and worked in silence.

Reaching under the right-hand floor mat, Bevz palmed a leather purse. He unzipped it to find a complete set of keys to the Oldsmobile.

While Yegerov took the keys to the Olds's boot, Bevz rummaged in the door's side pocket, finding a folder. As was to be expected, the folder contained the Hertz car rental contract, National Geographic maps of Illinois, Wisconsin and Iowa, a map of the forty-eight contiguous US states, a thousand dollars in cash, identity documents and forged driver's licences.

From where he sat in the front seat, Bevz felt a jolt as Yegerov yanked the boot open. After stowing away the luggage in the big recess, Yegerov banged the lid closed. When he got into the seat alongside Bevz, all he did was to nod: yes, inside the boot, packed away, were two sharp spades, lengths of rope, and a large, steel toolbox.

Yegerov had not looked inside the toolbox, but the contents included two strong torches, Colt .45s, a homing device, an M-54 automatic rifle, silencers for the .45s, and four hand grenades.

Immediately Yegerov nodded, Bevz retrieved the keys, worked the biggest key into the ignition and started the Olds's engine. If he was familiar with the American car's systems, this was not a coincidence either. Both he and

Yegerov had spent a few hours behind the wheel of a similar model Oldsmobile not ten days earlier.

In spite of it being his very first visit to Chicago, forty-five minutes after stepping off the Air France jetliner Bevz rounded the northern perimeter of the massive airport and drove unerringly, a little north of west, to Interstate 90.

He turned to glance at Yegerov. It annoyed him to see how Yegerov was composing himself, as if to nap again.

"Try and keep awake, comrade. I don't live here, you know. You watch the road signs, too."

"What the hell do you think I'm doing?" Yegerov snapped guiltily.

"There's a good comrade."

Still, Yegerov was all right, thought Bevz. Everything was fine, except the KGB colonels' plan for assassinating Yazov. The colonels wanted Yazov kidnapped, driven out of Spencer, then shot and buried. They had even given Bevz the burial place—in the soft earth beyond a forest track off Highway 18, near Ruthven.

A little unnecessary, unrealistic—and risky, Bevz and Yegerov had both agreed in Paris. After all, the Bulgarian was himself a notorious, dangerous killer. Neither of the Russians wanted to give him time to manoeuvre—time between the kidnapping and the killing, during which Yazov might do anything. Although it was unlikely that the Bulgarian could escape, provided the proper safeguards were taken, Bevz and Yegerov did not want to run any risk which was needless.

So they planned to kill him in his bed, where he slept. A surprise, quick, dirty shooting.

Back home in Moscow, they would explain to the KGB colonels that Yazov had resisted, and there was nothing for it but to . . .

Doing it their way, the Russians would give themselves only twelve hours to get out of the US, if they got Harvey Tyler, too. Both killings would be done this very Sunday evening—and at least twelve hours would elapse before anybody in Spencer wondered why the general store was still shut on Monday morning.

Twelve hours were enough. It would be an easy drive back from Spencer to O'Hare, and they would be safely aboard a flight to Canada before the killings were discovered.

Nonetheless, the assassins knew well enough that they could not openly disobey the KGB's directions. And the KGB would doubtless make routine checks through the Mid-West resident, who would surely inspect the grave. If there was no grave, albeit empty, their story would not stick; a grave would have to be dug, exactly where the KGB had ordered.

So Bevz had driven the route to Spencer via Madison, approaching Spencer from the east, through the lake country around Ruthven. The Olds swept past a "Welcome to Algona, we are proud to be Americans" sign. "Here's Algona, comrade," Yegerov proved that he was awake. "We're coming up to Ruthven. About thirty-five kilometres away."

Soon the Olds got to a couple of miles west of Ruthven, and Yegerov said, "Take the next turning to the right."

"You're really wide awake, eh? Sharp as the devil's tail," Bevz spoke in the Russian idiom.

"Okay, comrade. You never let up, do you? If you're not careful, you could needle me to death with that big mouth of yours."

As he turned on to a rough track, Bevz laughed.

The Olds bumped along, through a wooded area which fringed on the south finger of a small lake, and Yegerov called out, "Now swing left, comrade."

The Olds moved off the track, wheels bouncing.

"Stop here, comrade."

The Olds came to a halt.

About twenty metres from the car, the two Russians actually dug a grave. While Bevz held the torch, shielding it with his overcoat, Yegerov used the spade. The ground was soft and initially Yegerov worked easily, but it was not long before he leaned on the spade, expectantly. Bevz took over.

They even marked the place by hanging from a tree branch a small, battery-operated lamp over the hole. When Bevz took a black, flat plastic box out of his overcoat pocket and pressed a button, the lamp over the grave blinked a white light.

In order to make everything totally convincing, back in

the Olds Yegerov twisted the trip meter to read zero. If the KGB's resident took the trip meter reading, he would find that Bevz and Yegerov had done precisely as directed, and had worked the trip meter to measure the mileage from the burial spot to Tyler's store in Spencer.

So far nothing untoward had happened all the way from Moscow, through Finland, Sweden, France, Chicago to Iowa. But about ten kilometres from Spencer an oddity did befall the Russians.

As the Olds drove by a sedan parked on the side of Highway 18, the car flashed its lights, and someone blew its horn hard, long and disturbingly. The shrill sounds had hardly faded before a figure wearing a cream mackintosh materialized in the Olds's twin beams. Whoever was standing on the tarmac tried to wave the Olds down with a hand-held torch.

Bevz glimpsed a pale, wild face. Meanwhile Yegerov, who was now driving, accelerated the Olds, scuttling the apparition.

"What do you think, comrade?" It was Yegerov.

"I don't know."

"All I could do was drive on. Force him off the road."

"You did right."

"We don't want to be stopped."

"No."

"The police?"

"Could be anything. Breakdown. Didn't seem like the police."

"What about our side?"

"Could be us. Yes."

"On the other hand, a breakdown . . . ?"

"Or anything that we haven't thought of."

"Do we go in?"

Up ahead, the lights of Spencer showed clearly.

"We are here. Yes, we go in."

"That's what I say."

"Just look out for anything unusual."

"Like what?" Yegerov wanted to know.

"I don't know," Bevz shrugged.

The Olds crossed into Spencer via a bridge over the Little Sioux River. Almost immediately beyond the bridge, Yegerov drove on to Highway 71 and into Grand Avenue.

With a final twirl of his fingers, Bevz fixed a silencer firmly on to the Colt .45. There was a clear snapping sound as Bevz slid a bullet into the gun's barrel. Using his right hand, Yegerov reached for the gun primed by Bevz and slipped it into his overcoat pocket.

Now Bevz repeated the exercise with another Colt .45, arming himself, too.

The Olds crept along a cold, deserted Grand Avenue. Shortly before reaching Harvey Tyler's store, Yegerov doused the lights. The resident had done a good job in supplying the Olds, because when Yegerov applied the brakes there was no sound.

Yegerov switched off the ignition.

"Let's go, comrade," Bevz grunted.

Outside, in the open, they felt the cold on Grand Avenue, their hot breath trailing in the night air. Still, they were grateful for the near freezing temperatures, for the cold had driven all the residents of Spencer indoors. Along Grand Avenue there were a few lighted windows, but many of Spencer's citizens were already abed.

Bevz unlocked the door with two skeleton keys, items provided by the KGB's resident in Chicago. An agent had checked out the makes of the door locks after taking a special trip to Spencer.

A few soft clicks, and the door swung inwardly. Inside, a dim light glowed as the two men stepped off the board-walk.

Next, they had to deal with the dog.

How to handle the dog had been practised for hours in the KGB's unarmed combat gym on Belovitsky Street. Both KGB men were good at it, though Bevz had the best killing action. Accordingly, Yegerov prepared to offer his right forearm as bait.

The two Russians strained their ears to listen for the dog. They had listened in the semi-dark at Belovitsky Street, too, in the kind of dull light which Harvey Tyler let burn in the store.

A rushing sound came from the stairs. A soft growl. Pattering.

In the dim light, the dog was very quick. Boards creaked sharply the instant it sprang off the floor. The big animal sank its sharp teeth through the sleeve of Yegerov's overcoat, biting deeply into a thick leather pad wrapped around his forearm. Yegerov stood firmly planted on the floor, his chin tucked deeply into his neck.

Bevz did the killing. Already he had his right hand flat, raised to his right ear, thumb tucked against the bottom of his index finger. Now he slipped around Yegerov, his timing perfect, to snap down the flattened hand.

The joints in Bevz's elbow and right hip crackled crisply. The edge of the Russian's right hand was speeding at twenty metres per second when it whipped through the dog's thickish fur, depressing the flesh, impacting sharply on the bone.

For a split second the animal's vertebrae resisted the Russian's tough and tempered right hand. Then the bones splintered, and the pencil-thick cord in the dog's vertebral canal parted.

Yegerov went down with the charging animal, but only the Russian rose.

This all happened within ten seconds of Bevz unlocking the door. Also within moments the Russians ran silently across the floor, hardly making the floorboards creak. Bevz flattened himself against the wall at the foot of the stairs. He covered Yegerov, who rushed silently up the stairs on to the landing. Yegerov flattened himself against the landing wall, covering Bevz. He jerked an all-clear with his thumb.

This was twenty seconds after breaking into the store.

Bevz ran quietly up the stairs, taking them two or three at a time. He was halfway up the second set of stairs, those beyond the landing, when Harvey Tyler came around the corner, at the top, looking for his dog. Striker had taken off quickly and silently, without warning.

Bevz dug the Colt's sausage-like silencer painfully between Tyler's ribs and clamped his left hand over Tyler's mouth, stopping the sound in his throat.

Yegerov was already moving past them both, making for Yazov's door. It was slightly ajar, and Yegerov kicked it open, his Colt ready to spurt flame, knowing that Yazov had already moved out.

Obviously, it had been the resident's men who had flashed a warning, honked the horn, jumped into the highway outside Ruthven—to warn them that Yazov had bolted. He must have gone suddenly, probably only hours ahead of them.

Tyler would know where Yazov had gone.

The Russians exchanged glances, saying nothing. Bevz shifted the position of his hand, moving his thumb to a spot in Tyler's neck. The American's eyes went white with terror. Moments later he hung limply, in Bevz's grasp. Yegerov moved down the stairs into the store, walking quickly to the hardware section. He searched briefly, his eyes running over a pair of pliers, a clumsy blow-lamp, a small vice. They came to rest on a Miniflame kit.

Yegerov read the directions on the side of a slim, six-inch-square plastic box, and the legend, "Miniflames can reach 5,000°F." Moments later he pocketed the kit.

This was sixty-five seconds after entering Tyler's general store.

When they walked out of the front door together, tiny snowflakes had begun to drift down out of the dark. Yegerov opened the boot, then the right-hand door. While Bevz carried Harvey Tyler into the Olds, the other man dumped the dog into the boot.

Yegerov had a length of rope in his overcoat when he returned to lock the general store's front door. Then he climbed into the Olds's driving seat alongside Harvey Tyler, with Bevz seated behind the American, propping him up. Yegerov noted the trip meter reading, then he gripped the grooved boss between his left thumb and forefinger, clicking the tumblers back to zero.

Ninety-eight seconds after Bevz had swung open the front door to Tyler's store, the Olds was making a slow U-turn in Grand Avenue, starting a retrace of its route into Spencer. Tiny powdered snowflakes floated on to the windscreen. As the car moved faster, the light white powder was blown clear.

A few miles out of Spencer, Harvey Tyler regained consciousness. Slowly, he collected himself. The ticklish warmth on his neck, he realized, was the soft breathing of the man sitting behind him. Tyler was sitting on his hands, which were numb and tied together in some way. Every time the Olds braked slightly he felt something dig into the hollow of the back of his neck. He guessed that was the gun.

73

He knew he was going to die.

These men, whoever they were—probably Russians or Russian-hired—were taking him somewhere to make him talk, and right after that they would kill him.

These clear realizations made the man's heart hammer inside his chest.

He had already got through to the CIA about Yazov and had spoken to a man called Butterfly. The CIA would see to Yazov in New York, but there was nothing anybody could do for Tyler.

The Russians had not said a thing at any time. Really, there was nothing to say; when they were ready, they would ask what they wanted of him.

When the end came, Tyler hoped that it would be quick and sure.

Twenty minutes later, the American knew that oblivion was not going to be quick.

He rested with his head and shoulders on the front seat of the Olds. His hands were tied behind him. He lay across the two wide seats. Above him, both of his ankles were trapped through the right-hand door window, between the armoured glass and upper, metal window sill.

He had struggled, yelling as he struggled, but Tyler was no match for the burly killers. Though he had flailed his feet about, and they lost time in removing his shoes, they ultimately had his feet through the open window. Bevz had pressed the button and the top of the glass had risen, jamming the former CIA guard's ankles into place. When he tried to pull them back through the window, the bare skin had rubbed painfully against the window and the metal sill, but his feet were too large to be dragged back through the opening.

Thus the bare soles of Harvey Tyler's feet protruded into the night with its gently drifting flakes, and Tyler felt the cold.

From where he lay along the front seats of the Olds, Tyler could not see much of what was going on outside. Had he been given a clear view, the American would have seen that Yegerov was studying the directions contained in the Miniflame kit, while Bevz held the torch for Yegerov to read by.

The Russians could have asked their questions, of course, and listened to Tyler's responses. Given enough time, they could have extracted what information they required in a way that was relatively painless when compared with the use of the Miniflame kit. But there was no time to fence and parry with Tyler.

Possibly Tyler would have told them all of the truth, immediately. Since he was a former CIA agent, this did not seem likely, and the Russians did not want to waste time.

According to the instructions, the Miniflame kit was a small, hand-held device which worked off two small butane and oxygen cylinders. Each of these slim cylinders was only about four inches long and came with grooved knobs. Following the directions, Yegerov carefully twisted the knobs. Immediately the blow-pipe emitted a sharp hissing sound.

Though he could only guess what was happening outside—he had imagined that the Russians were going to beat the soles of his feet with a paddle or cane of some kind, a torture called *bastinado*—Harvey Tyler saw and heard the flame. It whooshed and exploded into four feet of fire.

Yegerov quickly worked the knobs with his fingers, and the long, gentle, yellow flame shortened into a fierce, blue fizzing incandescence.

Then Yegerov got to work.

In no time he burned the bare sole of Harvey Tyler's left foot with a flame intense enough to pierce a half-inch plate of mild steel. Under the fire, skin peeled off. It came away in tacky patches, flapping in a gust of whirling snow.

In between painful gasps, Harvey Tyler told all he knew of Yazov. During the brief interrogation Yegerov hovered with the Miniflame close by the old man's right foot.

Sometimes Bevz had to shout to get a reply. And at times, Tyler did not speak coherently, so that Bevz had to repeat a shout.

Only killers would be out near the lake on a bad, foul night like this, and Bevz could shout all he wanted.

Afterwards they tossed him in the hole, on top of the dog. And even then they took no chances, having tied his feet together.

The last of Tyler's consciousness was taken up by Bevz: a black, threatening, looming shape, silhouetted against the Olds's headlights.

And at last, it did come swiftly and certainly. Bevz pulled six times on the Colt's trigger. He was using heavy stuff. With every squeeze, the big gun bucked heavily in fingers locked in a two-handed grip over the butt.

Both Russians worked briskly to spade earth into the shallow grave. Not all the gravel would go into the hole, so the men had to spread the fresh earth. They covered the scars in the ground with a thin carpet of green, brown and rotting pine needles.

"If it snows hard, they won't find anything for weeks," Yegerov said.

"Weeks, maybe months, comrade," Bevz replied.

Soon they were back on Highway 18.

On their way back to the bridge over the Mississippi, this also being the Iowa/Illinois state line, Bevz and Yegerov took stock. It was Bevz who did most of the talking when they summed up.

"So, the Bulgarian is using a new model Chrysler."

"Chrysler Imperial," Yegerov added.

"Yes. He has sixteen hours' start, going to New York. If we drive hard, take turns, we could get there sooner, comrade. Not so?"

"Beat him . . . or cut the lead down to a few hours. Depends how hard he drives."

"Agreed. Very well, then. Tyler will be missed sometime tomorrow. Maybe the next day. Do you think the CIA will try to contact him in, say, the next twenty-four hours, Vladimir? I don't, I must tell you."

Bevz rarely used Yegerov's first name, and only when he was trying to persuade him to do something. Yegerov could see what was coming, but he said, "I agree. I don't think the CIA will contact Tyler that soon. Anyway, even if they did, they won't immediately suspect what's happened. A couple of days. At least that much will be lost."

"So far, good. Our cover is still intact, not so? We're still armed. We've got money. We could finish the job in another twenty-four hours and fly Aeroflot out of New York."

Yegerov was silent.

"The alternative, I suppose, is to take the British Airways flight out of Chicago as planned," Bevz said.

"I'm not sure we won't be blamed for not stopping when we were waved down by the resident's man."

"Precisely, Vladimir. You're getting the point. We could still see our arseholes over this business," Bevz used a crude Russian expression for getting the "chop," or losing their heads—and their jobs—figuratively speaking. "But if we complete the mission, what then, eh? A little success, and Comrades Bevz and Yegerov are heroes again. Big men."

"I suppose so," Yegerov admitted grudgingly.

"You suppose, Vladimir," Bevz warmed to it. "Suppose for a second we do a little wet work on the Bulgarian in the Taft, and we get back to Moscow, eh?" Bevz used the Russian idiom for a killing, the Taft being the hotel where they had learned from Tyler that Yazov was staying. "He is armed with a sawn-off shotgun, but what's that to us, Vladimir? We'll have surprise." The mechanics of assassinating Yazov at the Taft were not a problem to Yegerov. He and Bevz were trained to carry out assassinations, anywhere, any time—provided the risks were valid.

"The centre may not like it anyway, comrade. We're not strictly under orders to do anything but the business in Spencer," Yegerov said.

True, thought Bevz. Russian agents were told what to do, not to think for themselves.

"There's no time to clear it with the centre, Vladimir. The fact is that unless the Bulgarian is splashed in the next day or so, the centre may have to wait years. Once the CIA wake up to everything, our friend will be pulled into a safe place, indefinitely."

"That's so. No arguments."

"Exactly, Vladimir. Now we still have a chance at him. In New York, he is unprotected. We can do it."

"There are more risks. . . ."

"You know the risk factor is still good. Very good. It'll be the right decision. If we go back to Chicago, we could smell in Moscow. Failure smells. You know our people are not always reasonable. But if we pull it off, eh . . . ?"

"I've been studying this map while you've been doing

77

all the yapping, comrade. If we keep on Interstate ninety, bypassing Chicago, we'll get to New York fastest."

"You know, Vladimir, I could wring that thick neck of yours sometimes. I suppose you were for going to New York all the time, eh?"

"Your skull is not as thick as it often seems, comrade."

9

Bevz and Yegerov were driving as hard as they could, without stopping to sleep, all the way to New York.

Meanwhile, in Washington, the news of Yazov's departure from Spencer had angered Tarrant, who was having trouble with his own plans. Operation Brimstone took precedence over Yazov, but the CIA executive nevertheless found time to instruct Arnie Kruger.

"He's a menace, Arnie. Fix it. Soon as you can. I don't trust any of it. This could be the start of something. Redefection, something. Get it done."

Promptly thereafter Tarrant had got back to Brimstone. Had he but known it, Brimstone was more urgent than ever. But even the CIA had not yet learned of plastic explosives, made to look and smell identical to a famous brand of commercial toffee, that were being smuggled to Copenhagen in Arab diplomatic bags. The explosives were for use in a bomb to be constructed aboard the El Al Boeing which Commando Badawi was to hijack.

Three of Commando Marighella's team had already arrived in Johannesburg and were staying at the Carlton Hotel itself.

In Athens, a bus driver, the Front agent who would smuggle arms on to the airport apron for Commando Meinhof, had already stored his weapons in the attic of a small, modest house near Latakia airport.

The Front and Okan were closer than ever to launching their multiple outrages.

In New York, Yazov was unaware of how gravely he

78

had enraged Tarrant. He had thought of calling Kruger, to tell him that he was leaving Spencer. But he anticipated that the CIA would have told him to stay. In place of telling Kruger himself, Yazov had left it to Harvey Tyler, because he knew that the old man would call Langley as soon as he left, if not sooner.

The Bulgarian had decided that he would simply have to risk affronting the CIA. Surely it was not so hard to understand that he was hopelessly bored in Spencer?

He and Tyler had discussed where Yazov was going. The former CIA agent had been agitated, but had nonetheless offered some parting counsel: "If you want good advice, stay away from the Minnesota Strip. Keep away from the hookers, porn shops, and them massage places, too."

The Bulgarian had asked Tyler where to stay. Without hesitating, the other man had said, "The Taft, north of Times Square. All the theatres are right there. Suit your pocket, too."

That was why the Bulgarian had stopped first at the Taft. The hotel was too outdated for his taste, so he walked a block north to the Americana, where the prices sent him to the Hilton, and the tariff at the Hilton brought him back to the Taft. He booked into a room on the twentieth floor. It had a window which opened on to the rear of the hotel, with a murky courtyard far below. To Yazov's trained eye, the room looked safe enough, provided that he kept clear of the window.

Already the winter's daylight was fading as Yazov strolled the short distance to Times Square where he watched the news creep in big electronic letters along the side of a building. The news was that the outgoing secretary of state would in a couple of days be shuttling through eastern and southern Africa. Yellow, lighted letters marched electronically around a lowish, triangular-shaped building, spelling, "FACKMAN INITIATES SOUTHERN AFRICAN PEACE BID IN LAST DAYS OF OFFICE. PRESIDENT ELECT WISHES SECRETARY OF STATE WELL. . . ."

Yazov paused long enough in the square to read of the president elect's choices to head the state and defence departments, as well as the CIA.

By this time he was sufficiently hungry to want a meal.

79

He took it at a steakhouse off Times Square, ordering a bottle of Schlitz to wash down a thick, underdone T-bone and a fat potato baked in its jacket. Another Schlitz followed, and a third, and suddenly the Bulgarian was tired. It had been a hard ride from Spencer, and he had driven almost without stopping. Once he had catnapped for a few hours.

What he needed to do was to catch up on some sleep, so with that in mind he walked back slowly to the Taft. Yet again he caught himself worrying about not having called Arnie Kruger: the CIA very probably was not used to having defectors resettle themselves, and would be unhappy with his actions. Yazov made himself promise to call Kruger in the morning, at the latest.

Apart from making his apologies, he wanted a favour from Kruger. The Franchi shotgun was a good weapon, but he could not carry it with him, stashed in his overcoat, along the streets of Manhattan. Yazov required a small arm, preferably a Walther PPK, and Kruger could get it for him.

The more he thought about it, the more convinced he was that he ought to have called Kruger. After all, Kruger was his mainstay. . . .

Back in the Taft, Yazov took the lift to the twentieth floor, unlocked the door to his room and checked through it carefully. He found nothing untoward, except that the air-conditioning was malfunctioning. Whatever he did with the knobs, the room was too hot. Yazov thought of calling the management but decided against it. Rather than have the unit repaired, he reconsidered the risks of anybody climbing through the window; then he left it open.

The next thing he did was to pass an hour watching TV. He sat on the edge of the bed, clear of the window—and any shot aimed from a room on the other side of the courtyard.

Yazov watched the screen until he found himself yawning repeatedly. His body was ready for sleep, so he brushed his teeth, then switched off the TV set. From the wooden clothes closet he took out the sawn-off Franchi shotgun, breaking the weapon to check that it was loaded. He straightened the gun's barrels with a soft click and stowed it under the bed.

In spite of his intermittent yawns, Yazov could not drop off. Though his body craved rest by now, his mind was overactive, a variety of thoughts flitting through his brain.

Soon he was conscious of the room's heat—despite the open window—and it irritated him to hear the irregular crash of relays in the lift machine room, which was located not far from where he lay. Whenever a lift stopped, a relay crashed.

As more time passed, the irregular slamming of the relays worked badly on Yazov's nerves. Gradually he was conditioned to wait, silently, ears straining, for every grating crash.

Therefore he was very much awake, and his hearing was keenly primed, when he heard the handle to the door of his room squealing softly in its bearings.

It was what Yazov had been expecting, ever since he left the CIA's protection.

He knew exactly what to do.

He estimated that he had twenty or thirty seconds before the two locks were picked. Yazov took ten seconds to stuff two pillows under the blankets and smooth over the bedthings. He used the next ten seconds to retrieve the shotgun and pad quietly into the clothes closet.

Once inside the closet, he sat down carefully, resting his back against the wooden rear. It was pitch dark, and the closet smelled of stale mothballs. As Yazov moved his head he felt a jacket which was hanging in the closet brush against his temple.

The dull crashing of lift relays sounded through the closet's heavy wood. Somewhere water flushed, and pipes rattled.

Yazov cradled the Franchi. All he had to do was raise it slightly and he would have the rubber recoil guard against his right shoulder.

There was no sound of movement in the room, but the heavy wood blocked small sounds.

At last, the closet door opened, swinging very slowly on old brass hinges. Yazov dug the stock of the sawn-off shotgun into his shoulder. He knew the closet door was opening only because of a steadily changing shade of black ahead of his eyes.

A thin pencil of light shone from behind the door. Instantly, Yazov squeezed the trigger, plunging a firing pin into the rim of a Remington shotgun shell.

Fire erupted out of the Franchi's top barrel, singeing the trespasser's overcoat. A deafening roar battered Yazov's ear drums. The wood behind him cracked and split under the shotgun's heavy recoil.

The trespasser was illuminated for a fraction of a second by the Franchi's massive, bright, muzzle flash. Then pellets minced into him, and he was removed by the blast—uprooted from where he stood—and dumped across the room.

Yazov twisted out of the closet, nitrous fumes burning his throat, ears ringing. With the shotgun held in his hands, he wriggled over to the passage door on his elbows and knees, moving fast. No sooner had he reached the doorway than his hand was up to turn a key. He rounded the bed in the same, quick wriggle, stopping by the telephone. Still holding the gun, he managed to drag the telephone off the bedside table. Then he propped himself against the wall, ducking his head under the window sill.

When the telephone operator came on the line, Yazov put through a call to Washington.

"Good evening," the CIA man's voice crackled in Yazov's ear, and he repeated the series of digits which Yazov had given the Taft's operator.

"This is Crystal, Reassignments, Department 12."

"State your location."

"Room 2006, Taft Hotel, New York City."

"You using the Taft line?"

"Yes."

"Report your status."

"One hostile dead. I've got a twelve-bore Franchi covering the door. I'm under the window sill. Safe for now."

"You injured?"

"No."

"Okay. Wait in position. We'll call back soon. That suit you?"

"Yes."

"We'll have to clear things with the hotel civilians first. No sweat. We'll get you out safe. Understood?"

"Got it?"

"Any requests?"

82

"Call Butterfly."

"Will do. Wait quietly. Keep under control. Keep away from the window. Don't open the door to anyone, until we fix a code later."

"I think anybody else is scared off."

"Sit tight. We'll do the thinking."

"Yes."

"And, Crystal. You should be in Spencer, it says here."

A click in Yazov's ear, and the line went dead. The Bulgarian replaced the handset, set the phone down by his left leg, and reached for a box of Remington cartridges under the bed.

He wondered who the dead man was.

Had he stayed in the Americana Hotel, which is just north of the Taft along Seventh Avenue, Yazov could have walked over to Arnie Kruger's room. He would have found Kruger dressing impatiently in his plush, nineteenth-floor suite.

Kruger had just received an urgent call from Mike Tarrant—a call ordering him to a call box on Times Square, seven or eight short blocks south of the Americana, which would take him past the Taft.

Now that he was warmly dressed against the cold, Kruger checked that he had sufficient small change. It struck him that Mafia bosses and CIA field agents always kept small change handy. After switching off the room's lights, he pulled the door closed and then hurried out of the Americana.

Outside, tiny snowflakes melted on hitting the sidewalk and street, making Seventh Avenue glisten wetly.

As he walked by the Taft Kruger paused to stick his head around the lobby. Nothing unusual seemed to be happening.

Although the weather was cold and foul, the streets around the square bustled. Kruger reckoned himself lucky to find an empty call booth. As he dialled the numbers, coloured lights reflecting off the shiny, wet asphalt played on his white face.

He and Tarrant ran quickly through the preliminary identification talk.

"Sonofabitch, Butterfly," Tarrant got to the point

straightaway. "As if I'm not stuck with enough problems already. I give you something . . ."

"And it gets balled up," Arnie Kruger cut in. He had heard the sound of the explosion come over the small wristwatch of a transceiver that his man was carrying when Yazov had fired. Immediately, Kruger had known that something had gone very badly wrong.

"Screwed, Arnie. Screwed."

"I've got the picture, Mr. Tarrant."

"This may just cost you a big piece of your arse, Arnie. You wouldn't like that, would you?"

"No, sir. I wouldn't." Kruger spoke calmly, in a flat, unemotional tone.

"Damned right, you wouldn't."

"So what's he doing now?" Kruger ignored the remark.

"He's sitting with his back to the wall. A shotgun in his hands. Your man is dead, Arnie. Whoever he was, he got blown up."

"Like you said, Mr. Tarrant, assassination is an art. . . ."

"So I'm learning, more and more."

"Has he got it figured? I mean, where CIA comes out in all this?"

"Not sure. Don't think so."

"Then we take him now? He could be vulnerable."

There was a chuckle in Kruger's ear. "What I like about you, Arnie, is that you never give up. The man in you is willing, all right. I thought along those lines already."

"I'm listening, sir."

"You keep listening, Arnie. Listen for five minutes. Maybe we can save most of your arse."

Kruger held the handset close to his ear. His face was expressionless until near the end, when fleeting surprise showed on the otherwise impassive countenance.

"You're a genius, Mr. Tarrant," he said drily.

Tarrant spoke again. This time Kruger's handsome features clouded. He had even white teeth except for the single, gold left canine, and blue eyes under a mop of Kennedyesque hair. As Tarrant talked, the eyes narrowed unpleasantly.

"Thanks, Mr. Tarrant," he said in that flat, matter-of-fact way of his. "I'm touched by your concern with my

84

love life. I appreciate it very much." He could imagine the sly leer on Tarrant's round, pockmarked moonface.

The CIA agent replaced the handset, then he dialled another number. He got through to the Taft, and the receptionist connected him with Yazov's room.

"Crystal?"

"Yes."

"Butterfly." Kruger spoke with a soothing, throaty chuckle.

"Good to hear you, Butterfly."

"Okay. What's your situation?"

"Secure."

"No trace of any hostiles?"

"Nothing I can tell."

"Any civilians bothering you?"

"No."

"Okay. Sit tight. We're coming for you."

"Yes."

"I'm coming with two friends. You remember the panic code?" Kruger was talking about a code that he and Yazov had settled on for precisely this kind of emergency.

"I do."

"Okay. I'll have a medium-big Kevlar, too. Would you like that, Crystal?"

"I'd like a Walther PPK, too, Butterfly."

"Later, maybe. What shape is the hostile in? Have you examined him?" Kruger worried that the Bulgarian might have searched the body, picked up something.

"He's lying where he bounced. Very dead. You'll need a large, plastic bag."

"One large plastic carrier bag coming up," Kruger laughed out loud. "Be with you in ten minutes, Crystal."

"Get the code right, Butterfly."

"Don't make me nervous."

Kruger downed the handset for the last time. He stepped on to the pavement and under the light, powdery snowflakes.

In his room, Yazov propped himself against the wall more comfortably. He felt for the box of Remington 12-bore cartridges and lined up four on the fraying carpet, by his left thigh. Two other shells were clasped in his left hand, in case he had to break from behind the cover of the upturned bed.

It was now 10:03, and by this time Yegerov and Bevz were closing in. Having used the Verrazano Narrows bridge to cross from Staten Island into Brooklyn, they were moving on to Manhattan Bridge to get into Canal Street.

"We drive up Canal Street, comrade, on to Broadway, and turn right," Bevz had consulted the tourist map of New York upon which he had marked a broken trail, using a red felt pen. "Ride along until we get to Seventh Avenue, a one-way going south. Drop me close by the Taft. Find parking. We'll meet in the Taft's lobby."

"Yes, comrade."

"Yegerov and Bevz. Big men, you'll see."

The man at the Olds's wheel said nothing.

A compulsive checker, Bevz stuffed his left hand into the inside pocket of a dark, French-tailored suit to extract yet again his wallet, and all the cards: ID and social security cards, driver's licence, credit card, passport.

The next thing he did was to go over the Colt .45. To eject the magazine, he pressed a button high on the handle. Then he thumbed seven cartridges home and shoved the magazine back into the butt. After pulling back the slide, the Russian cocked the hammer to line the topmost cartridge with the breech block. Finally, he released the slide, allowing the Colt's recoil spring to drive the big bullet into the chamber.

Each operation was accompanied by the well-oiled, efficient sounds which Bevz had heard countless times.

The gun was ready. What of the plan?

The plan had been worked out in detail during the nonstop drive from Spencer. To keep going, each man had taken his turn at the wheel, while the other had napped uncomfortably in the rear seat. Sometimes, when they were both awake, they had listened to the radio. Otherwise they thought and talked about killing Yazov.

Despite the hazards, both were confident. Provided that they surprised the Bulgarian, the risks were tolerable.

Yazov would either be in his room—or not. If he was

not in the room, he would be somewhere in the Taft—or not.

To find out whether or not Yazov was in the Taft, supposing his room was empty, Yegerov suggested pageing him, calling Yazov to the nearest lobby phone. Then Yegerov would cross over, a newspaper hiding his Colt, to gun the Bulgarian where he stood. Bevz would cover his escape.

"I hate being paged," Bevz had squashed this idea. "He could be suspicious. Probably nobody knows he's at the Taft, except Tyler. Pageing will put him on guard."

Instead of pageing Yazov, they would ambush him from the room closest to his. If they were lucky, they might even be able to hire the adjoining room.

Having decided on this method, the Russians worked on the details for over an hour before they were satisfied.

But what would they do if Yazov was in his room? This was the likeliest of the alternatives: Yazov would be in bed—asleep or awake—with the Franchi in easy reach.

How would they do *that* killing?

"Then we do it with grenades," Bevz proposed. "We get them in through the door, or through a window. We trick him to open the door, or we break it down."

The Russians considered all the variables until they were satisfied with the details of this plan, too.

"The devil take you if you forget the grenades," Bevz warned Yegerov, trying to check Yegerov's part in the business, too, as the Olds approached the drop-off point near the Taft.

"I'm not that stupid, comrade." Nonetheless, Yegerov carefully removed two grenades from the right-hand side pocket. They were US Army grenades, and he slowed the Olds down to drop a grenade into each overcoat pocket.

Bevz glanced at a thick, gold Rolex: it was precisely 10:13 p.m.

"Drop me here. I'll walk the rest."

"See you soon, comrade."

"Don't forget the gun, either."

"I won't, papa."

Bevz walked in through the Taft's Seventh Avenue entrance. In the lobby, he looked to his right and saw a public bar. Ahead of him were the lifts, and a stall where theatre and tourist bookings could be made.

No sign of Yazov anywhere.

The Russian briefly explored each of the public restaurants and bars. Returning to the lobby, he walked up to a long reception desk. Bevz asked the duty girl for John Hardacre's room number.

Her immediate reaction—the manner in which she flustered—was a warning.

"No matter," Bevz said quickly, backing away.

Something was up. All he wanted now was to get out of the Taft. Turning on his heel, Bevz strode towards the doorway through which he had entered.

It was 10:24 when Yazov, Kruger, and a CIA bodyguard reached the lobby level in their lift.

"If anybody shoots you, don't duck. I'm right behind," Kruger cracked, as the lift doors slid open.

"I won't."

"It's exactly twenty-seven paces to the doorway. The car is an unmarked Chevy. Don't flip if the back door opens as you approach. Just get in."

"Okay. I've got it."

Yazov was halfway through the lobby, walking by a thin crowd of hotel guests.

Bevz had seen him as soon as the lift doors had opened.

Bevz glanced at the Rolex. It all depended on how quickly Yegerov had managed to find parking.

Already he was clicking like a computer, so well had he been trained. What he saw was the geometry of an assassination: angles, distances, strategic positions. If it was going to work, the geometry would have to be right.

He dared not look back into the reception area. All he could do was walk casually, not even break his stride or turn to watch Yazov again. He hoped the girl was not going to react.

During the time that Bevz had walked into the Taft and checked out the public bars and dining rooms, Yegerov had parked the Olds a few short blocks away, north of the Taft. He had got into Seventh Avenue, a block north of the Taft, when he noticed an unmarked car. Its headlights were doused, but somebody was sitting on the brake, and the rear of the car was a blaze of red.

An unmarked car, double-parked outside a target hotel—these were signs Yegerov was programmed to recognize as possible snags.

Very probably, it meant nothing. A hundred unmarked, double-parked cars outside the Taft could have nothing to do with Yazov inside. But provided that he could play it safely, he ought to. For one of the many possibilities was that Yazov could be about to leave.

So as he neared the Taft, from the opposite side of Seventh Avenue, he watched the entrance closely. Thus he saw Bevz as soon as he emerged from the Taft. And Bevz saw him.

Without hesitating in his stride, Bevz walked to the south corner, alerting Yegerov all the more.

Yegerov also saw Yazov the instant he stepped beyond the Taft's swinging doors on to the sidewalk.

Yegerov was already crossing Seventh Avenue, dodging cars easily, unhurriedly.

It was Yazov, all right: Yegerov had studied the KGB's photographs long and often enough. And the lightly falling snow did nothing to obscure Yegerov's fine view of the Taft's main entrance.

It was only seven, maybe eight, paces to the unmarked Chevy.

He was well armed, his victim was only paces away— and he had surprise. He also knew that Bevz was preparing to cover his escape.

Could anything be more simple?

Yegerov reckoned he could get in one, probably two, shots.

He had only two seconds before Yazov would duck into the Chevy, the windows of which were probably bulletproofed.

Two seconds was all the time in the world.

Yegerov got to the left-hand side of the Chevy. The right-hand back door opened. Yazov was five paces away, over the roof of the Chevy.

Yegerov had timed it so beautifully that he got to the car without arousing anybody's suspicion. He was just a man crossing Seventh Avenue to get to the Taft.

Yazov only saw him when Yegerov had the silenced Colt .45 up, shoulder high, over the Chevy's roof. Nobody else had seen it yet—not Kruger, nor the bodyguard, nor the man in the Chevy.

As he looked straight at his attacker Yazov's face twitched involuntarily.

Then Yegerov fired. His gun sounded like a dry cough.

Simultaneously, Bevz banged five shots up into the drifting snow and black sky. He was standing at the corner of Fiftieth Street and Seventh Avenue. The big, booming sounds of the 250 grain Kleanbores scattered people in fear and confusion.

Yegerov's bullet hit Yazov high in the chest, the classic, killing shot for the heart. The slug was stopped by the Kevlar, a bullet-proof vest of thick, fibre-glass cloth.

After going for the bigger, easier target of Yazov's chest, Yegerov tried to snap in a brain shot. But his first had bounced Yazov off his feet, making the second whizz harmlessly between Kruger and the target. The bullet finished high up on the Taft's glass door, shattering it.

Everything happened all at once.

Yegerov started running. Bevz was already sprinting for corners, changing direction.

Yegerov rushed north, along Seventh Avenue, along with others who had been scattered by Bevz's bullets.

It was a testing time for Kruger's reflexes. Between Bevz's first and second shots, Kruger had reached for his own firearm. The CIA agent's hands were a blur of movement. And he had a lot of experience on moving-target ranges.

From where Yegerov's bullet had knocked him on the pavement, Yazov watched Kruger's smooth, professional performance.

Kruger froze for a fraction of a second. His feet were spread apart, his knees were bent. The Walther PPK was gripped with both hands—the shooting hand clasped in the supporting hand, in the double-action style.

What Yazov could not see was how Arnie Kruger's guts were knotted, and how hard blood was pounding in his skull.

Kruger fired with the Russian running hard, fifteen paces ahead.

Yegerov wanted to sprint up West Fifty-Second Street, by the Americana. Kruger's slug crashed into the back of his right shoulder, knocking him down. The Russian slid three paces along the slippery pavement. In an instant he had the slide under control, and he rolled into the doorway of a busy restaurant.

The people in the restaurant, who were heading for the doorway after hearing Bevz's gunfire, rushed back into the dining area, overturning tables.

Yegerov's right shoulder hurt badly. He knew there was little time left. A week previously, he had been in Moscow. Now he was bleeding, tucked away in the entrance of a restaurant that sold fast foods and snacks off Seventh Avenue, Manhattan Island.

The whole thing was unreal, as unreal as killing Harvey Tyler, or the editor in Kabul.

Escape was impossible.

Unless they took him dead, he would talk . . . because everybody talked sooner or later. If he died without talking, he could still be a big man in Russia. Not that being a big man would help him any longer, but it would assist the family.

Yegerov placed the Colt gently on his lap, felt in his pockets for the US Army grenades. After searching both pockets, he could find only a single grenade. He looked up and saw the other blue-green oval sphere of indented metal lying close to the curb, where it had rolled free.

"Grenade! He's got a grenade!" Yegerov heard a shout. From inside the restaurant came the sound of more tables being toppled, of people cramming as far away from the entrance as possible.

First he would burn all his identity documents. He made a neat pile of shredded pages from his passport, threw in the plastic credit card, and even tore up a few dollar bills. He used a Ronson gas lighter to get the flames going.

He heard the sound of a siren. It was a warning to get on with it. The KGB hated to see any of its agents taken alive, and in particular it was against orders for anybody from Department V to be captured. Department V did not exist, said the KGB.

When he was sure that the documents were burnt out, Yegerov used his feet to scatter the black ash. Then he leaned against the side of the doorway and reached for the M-26 grenade. He pulled the safety pin.

"Don't be crazy! We can work something!" Yegerov heard but did not know Arnie Kruger.

Allowing the safety lever to spring in the palm of his hand, the Russian tucked the grenade under his chin.

Taking no chances at all, Kruger retreated behind the Chevy, into which Yazov had already been dragged. Just as he peeped above the level of the right-hand door window, a great orange incandescence billowed from the doorway, and a huge boom sounded.

Kruger's eyes were too slow to record the collapse of the restaurant's doorway. Nor could he follow the path of a round, dark ball, spinning against a screen of snowflakes: Yegerov's head bounced on to the opposite curb of Seventh Avenue.

Very shortly thereafter, Yazov was on the floor of the Chevy as the car sped down Seventh Avenue, cutting wide swathes in traffic that had already been cleared.

Arnie Kruger was one of the two men who lay on top of Yazov—for extra protection.

10

Yegerov committed suicide, but Leonid Bevz escaped easily enough.

Bevz had all the confidence of his training, from which he had emerged well able to elude pursuers in a busy place like Manhattan. The many buildings, streets and side-streets all gave excellent cover.

After dropping both grenades at the corner where he fired his covering shots, Bevz had ducked about, on the run. He made half-a-dozen turns, walked briskly in and out of a couple of buildings, then hailed a taxi. He was already safe when he made the first change-about, for nobody had reacted in time.

Prior to booking into a hotel for the night, Bevz got rid

of the gun. After wrapping it up in that evening's *New York Post,* all he did was drop the weapon, casually, into a dustbin on one of the pavements.

His identity papers were forged, but superficially in order, and he had enough money, so a stay in one of the hotels presented no problem. He spent the night at the Summit, on East Fifty-Second Street.

How to get back to Moscow was also simple, and Bevz had no need to contact anyone to do it. He would use Aeroflot. Besides being the biggest airline in the world, the Russian carrier is also used as a KGB agent's best means of quick escape. Aeroflot captains are under KGB orders to bring home any escaping spy.

If the emergency warrants it, an Aeroflot captain can take off as soon as he can clear it with the airport control tower, and he is authorized to abandon other passengers at the terminal.

Bevz had it in mind to take the regular Aeroflot flight out of John F. Kennedy airport to Moscow. The only hitch lay in the timing: flight SU 316 would leave JFK at 17:00. This meant that the Russian would have to keep out of harm's way for the next morning and most of the afternoon, before taking a cab out of Manhattan.

Bevz managed it without any trouble. After checking out of the Summit, he lingered over a four-course breakfast—and also read *The New York Times* report on the happenings outside the Taft. He had already picked up the news of Yegerov on TV the previous night, so it did not come as a shock to read about it.

Although the news story mentioned Bevz's escape, it appeared that the authorities had no adequate description of him. He assumed that the receptionist at the Taft would have given them something to go on, but all that she could have accurately described was the colour and style of his overcoat. Consequently, after completing his breakfast, Bevz tried on a new overcoat at a men's outfitters. He left the old overcoat in a locker at Grand Central Station.

For the rest of the day the Russian kept to the big department stores, browsed in a bookshop, took a long time over a late lunch—or walked purposefully through the streets.

At 15:30 he took a cab to JFK.

He was so relaxed when he approached the Aeroflot girl, who was checking passengers on to SU 316, that he was sure any watcher would not suspect him. The girl was good, too. When he gave the passwords she never batted an eyelid. Without any fuss at all, Bevz was issued with a ticket and boarding card.

Once the IL-62 was safely in the air, Bevz got the captain to transmit a brief, coded report to KGB headquarters.

Thereafter he slumped across a full row of empty seats and tried to sleep. He got little rest, and instead anxieties gnawed at him, all the way to Moscow.

Flight SU 316 landed at Sheremetyevo airport, at 09:25, local time.

The airport was bleak and cold. As the aeroplane taxied towards the buildings, Bevz watched the dozens of blue, white and red Aeroflot planes that were parked in the slipways. Through the gloom, he caught sight of a banner hung on a huge, modernistic structure. Unless he was mistaken in the bad light, the flapping banner proclaimed:

Welcome to the Soviet Union, the world's founding Communist State. Forward to final victory over Capitalism.

A KGB man was waiting to take him straight to Dzerzhinsky Square. If anything, Bevz's worries worsened, and the ride to KGB headquarters was his most uncomfortable in ten years with the Russian spy service.

Inside the KGB building he had his papers perused twice, painstakingly. Tired and worn as he was, Bevz stood patiently, stoically. He knew very well that any resistance, any argument, would prolong the inspection—or provoke his arrest.

Ultimately he got to the Department V debriefing room. Bevz knocked on the door, his stomach knotting.

"Come in," someone called from behind the door.

Bevz walked in, stepped up to the desk, saluted smartly and said, "Leonid Bevz, Department V, special agent, sir. Reporting from New York, as ordered."

The lieutenant-colonel got up from his desk, walked around it, shook his hand with a friendly smile. "Yes,

94

Comrade Bevz. We know all about it. No need to look so worried. These things happen."

Instant relief flooded through Bevz: his worst fears were unfounded.

"We're glad to see you back."

"Thank you, sir."

"Well, then, why not sit down? Did you have a good journey, comrade?"

"Very tiring, sir."

"Yes, I know. Those big engines are too noisy, for the rear passengers especially. I hope you got some sleep."

"Thank you, I did, sir." It did not amaze Bevz to learn that the lieutenant-colonel had known even where he had been seated.

"We've had a full report from New York. Of course, you'll file another. Even fuller, I'm sure. But overall, our view here, provisionally, is that you had a lot of bad luck." The KGB officer sipped lemon tea and offered Bevz some.

"Yes, bad luck. A few hours this way or that, and all would have been fine. Anyway, Comrade Yegerov's sacrifice will not go unrewarded. His family will not suffer. In fact, they will be grateful. A brave thing he did, don't you think, Comrade Bevz?"

"Indeed, sir."

"Yes, we all think so. Anyway, let's hear your story."

Bevz spoke for twenty-five minutes. Occasionally, the lieutenant-colonel stopped him, asking Bevz for more details or to clarify something he had said.

"All right," he told Bevz after his verbal report was done. "Now get all that on paper. And then get some rest. Plenty of it."

"Thank you, sir," said Bevz.

"We've got new orders for you."

"Sir?"

"You'll need new papers, that kind of thing. In fact, I have them already." The lieutenant-colonel tapped a set of documents, bound with a tightly stretched rubber band.

"Very good, sir."

"We want you to go to Kampala, Uganda. You've heard of the place, I take it?"

"Indeed, sir."

"We have something on our opposition trying to assassinate Okan. Nothing absolutely definite, comrade. You know, Okan is very well guarded. And our opposite numbers are not supposed to be in the assassination business at all, these days."

"I know, sir."

"Who would you use, if you could, to kill Okan? I mean, supposing you were the CIA?"

"Yazov?"

"There you have it, Comrade Bevz. Not impossible that they'd consider Yazov. Anyway, Okan has himself asked us, the Komitet, to make a fresh assessment of his own security arrangements. In case you've not noticed, relations have recently warmed between the Soviet Union and Uganda. In fact, for reasons you need not know, at this moment it is vitally important to keep Okan alive. And I can't think of a better man for the job than you."

"I'm flattered, comrade colonel."

"I'm sure you are, comrade. You know, I don't want you to fly away thinking that you did a wonderful job in America."

Bevz was unsmiling.

"We've been more than fair to you, Comrade Bevz. I'm sure you can now see why."

"I see perfectly, sir."

"Very well. Your orders are to proceed to Kampala as soon as possible. Within a day or two at the latest. You will report to the directorate of our Special Section in the Kampala embassy. Your primary mission is to protect Okan. You'll study his security precautions. I'm sure you'll think of improvements. Perhaps you'll run into Yazov."

"I see no problem, sir."

"You know, set a killer . . . to catch a killer. So to speak."

"Naturally, comrade colonel."

"I'll want you here tomorrow, Comrade Bevz. To discuss your mission in much more detail. Meantime, get your report in."

"Yes, sir."

"Dammit, comrade. Your tea's gone quite cold. Do you

mind if I don't ask for another? I've got a pressing time today."

"Of course not, comrade colonel." Bevz got up and turned for the door.

11

During the time that Bevz got away, Yazov was taken to a safe house in Greenwich Village. While Bevz slept in a room at the Summit Hotel, Yazov was on his way to the 250-acre estate at Brushy Hill, Maryland, where he had previously stayed safely, the place of his many debriefing sessions.

He and Arnie Kruger flew there from LaGuardia airport, in a CIA executive jet. Arnie Kruger was elated. Following Tarrant's instructions, and using some of his own arguments, he had persuaded Yazov by the time they reached the CIA's airport outside Langley. Kruger's had been a good act, compounded as it had been of apparent sincerity, sympathy, and plain common sense. And now Tarrant had his assassin for Brimstone.

Not that it had been all that difficult to bring Yazov around. He had been overwhelmingly bored at Spencer, and the prospect of another year or two in a safe house was also very unappealing. Yet he was in obvious danger, having had two attempts made on his life so soon after quitting the CIA's protection. He needed help to stay alive.

"You need us, we need you," Kruger had summed up. The case officer had skilfully hinted that the CIA would overlook Yazov's indiscretion in leaving Spencer without permission, on condition that the Bulgarian volunteered to help Tarrant. "Mike Tarrant's in a jam. I know he'd appreciate a little help," Kruger had said.

"What kind?" Yazov had asked.

"Oh, hell, pal. You know what I mean," Kruger had smiled engagingly. "Your kind of thing. I'm sure you've got the drift. I don't want to be crude and spell it all out. . . ."

"Who is it going to be?"

"I don't know, I really don't." Kruger had known in that moment that he had won. "But you'll find out soon enough."

Not once had Kruger applied any obvious pressure on the Bulgarian, and he never referred to how he had got Yazov out of the Taft and saved his life.

In the morning, the subtle game continued. Kruger and Yazov breakfasted alone. But promptly after finishing the meal, Yazov was shepherded by Kruger into a large, semi-darkened room of the big mansion.

Tarrant rose from a chair to shake his hand warmly. "It's really great you're working with us on a big project. Glad they never got you. The sons of bitches. But they got Tyler." This was all he said before motioning Yazov into a seat.

Yazov was still settling down when an image flashed on to the makeshift screen in front of him. Obama Okan's round, black and smiling face illuminated the white surface. It was a face well known to Yazov, who instantly realized everything. His bullet would remove Okan, enabling a few insiders in Uganda to take over.

The next slide was another image of the Ugandan president. He was third in a chorus line of dancing ministers and military officers. Looking jovial and something of a clown, Okan had his left leg up in the air, in the middle of a high-stepping dance.

"Don't let all that soft-shuffling fool you. Our assessment is that he is quite sane, totally shrewd, and he knows exactly what he's doing. Also he has survived thirteen attempted assassinations."

Another click brought a fresh slide flashing on to the screen. "That's Okan with Zagorin, Soviet ambassador. Taken at a State House ceremony when Zagorin handed over his credentials. Okan called the Soviet Union Africa's best friend and saviour. Incidentally, the move has caused anti-US feeling. Okan's press is full of charges about the CIA launching invasions, preparing for a coup, even killing Okan."

"No kidding?" Arnie Kruger made them chuckle.

Tarrant's next picture was a composite photograph of four young women, each of whom had a number plate tied about her neck. "What we're really worried about, though, is a massive terrorist attack. A pending assault on US, European and Israeli targets. It's all starting to tie in."

"Who are they, Mr. Tarrant?" Kruger asked.

"I was just coming to that. They're West German terrorists who recently escaped from a maximum security prison. Glad to say the girl on the far right was cornered in a Bonn car park. She pulled a gun and wounded a cop, but she's back inside. The others are all on the loose. It's this kind of information that's been steadily accumulating."

"And you think Okan is about to help?" Kruger asked.

"No doubt. When it's all in, the conclusion hits you over the head. And intelligence just keeps flowing. As of this moment we've got untriangulated reports of a meeting deep in Sahara between the heads of Libya, Uganda and the Refusal Front." Tarrant meant to convey that the reports had not come from separate, independent sources. "A fact is that all of them disappeared for up to twenty-four hours very recently."

"What's the latest?" Yazov asked more out of curiosity than anything else. The possible attacks did not stir him morally, one way or the other.

"Lots of suspicious movements. A team of trainees from Libya has vanished in Bagdad. Hassan Jabril, the Front boss, has holed himself up in his Aden hideaway, doubled the number of guards. Okan's guard has been increased, too. The underground is alive with rumours. Of course, we can't check everything. . . ."

In fact Tarrant did not know just how close the Front was to launching its triple assault. Almost all the members of Garst's eight-man Commando Marighella had arrived in Johannesburg. Garst herself was even then reclining in a chair on the roof-top swimming-pool deck. As she ate a hotel snack she satisfied herself that it was possible for a Westland Wasp helicopter to land on the pool deck.

Two of the four-man Meinhof squad had that very morning flown into Latakia airport in Athens, aboard a Singapore Airlines 747. The man had waited by the baggage rack for their luggage, while fifteen paces away the

99

girl had studied the National Tourist Organization of Greece's signboard to find out what accommodation was available for tourists who arrived without bookings. She decided to spend two days on Milos, before returning to Athens. If flights off Milos were cancelled for any reason, she and the man could take a short boat ride to the mainland.

And in Copenhagen a member of Commando Badawi had gone to one of the Arab embassies to collect the plastique—an explosive mixture of hexogen, trinitramine, TNT, and wax, all disguised as a slab of toffee. He was told to come again. With three days in hand, he could afford the delay.

Tarrant was pressed for time, more than he would ever know.

Watching the screen, Yazov saw a detailed aerial photograph of a small city. It was Kampala, he guessed correctly. Already inside Uganda would be a few CIA logistics experts, who were smuggling arms from a base just inside the borders of a friendly, neighbouring country.

"Now let's see what we're up against." Tarrant had Yazov's attention again. "Most of the time Okan is surrounded by special security men. Screens of guards in three roughly concentric circles. Almost all are drawn from the State Research Bureau, PLO Palestinians, Nubian mercenaries, or blood relations from Okan's Kakwa tribe."

Tarrant clicked the button in his hand. "By the way, that was Kampala you just saw. From the air. We'll come back to it. But here's Okan's Mercedes."

The image of the president's black 350 SE flashed on to the screen.

"The car's bullet proof. And what you don't see is the reinforced steel floor. It could probably survive a mine blast. Okan prefers the Mercedes to his helicopter. Reckons that a chopper is too vulnerable up in the air. It can get shot down, you see. What he hasn't reckoned on is his Mercedes being *shot up*." Tarrant emphasized the last two words.

"I get his point," Yazov was suddenly more interested, now that Tarrant was talking about ways and means of assassination. "A helicopter you can put down from a

100

dozen different ground stations, at any one time. A car is different. . . ."

"Take the reverse," Tarrant interrupted. "What if we're in the helicopter? Down below we've got Okan's Mercedes covered."

"A helicopter? Where would we get . . ."

". . . a damned chopper anyway? But what about a high building, with you under cover? Armed with an anti-tank missile. And Okan's Mercedes passing within a thousand metres?"

Yazov was silent as Tarrant changed frames again.

"Kampala, Uganda," Tarrant intoned. "Same photograph, but this time we've got some street and building names. And the map on the right is based on the photograph. The points marked A, B and C mark a regular route Okan is stuck with whenever he has to travel by road from Command Post to State House or Entebbe airport. Is it all starting to make sense?"

For both Yazov and Kruger, it was.

"Maximum chance of success. Take point C. That's where the main road takes a sharp, 120° hairpin bend. And naturally, whenever Okan travels the road, that danger spot is guarded by a dozen SRBs, packing AK-47s. No possibility of getting near. . . ."

"But Okan's car has to slow down at the bend. Just enough for me to fire an anti-tank missile. I'm up on a building somewhere."

"Exactly. Before that time, the Mercedes is travelling much too fast. The catch is that there's time for only one shot, between two buildings. For a while the Mercedes is hidden, it emerges into view for maybe fifteen seconds, then it's behind another building again. So there's a lot of pressure on the man making the shot. We don't want anyone on that roof, shaking. . . ."

"I think I know what Mr. Tarrant means," Arnie Kruger spoke, ending a long silence.

"Yes. Think you do, Arnie. We don't want anybody up there who's liable to choke on the shot. That's why I hoped so hard this feller here would oblige us. . . ."

"Where's the building?" Yazov offered no comment.

"That's marked D. The International Hotel, the only

101

liveable place in Kampala. Where you'll be staying, along with Kruger."

"You mean he comes, too?"

"Sure he does. He goes along and gets to warn you when the Mercedes gets near the bend. That way, when you break cover on the International's roof, you'll be exposed for minimum time."

"Say, nobody asked . . ." Arnie Kruger said complainingly. He was very convincing.

"That's the great thing about it, Arnie. You, I don't have to ask. Of course, we have a feller in Command Post who'll signal when Okan is ready to leave. The trip to the bend takes about ten minutes, on average. Bad average, though. Can be as low as six minutes thirty-six, and as much as twelve minutes ten. We can only have you exposed on the roof for twenty, maybe thirty seconds. Anything more than that, we're looking at a disaster."

"How do we go in?" Kruger asked.

"You'll go in as East African Airways technicians. We'll have a 737 grounded at Entebbe airport, courtesy of the Kenyans. Okan is still threatening them with a whole lot of things, including grabbing huge areas of Kenya's north-west."

"It could work. And what about getting out?"

"It'll work. Don't worry. And escape, why, that's the easiest thing of all." Tarrant turned in his chair to smile at Yazov in the semi-dark. "It's all set up. Now let's get down to details."

Tarrant used the afternoon to familiarize Yazov with his weapons. For that purpose he took the Bulgarian and Kruger to a heavily wooded area about twenty miles north-west of Williamsburg, past the Colonial National Historic Park. It was less than an hour's ride away from Brushy Hill in the CIA's Bell 212 general-purpose helicopter.

When he was in the Bulgarian MGB, Yazov had known it as the Farm—480 acres of ranges for training agents to use weapons, cross borders, sabotage factories, and lay ambushes. As the helicopter approached the area, he caught sight of a high fence which he knew to be chain-linked, mounted with barbed wire and patrolled by guards who used rifles, dogs and walkie-talkies.

The helicopter settled down on the pad, close to a waiting jeep. With a military policeman at the wheel, the small party rode to a wooden T-framed building.

The weapons were inside, displayed upon a long table; a CIA weapons expert already stood at attention. When Tarrant came in he broke into a warm smile of recognition, and the two men shook hands vigorously. Tarrant introduced Yazov and Kruger, and the men all gathered around the long table.

"Soviet AT-3 missile. AT stands for anti-tank. Also known as Sagger missile or PUR-64." The weapons expert began a short lecture by pointing to a stubby, compact flying bomb with small wings mounted at the extreme rear.

"The rifle is a Soviet Dragunov, used by snipers. Self-loading, fires a 7.6-mm rimmed cartridge," he described the other weapon. Yazov nodded, because he was familiar with the Dragunov and could have told them that it used a four-power scope and a ten-round magazine.

Having seen Yazov nod, Tarrant asked, "Have you ever used a Dragunov?" And after the Bulgarian nodded in reply, the CIA man grinned broadly. "Well, that's great," he said. "And I promise you, feller. Once you've sighted this little gun, we'll get the very thing into Kampala for you."

Tarrant turned to the weapons specialist, saying, "Chuck, don't worry about the Dragunov details. We'll save more time by working on the missile. . . ." There was a short pause before Tarrant's expression changed slightly, and he addressed Yazov again, asking, "Say, have you ever fired any of these Saggers?"

"I've fired the older, AT-2." The AT-2 was Sagger's precursor.

"No kidding?" Tarrant's eyes narrowed slightly. "Then why didn't you tell us in any of your interrogations?"

"I'm sure I did. I told them I underwent weapons training."

"The Dragunov I know about. That's in your record. I don't recall any mention of training on an AT-2. . . ." Tarrant's eyes misted over very briefly, then he suddenly brightened. "Anyway, it's good news. They sure as hell train you fellers, don't they?"

Yazov shrugged.

"Okay, Chuck. Over to you. This is not going to be the sweat I once imagined. The weapons familiarization, I mean."

"Yes, sir, Mr. Tarrant. The AT-2 and AT-3 are closely related." The weapons expert looked up at Yazov, a quizzical, unsure look on his face.

"Hey, Crystal." Arnie Kruger wrapped an arm around Yazov's shoulder, trying to rescue them all from a curiously uncomfortable moment. "It's like you've committed some kind of crime, knowing about this anti-tank missile stuff. Well, I'm glad about it. Very happy for us all."

"So are we," Tarrant smiled thinly at Kruger. "So are we, Arnie."

It was the weapons expert's cue to carry on with his discourse. "The Sagger is much like the AT-2. Both are wire-guided and carry hollow-charge explosives. Much the same explosive power. The missile is also controlled by electrical signals along the trailing wires. Same kind of control box, similar to that used by radio-control model aeroplane fliers. The major differences are in the size, Sagger is more compact. And the AT-2 uses an infra-red terminal guidance system that is unlike . . ."

Later, out on the open weapons range, Yazov fired four Saggers from ground level, putting the last two into a couple of junked M-62 tanks. If the first of the missiles had flown a little wildly, by the time the fourth exploded into the tank, the weapons specialist was saying, "That's pretty good. You'll know from the past, Mr. Tarrant, this kind of thing takes getting used to. And some skill."

"Don't I know it, Chuck?" Both men laughed as they recalled their frustrations of the previous ten days, and the poor weapons performances of some of the men previously tried out for Operation Brimstone.

Next, Yazov mounted a gantry which rose up toward the sky to the precise height of the International Hotel's twenty storeys. The gantry creaked in a chilly wind, and shortly after a World War Two B-26 passed overhead to lay a pattern of bombs over the next hill—practising for yet another CIA mission—the gantry swayed with the concussion of the explosions.

"It'll be easier in Kampala, Arnie. On the roof. No swaying," Tarrant told Arnie Kruger.

"Any problem getting the missiles?" Kruger asked.

"We're using stuff taken by the Israelis in the 'seventy-three war. No problem there. And we've got good logistics to Kampala. The usual kind of network."

Tarrant signalled with his right hand, and an old, second-hand Dodge moved toward the hairpin bend painted in whitewash over the cold, dying turf. The Dodge was driven by remote controls which programmed it to go around the bend at fifteen to twenty miles an hour, the speed the CIA had estimated for Okan's Mercedes. And the distance from where Yazov stood on the gantry to the painted marks on the turf was almost exactly the distance from where he would be standing on the International's roof to the bend in the Kampala road.

As the Dodge came out of the painted bend it blew apart with a thumping whoosh, under Yazov's direct hit.

"What a gift!" Tarrant exclaimed. "That's the third car the sonofabitch has taken out in a row!"

From far below the gantry, Kruger enthusiastically signalled Yazov by clasping his hands high above his head. In the target area firemen doused the flames, and somebody used a breakdown truck to fish the Dodge's burnt-out hulk from the site.

"Okay, Arnie. You're on next," said Tarrant.

In Kampala, Kruger would have a part in the killing, too. He would warn Yazov of the black Mercedes's approach to the bend, which was otherwise screened off by two tall buildings. The warning would give Yazov time to break cover, set up the missile, and stand briefly as he sighted through the gap between buildings on to the hairpin.

The plan called for Arnie Kruger to signal Yazov once Okan's Mercedes reached a point marked X on the briefing map—the same point was identified by a tall tree on the road in Kampala. Okan's Mercedes normally approached the bend at about fifty to sixty miles an hour, before slowing down sharply. The X mark on the map—or tree on the road—was 270 yards from the turning, so that Yazov would have at least ten seconds to act from the time of Kruger's bleeping signal.

Kruger pressed the button to a small, plastic-encased radio transmitter. Up on the gantry, the pips sounded in the tiny receiver the Bulgarian had plugged in his ear.

Galvanized into action, Yazov locked a missile case into position, resting the tubular guides on marks filed into the gantry's steel railing.

A broken-down, black Mercedes moved around the whitewashed hairpin. Fourteen seconds passed between Kruger's signals and the sound of the target Mercedes exploding in sheets of flame and chunky metal fragments.

"So simple, eh, Arnie? Those hollow-charge warheads are really something. I'm starting to think it's going to work."

"You reckon, Mr. Tarrant? I thought that was the whole idea, to get it to work." Kruger used his flat, matter-of-fact voice.

Another two smashed test cars and Tarrant was satisfied—even happy. While the last of the destroyed sedans smoked and burned, Tarrant motioned delightedly to the Bulgarian that his practice with the missiles was completed. We are bringing you down, his hands told Yazov.

Almost as soon as his hands were back at Tarrant's side the mobile gantry's huge pipes started to telescope, one into the other, steadily, section after section.

"What a talent, Arnie. You have to say it."

"He's a good man, Mr. Tarrant."

The other man swung his head sharply round to observe Arnie Kruger closely. Tarrant paused before speaking. "You know he's still got to go, don't you, Arnie?"

"Yes, sir, I do."

"Good, for a moment I thought you were . . ."

". . . Having doubts? No, sir, I don't. I do what I'm told."

"He should never have left Spencer, Arnie. Makes him unreliable. When that happened, all the old suspicions came back. Don't mind telling you, I near panicked. Thought he was going back to the Russians, setting us up for something. . . ."

"I understand, Mr. Tarrant."

106

"In the longer run this sonofabitch is unpredictable, un-controllable. He could become a big danger."

"You're convinced he won't settle down?"

"Absolutely. This guy will go his own way, do his own thing. Can't be trusted. He never ever told us about training with that AT-2 missile. I went through his record with a fine comb. I was specifically looking for any training on missiles."

"You never found it?"

"He never told us, Arnie. He's been lying about some things, I'm sure of it. He could easily turn on you, me, CIA. Any time. He's capable. I'd not be a bit surprised if he suddenly turned a Sagger on us from the top of that gantry."

Kruger looked up at the gantry and saw the Bulgarian's dark, lonely figure framed against a grey sky.

"You do what you like with him. Only make sure he doesn't get back from Kampala. Want a tip? Put a bullet in his back straight after he takes care of Okan. That way you won't take chances."

"I'll work something out, Mr. Tarrant."

The last of the gantry's sections finally hissed into silence. Yazov swung a leg over the steel rail and clambered down a short ladder. Tarrant rushed to meet him, clasped the Bulgarian's hand and pumped it rapidly.

"What a talent, what a gift," Tarrant bubbled happily. "And when this is all over, it's going to be wasted. All we can do is give you a big bundle of dollars, then it's over to you. Take a tip from me. Get out of the States. Get lost in Latin America. And don't tell anybody, not even us. Especially not me, eh?"

The three men stood stamping their feet on the cold earth, laughing.

"Come on. Let's get something hot down our throats. Then you'll sight the Dragunov. There's not much left after that. A little homework, another briefing on your getaways."

During the last part of the afternoon, in the rapidly shrinking daylight, Yazov sighted the Dragunov. He did it from the gantry, and he fired 53 shells before he was satisfied.

As he fired his rounds in quick succession, the last two magazines emptied fast.

"The Office of Logistics will get it into the hotel room," Tarrant told him. "In between carting office equipment and household furniture for all of us, Logistics gets to do this kind of thing."

"That'll be fine." Yazov felt he had to say something.

The Dragunov was insurance against a special contingency arising: it was not impossible for Okan to survive the missile warhead's blast, even if that was very unlikely. Should that happen, either Okan would try to get out of the Mercedes, or the guards stationed at the bend would struggle to free him. The sniper's rifle was for them. "Besides, a hail of accurate fire into the bend will help stir things even more," Tarrant explained. "You know. You see men dropping all over the place. More panic."

They would use Russian-made arms, and Yazov would leave them behind on the International's roof "to afford a plausible denial." "Hell, nobody's going to believe it, anyway. But that's going to be a lot better than finding US Army gear."

Back at the Brushy Hill retreat there was more homework on Kampala, more details on the planned assassination—and the latest intelligence from the CIA's Ugandan network.

The roaring log fire had burned itself down to bright red, glowing embers, and Kruger was about to put on the last of the logs when Tarrant indicated that the final discussions were done. "You get some good sleep," Tarrant yawned. "I want you on a flight out of Washington tomorrow. I'm turning in now." A check on his wrist-watch told him it was past midnight. Tarrant got up, stretched, and walked out of the room.

It was Arnie Kruger who suggested that he and Yazov use the mansion's sauna bath. The Bulgarian thought that was a good idea, and he and Kruger still had things to talk about.

Later, they lay on bunks in the hot, airless sauna room, towels thrown loosely over their hips.

A lot depended on how much chaos would follow the assassination, and Yazov was worried about Tarrant's somewhat makeshift arrangements for their escape. The

Bulgarian's anxieties had been noticed by Kruger, and he had decided to reassure Yazov at the first opportunity he got when they were alone.

"Hey, I'm not supposed to tell you all this. Things I got from Mike Tarrant while you were swaying up there on that gantry," Kruger began.

"What things?"

Kruger hesitated deliberately before replying. He just lay quietly in the heat. Then, when he thought he had paused long enough, he said, "Dumb thing you did, leaving Spencer like that. Very dumb."

"I upset Mr. Tarrant?"

"Very much. He didn't like it one bit."

"He doesn't trust me?"

"Not exactly. Let's say, he doesn't want you to know everything. He's not telling, if you don't need to know."

"So why are you telling?"

"Me, I think you need to know some things. I figure you're worried about how we're going to make it out of Kampala, after the shooting's over."

"You see a lot. . . ."

"I'm your angel, remember. I get to hold your hand," Kruger chuckled. "I get paid to know these things. Anyway, there's going to be much more chaos than you think."

"Enough to make it easy to get away?"

"Five or six detachments of shocktroops going for strategic points enough? They'll hit the airport, radio, power stations. They don't even know they're going to do it yet. It'll be normal after Okan's killing to go for the strong points and hold them. They'll just be following our man's orders."

"And he is . . . ?"

"That you don't need to know. But he's been cultivated and recruited over six months. He's confident—provided we take Okan out," Kruger said. "What's more, we're going to have a secret radio station going. It'll sound like they're broadcasting from inside Uganda, even though we'll be beaming the stuff in from across the border. On short wave. All the rural people have short-wave sets. If our man runs into opposition in taking over Radio Uganda, our service will broadcast on a frequency right next to Radio Uganda—sort of snuggle up and confuse the listeners that they're listening to an official broadcast."

"Sounds good." From the way he said it, Yazov was impressed.

"They've even got tapes of a guy mimicking Okan. You'd never tell the difference. All kinds of fake orders. If you want a covering disorder to get out, you've got it."

There was no reply from Yazov.

"Satisfied?" Kruger wanted to know.

"Sounds good, Butterfly."

Kruger heard sounds of the other man climbing off the sauna bunk. Yazov's towel had slipped off his hips, and he held it in his hand. He stood naked, sweating. "Hey, man," Arnie shook his head approvingly, "that's what I really call well hung."

Yazov stared at him with a blank look on his face.

"Okay, skip it. I'll tell you another time."

They left the sauna, and as Yazov got under the cold shower, Kruger barged in with him. "Isn't this great!" the CIA man shrieked as the icy water pounded on to them, making both men gasp. When Kruger came too close, the Bulgarian gave way.

Later, Kruger offered to help towel down Yazov, but the latter declined.

"What you really need now is a body massage, up on the table," Kruger nodded at the long, low bench used by the masseur when he was in residence. "Anybody willing to try?" He gave a lopsided, speculative grin.

"It's long past midnight, Arnie," Yazov brushed the mock-serious proposition aside. If he was aware of how much Kruger was attracted to him, he made no show of it at all. "We've got a long trip ahead."

"Whenever you need that sonofabitch masseur, he's never around," Kruger said with a trace of viciousness. Then the CIA man's features, which had contorted for a fraction of a second, returned to calm. "I guess you're right. It's going to be a long haul. Let's both turn in."

They would soon be taking a Pan American aeroplane from Washington to Accra, Ghana, where they would wait in transit to take the earliest available flight to Entebbe.

12

From Accra, the two CIA men boarded an Ethiopian Airlines Boeing 707 for the 2,500-mile trip to Entebbe, stopping over briefly at Lagos, Nigeria. The flight then continued over Cameroon, the south-western corner of the Central African Republic and both the Congos, before they reached the swampy areas north-west of Lake Victoria.

The Ethiopian Airlines jetliner was scheduled to land at Entebbe shortly after 1 p.m., local time.

Within six hours of this landing, assuming all went according to plan, the Refusal Front would have struck in Johannesburg, in an El Al aircraft between Copenhagen and Tel Aviv, and aboard ICA Flight 881 out of Athens. To ensure maximum surprise, all the assaults were to be executed between 1800 and 1900 hours, East Africa Time. The Front's plan also called for all the hijacked aircraft and hostages to be at Entebbe airport by 1200 hours on the following day.

None of this was known to Yazov and Kruger. If they kept to their own schedule, Obama Okan would be dead within forty-eight hours of their own arrival at Entebbe. In fact, the sooner the assassination was done the better. The longer they remained at the International in Kampala, the greater was the danger of their detection and arrest. Kruger hoped to have everything done inside twenty-four hours, and that included sodomizing and killing Yazov.

Provided that the mood was congenial, he wanted to go about his seduction that very night: once Okan had been killed, he would probably barely have time to dispatch the Bulgarian.

Thus far his persistent, cautious wooing of Yazov had not got anywhere. Both during the hop over the Atlantic and after the Ethiopian Airways Boeing had lifted off from Lagos airport, Kruger had snuggled his head against

111

Yazov's shoulder, pretending to doze off. From time to time, Yazov had reacted by pulling his shoulder free. Unabashed, whenever he could, Kruger tugged at the Bulgarian's sleeve, gently squeezed his upper arm, or brushed against him while he engaged Yazov in soft and intimate conversation.

Now, as the Boeing 707 steadily lost height during its approach to Entebbe, Kruger again felt Yazov shove his head clear of the Bulgarian's shoulder and pretended to wake with a start.

As the aircraft dipped into the final approach to the airport's north–south runway, Kruger gathered together a few personal items, such as a pen he had been using for the crossword puzzle in the *International Herald Tribune* and the Ethiopian Airways in-flight magazine. The maps in the magazine could be useful, and nobody would query them when he passed through customs or immigration. But the copy of *Time* magazine he slipped under his seat: Kruger was not prepared to risk any trouble from the tough immigration people with whom he would soon be dealing. And the Ugandan authorities were likely to be even more prickly, for Kruger had learned from the last of the CIA's reports, which had reached them in Lagos, that Okan's troops had intensified security operations. Fresh roadblocks straddled Uganda's major roads and street searches were common in Kampala.

As the Ethiopian Airlines jetliner bumped on to Entebbe's main runway, the TU-154 which had carried Leonid Bevz to that same airport prepared to take off.

Kruger gave the Russian aircraft no more than a passing glance, but Yazov turned his head to watch the blue and white Aeroflot jet with a Russian flag painted on its tail. It accelerated down the runway, whistling into an ever increasing pitch. Then the TU-154 burst into the air with a huge roar which reverberated over the hot, muggy, flat spaces of Entebbe airport.

The presence of the Russian jet reminded Yazov very forcibly that he was on dangerous, hostile ground. As Okan's assassin he was a thousand times unwelcome: a miscalculation, a bad break—and he was dead.

Few passengers stopped over at Entebbe, and it took the CIA assassination team only fifteen minutes to reach the top of the queue of disembarking travellers. A Ugandan immigration officer sat at a wooden desk, under a big portrait of a smiling Obama Okan. It was hardly a degree north of the equator, so the black official sweated profusely through a damp, tired-looking white shirt. He wore white shorts, his woollen socks were pulled up to within an inch of his knees, and dark glasses hid his eyes.

"Iko wapi passaporti?" he asked, speaking Swahili.

"Sorry?" It was Kruger who responded.

"Jina lako nani?" The black man wanted to know Kruger's name.

"I don't get that. I'm American. United States citizen."

"Unatoka wapi?" Now the immigration officer wanted to know where Kruger had come from.

"Sorry, pal. I don't get you at all. I only speak English. English, okay?" Kruger talked quietly, patiently.

"I see, yes. You come to Uganda, but you only speak English. Your passport, please."

Kruger handed over the document in its green plastic cover.

"Where were you born?"

"June 6, 1939."

"I said where. I didn't say when."

"Dallas, Texas." These two details, along with a recitation of Kruger's physical characteristics, and the photograph, were the only true pieces of information contained in the passport.

"Where have you come from?"

"Accra, Ghana. In transit in Lagos, Nigeria."

"Yes, naturally. But where, before that?"

"Seattle, Washington State, United States."

"What is your business here?"

"My buddy and I are here to do special repairs on that aircraft." Kruger turned his head, jerking a finger at an East African Airways Boeing 727 which was parked on the tarmac, just visible from where the immigration man sat.

"We are both mechanics with Boeing, flying an emergency repair service for EAA," Kruger finished what he was saying.

"What kind of repairs?" asked the black man.

"Trouble with the hydraulic system. Not enough pressure. Nobody here knows why."

"I see. Yes."

The Ugandan flicked through Kruger's false passport. He stared for several seconds at the photograph. Then he ran his eyes over the stamps on some of the pages. Whether he could read or not was not clear to Kruger. Probably he could not, for the CIA's intelligence was that many of the Ugandans who manned immigration control points were illiterate.

Finally, the official looked up again at Kruger. He nodded his head, wiped his hand over his unsmiling lips, then he slapped the plastic outer cover of the passport against the table with an impatient snap of his wrist. "You wait here. Just wait here," he said ominously. "I have to clear this matter with security. Only a formality."

After getting up from the wooden chair, he sauntered across the room and stopped alongside a concrete pillar about twenty paces away. It was then that Kruger noticed the man leaning against the support, half hidden. He wore a gaudy, flowered shirt, he had dark glasses wrapped about his eyes, and he was dressed in bell-bottomed trousers.

Undoubtedly a member of the State Research Bureau, Arnie Kruger thought with well-disguised alarm. Were they on to him and Yazov? Had everything gone wrong so soon?

There were other ways of getting into Uganda, and suddenly Kruger regretted very much that he and Yazov had not taken another route. They could have slipped across Lake Victoria from the friendlier shores of Rwanda, Burundi, Tanzania or Kenya. CIA agents had often enough in the past landed on the shores of target countries, using a high-powered Johnson or Mercury outboard on a rubber boat. He and Yazov could have hidden the boat in a pre-dug hole along a deserted beach, or in the luxuriant tropical growth which overhung parts of the lake. And Kruger could have taken the boat when he got out later.

Kruger felt the tension in Yazov, who stood right behind him. He placed a comforting, restraining hand on the Bulgarian's wrist. The Bulgarian shook his wrist free, lightly.

114

A drop of sweat trickled down the ridge of Arnie Kruger's spine. He could feel it roll into the elastic top of his underpants. Then another started down his skin. . . .

If the Ugandans were on to them, Kruger estimated that their prospects of escape from the airport were very poor. Trying not to attract any attention, he looked casually about the big room. There were more armed black men present than travellers. Even supposing he and Yazov were able to dash out of the building, what then? They would simply be cut down outside, in the boiling sun.

Another moment and the black man with the colourful shirt, upon which were silk-screened large green and brown palm trees, stood alongside Kruger. The immigration officer sat down on the wooden chair, on top of a torn, irregular piece of foam rubber which served as a cushion.

"Good afternoon, gentlemen. How do you do?" The SRB officer began, very quietly and politely. Without waiting for a reply, he thumbed a yellow plastic card from the pocket of his shirt. "Special security," he announced, holding up the identity card. It had a photograph in the corner, but unless the SRB man removed his dark glasses, neither Kruger nor Yazov would be able to check whether the photograph matched the likeness of its bearer.

"Sorry about the checks, gentlemen. I'm sure it's nothing. And I don't want you to have a bad experience. But President Obama Okan is highly anxious about spies infiltrating our country. Just a few formalities. It will soon be over. I hope you don't mind. I'm sure you understand these things. . . ." The excessive politeness carried with it a peculiar menace.

"No problem, Mr. . . . er . . . ?"

"Sorry. I do apologize. I am Major Wakholi, State Research Bureau. You know the State Research Bureau . . . ?"

"We do, major."

"Very good. Then we understand everything, not so? We enjoy a fine reputation," Major Wakholi smiled. "Try and assist, please."

"Anything to oblige, major."

"Of course. Your papers please, sir." It was to Yazov that Major Wakholi addressed himself.

Yazov nodded and handed over his forged passport.

115

Major Wakholi studied the document carefully, taking his time over each page. He studied the photograph especially closely. After turning the last page, he closed the little booklet with a snap. Then he looked very levelly into Yazov's eyes, the trace of a smile flickering about the edges of his lips. "A very good document, sir. Very good indeed. You may both enter the Republic of Uganda."

"Thank you, major," Kruger said, his relief overcoming his slight discomfort at Wakholi's enigmatic smile. He had, for a few seconds, the sensation of his taut muscles suddenly relaxing. The American was still stuffing his passport away when Major Wakholi asked politely, "Do you have any luggage, gentlemen? I suppose you must. Do you mind stepping this way so that we can make the necessary inspection?"

Prickling started again at the back of Kruger's neck.

Yet his prompt reaction was to volunteer waspishly, "Sure, major. You can never be too careful." Almost as promptly, Arnie Kruger wanted to bite his tongue. Given the circumstances, any sarcasm was unforgivable. Major Wakholi could be much funnier than Kruger could ever hope to be. The last people to bait at the entry—or exit—point of any target country were the officials.

In the second that followed, while Major Wakholi arched an eyebrow, an image of the police station close by the Smile Fancy store in Kampala flashed in Kruger's mind. Down two flights of stairs, into the basement, along a way lit by dim lights, was a room where patches of dried blood stuck to the floor and walls like paint. Electric shock devices hung on the walls. An agency man had died there, arms and legs tied to a chair, begging four of his captors to stop.

Beads of sweat broke out along Kruger's spine yet again.

"We can't be too careful, you are very right, sir," Major Wakholi smiled. He turned to the immigration official, saying, "You know, this man is the most brilliant repairer of jets I have ever met. What do you think, my friend?"

The other man's face creased with a wide grin.

Kruger and Yazov accompanied Major Wakholi, as well as the immigration official, to a series of low benches, upon which were neatly placed the few items of luggage

116

that had come from the Ethiopian Airways flight. The two men identified their pieces of baggage.

"Would you open your cases, please? Slowly, if you don't mind, gentlemen," Major Wakholi asked politely.

Kruger's hands were slippery with perspiration, so his fingers slipped a little over the brass catches before he got the cases open. Yazov undid a pigskin holdall.

"Will you be staying long?" Major Wakholi asked as he removed articles of clothing from Kruger's cases, stacking them on the plastic, non-scratch surfaces of the benches.

"A day, maybe two. Until we get the job done."

"What kind of work will you be doing?" The SRB officer smiled a tiny, mysterious smile.

"We'll be repairing. . . . At least, we'll help repair that Boeing 727 that's been grounded here for the past few days. . . ."

"Yes, of course. Will you start today?"

"Nope. Hope we'll get a little sleep before that. Jet lag. Kind of takes it out of you. . . ."

"Yes. Jet lag, I know that very well. Especially when you go west-east. You'll need some rest," said Wakholi. "That's a very good excuse for not starting work on that aircraft today. . . ."

"I don't exactly know what you're driving at, major . . . ?"

"What do you think of our beloved President Obama Okan?" Major Wakholi went on as if he had not heard.

"Boeing's policy is not to talk politics. We're engineers, not politicians. All we're interested in is getting on with the job . . ."

" . . . of repairs. Yes, naturally. Very good policy, gentlemen." Major Wakholi dipped his hand into Yavoz's pigskin holdall and came up with a few technical manuals which dealt with certain kinds of repairs to the 727. He affected a study of some of the pages in the manuals before glancing up at Yazov, saying, "You know all of this, sir? Amazing. Truly amazing. . . ."

"Not when you've had all the training we've had, major," Kruger spoke for the Bulgarian.

Meanwhile the immigration official held up one of Kruger's white silk shirts, as if speculating on whether the shirt would fit him.

"My friend, you must put that down," Major Wakholi addressed the immigration man almost absently. "We are all friends here," he waved at Kruger, Yazov and the other man. "And a friend does not get jealous about another friend's shirt."

With that mild rebuke, the immigration officer put down Kruger's shirt.

"Where are you staying?" Major Wakholi wanted to know.

"The International," Kruger replied.

"Quite right, the best place in town. You can get steak—or even chicken. You must try the *waragi*. You know *waragi*? Strong banana vodka. Made in Uganda. Good for the nerves." The corners of the major's mouth curved slightly upwards again.

"Let's go together to the International. By the way, how were you going to get to the hotel?"

Kruger shrugged. "Bus—or taxi, I guess."

Major Wakholi roared with laughter. "Bus or taxi. Does this friend know about buses and taxis?" he beamed at the immigration official, who was himself chuckling.

"No," he said, still laughing, "we'll have to give these friends some VIP treatment. We'll take them to the International ourselves."

When he said that, the Ugandan immigration official suddenly sobered. For a moment, his expression froze.

Kruger had noted the changes in his face, which confirmed Kruger's own forebodings. The American felt his spine icing over. For he understood the meaning of VIP treatment in Uganda: VIP treatment was death after torture.

"Come, gentlemen, please let us make haste," Wakholi grinned. "You are VIPs in Uganda today."

Wakholi nodded in a direction between Kruger and Yazov, where two guards waited. They joined the small party, which then proceeded out of the arrivals lounge of the airport building.

They walked out through the exit and towards a black, dilapidated and ancient Chevrolet Fleetline, which was parked in a no-parking area. The two-door sedan was at least twenty-five years old.

118

While Major Wakholi and the two armed guards watched, Kruger and Yazov stuffed their luggage into the large luggage compartment. Thereafter Wakholi got into the back of the Chevy with one of the armed men, and he motioned the two CIA agents to climb into the front seat. They did so, squashing in next to the driver, who was a taciturn SRB man, wearing the inevitable opaque, silvery glasses.

The next thing Major Wakholi did was lean forward. He had his pistol drawn. It was a Russian Tokarev, and he held the gun so that it brushed against the side of Yazov's head.

A click told Kruger that the guard sitting behind him had slid the barrel of his pistol, too.

"Uganda is very dangerous these days, gentlemen. Full of spies," Major Wakholi said by way of explanation. "We must be armed at all times."

Looking through the open window, he said to the immigration controller, "Don't you worry. These friends are in safe hands now."

After saying that, Major Wakholi locked the Fleetline's door next to Yazov by pressing down the plastic knob.

"Drive safely, brother," he told the driver. "We've got VIPs here."

The Fleetline, registration number UUU 173, rolled forward.

As it twisted through a region frequently lashed by tropical downpours, the road outside Entebbe almost ran along the equator. Wild poinsettias, bougainvillaea and hibiscus grew by the verges of the road, colouring the countryside vividly. There were potholes in the tarmac, and in places hundreds of paper bags of cement lined the edges of the tar: most of the bags were dried solid as rock, the aftermath of a heavy rainstorm. Often, broken-down motor vehicles littered the way to Kampala: buses, motor cars, bulldozers, earth scrapers. A huge, heavy roller had tumbled down a steep slope, and it lay on its side.

"No spare parts, gentlemen," Major Wakholi explained apologetically. "What has Uganda done to deserve all this?"

At the same time he held the Tokarev in his left hand against the side of Yazov's head, just behind the left ear. The gun scarcely wavered.

Yazov was always conscious of the weapon, but despite this, the Bulgarian's mind was constantly measuring risks.

Though he was closest to the left-hand door, no escape was possible unless he flipped the plastic knob. Even if he rolled out of the front seat through the suddenly wrenched open door, the chances of getting away without serious injury—or evading Major Wakholi once the Fleetline had stopped—were virtually nil.

There had to be other, less dangerous possibilities.

Already he had considered a blow to Major Wakholi's Adam's apple, using the flattened palm of his left hand. But that was also much too risky. The gun was there in the way, as was the Fleetline's inside door jamb: no room was available for movement.

If he had to move quickly in the restricted space, a backward jab with his right elbow was feasible. He could try to smash his elbow into the suture between Major Wakholi's zygomatic process, which was a little left of the SRB man's right eye.

He could also butt his head, snapping it backwards, slamming into the soft, nasal bones of Wakholi's face. If he jerked back quickly and forcibly enough, he would put Major Wakholi out. All he had to do was plant his feet firmly against the Fleetline's sloping floorboard, so as to get a good purchase, and get the timing correct. . . .

At the same time he would fling his right hand past Arnie Kruger's head, bending it at the elbow. With some luck he could take the other SRB man with a flattened right hand. The hand would need to whip through, with enough pace on it to break the other man's cervical spine.

Arnie Kruger would have to deal with the driver.

Kruger sat between Yazov and the driver. He had a bad time of it, keeping his nerve. For the CIA agent was aware of a whole range of facts, possibilities and probabilities.

Beside him, Yazov was coiled like a spring. He could feel that the Bulgarian was a hair's breadth from striking out. If Yazov tried it, they were probably dead. In any event, the mission would almost certainly be over.

Yazov was a little fat and out of condition. Kruger had

120

noticed that even the callouses were softening on the edges of his hands.

Kruger's assessment was that the risks were too great. Yazov could easily get them killed. That being so, Kruger gently gave the Bulgarian's knee a warning squeeze. Under his fingers, Kruger could feel muscles that were like knots.

Very few options were still open to the CIA agents. Kruger tried one.

"What do you want?" Kruger asked Major Wakholi.

Wakholi did not bother with a reply. Instead, after a full minute's silence, he called out an urgent warning to the driver, "Road block ahead, brother."

Ahead of them, Kruger could see 44-gallon drums, presumably empty, strung across the tarmac. Ugandan troops in shoddy uniforms waved their Russian AK-47s at the oncoming Chevy Fleetline.

"Stop, this is a check point!" A soldier's scream slowed the Fleetline to a stop.

The leader of the gang pushed through an untidy group of soldiers. He wore a patch over his one eye. After glaring at the occupants of the Chevy with his good eye, he demanded, "ID papers, quickly!"

It was Major Wakholi who leaned out of the left window and showed the yellow plastic card. "Don't worry, my friend," he told the one-eyed sergeant politely. "Take it easy. We've got some VIPs with us, as you see. We are all friends here. All of us are on good terms."

Whether he could read or not, the gang leader recognized the authority of Major Wakholi's yellow card. After hesitating briefly, he shouted orders to his troops. They promptly rolled two big drums on their rims and off the tarmac.

"Sorry for the trouble, brother," the sergeant apologized to Major Wakholi.

"Of course, my friend. Don't you be worried. We'll look after these VIPs."

The one-eyed soldier gave Major Wakholi a ragged salute.

"You see, what did I tell you? Uganda is a dangerous place," Wakholi chuckled as the Fleetline picked up speed.

"What do you want?" Kruger asked again.

121

"Uganda is a good country. Plenty of bad people," Wakholi sighed. "Too many people looking for spies. In Uganda you can easily disappear."

In front of the Fleetline Kampala rose on flat-topped hills which were bathed in bright, hot sunshine. The Chevy sped by a row of shops that were all shuttered. "No more salt, no more sugar," said Major Wakholi. "No soap, even."

The Fleetline headed for Nakasero Hill, one of seven upon which Kampala is built. Kruger noted that the gates to all the light industrial factories which they passed bore the same sign in Swahili and English: "Hakuna Kazi—No work."

"What do you want?" Kruger was more insistent than ever, now that the Fleetline had at least reached the relative safety of Kampala, even though they might be going to the Bureau's torture chambers.

"All we want is the fare from Entebbe airport, gentlemen. You are VIPs, you know," Major Wakholi exploded into a laugh. "No taxi from Entebbe any more, you know."

"How much?" Relief flooded through Arnie Kruger. All that Major Wakholi was up to was a little armed robbery.

"You have United States dollars?" Major Wakholi said it more as a fact than a question, reaching over for the wallet proffered by Kruger.

When the wallet was returned it was thinned down to carrying the CIA agent's American Express card.

"What's that?" Major Wakholi asked, pointing to the heavy, gold Rolex watch on Kruger's left wrist.

"A gold Rolex watch. Fully automatic. Anti-magnetic, waterproof."

"I see. Very good watch. I like it. What do you think of this?" The Major stripped off his own wrist a tinny timepiece with medals and no jewels.

"I'd prefer the Rolex, if I were you, major." Kruger sighed inwardly.

"Good idea. You know, this man has arrived in Kampala with some of the best ideas. . . ."

"You take it, major. And give your watch to your pal in the back."

"No, I have one," beamed the man seated alongside Wakholi.

"You see, my friend here does not need a watch. You paid a taxi fare. We exchanged watches. Now what about a present for me?" Wakholi grinned. "What's that?" He pointed at the slim, gold, Cross ballpoint pen sticking out of Arnie Kruger's shirt pocket.

Then they started on Yazov, beginning with his wallet.

From far away Kruger heard the sound of a distant chime. Almost simultaneously he caught a high-pitched wail in his ear. Correctly, he took the sounds to be the chime and muezzin's cry, calling the faithful to prayer at Kibuli mosque.

It was going to be all right, after all. He and Yazov were going to be safe.

Later, when they stood outside the Chevy Fleetline, on the street, with their three pieces of luggage, Major Wakholi had his last say. He poked his head out of the left window and said: "We like capitalism people in Uganda. Capitalism people, but not spies. It is very bad to be a spy, not so?"

Kruger nodded.

"President Obama Okan has told me personally that a spy very often has lots of money, a good wife—and a black dog. Do either of you friends own a black dog?"

Both Yazov and Kruger shook their heads slowly.

"Good. Then you can't be spies."

With that said, Major Wakholi pulled his head back inside the sedan. The Chevy rumbled forward, trailing black, oily smoke.

The two CIA men wrapped their fingers around the handles to their cases and the pigskin holdall and walked across the street to the International Hotel.

"Sonofabitch! Sonofabitch!" Kruger muttered viciously, locking his eyes on to the Fleetline until it rounded the corner.

Major Wakholi had played his part so brilliantly that neither Kruger nor Yazov realized that he was Colonel Oyok's man. Major Wakholi and Colonel Oyok would take over Uganda once Obama Okan was assassinated. Then it would be President Oyok and Vice-President, or Prime Minister, Wakholi. It was Colonel Oyok who had

123

been adamant that Major Wakholi ensure that the CIA assassination squad arrived unscathed at the International Hotel.

But as the Fleetline drove toward Makindye Hill, Major Wakholi was having yet another round of unsettling thoughts. He had been impressed with Yazov, but not with Kruger. Kruger was much too nervous.

If Kruger's was the crucial role in the assassination, Major Wakholi would not be happy. He was unhappy that Colonel Oyok had not given him all the details, though Oyok protested that he himself was not aware of the killing.

"I have to trust in our friends, Wakholi. And you have to trust in me," Oyok had told him.

And the Russian, Bevz, had already requested an audience with Okan to discuss new precautions. So far, Major Wakholi had held the Russian off, but soon he would have to get Oyok to arrange something.

It was also not impossible that once Oyok was installed as president he could get rid of Major Wakholi. He did not trust Oyok completely. He was also quite sure that Oyok was mistrustful in his turn.

If the Americans bungled the assassination, Okan would have them all killed, mercilessly. There was no doubt about that at all.

Major Wakholi could feel events closing in on himself. Being so afraid, he knew that he was a danger to the whole plot.

Perhaps he ought to lead a raid on the International tomorrow. He might grab the Americans with their weapons. Possibly the weapons were already smuggled into their rooms.

All he had to show for himself so far was the Rolex, a gold ballpoint and a few hundred dollars.

"Let's go to headquarters, brother," Major Wakholi stopped the patrol. Then it struck him that he would probably find a message from Bevz to call him at the Russian embassy.

"On second thoughts, brother. Back to the airport. . . . No, let's report to Colonel Oyok. . . ."

13

By 1800 hours that same day, the weapons had still not arrived at the International Hotel. "No sweat. Not yet," Arnie Kruger said. "We've got time. They'll be here."

Leonid Bevz had left three messages for Major Wakholi, all of them at the State Research Bureau headquarters. Unless he got a reply soon, Bevz was determined to contact Colonel Oyok, and bypass the ordinary channels. He was also considering going directly to Obama Okan.

Meanwhile the Ugandan president was at Command Post, under an even heavier guard than usual. He would remain at Command Post until he was needed. So far there was no news from the outside world of any of the Front's attacks, which could take place any time after 6 p.m., East African Time.

Hassan Jabril had failed to pass on some bad tidings to the Ugandan head of state. Certainly Commando Meinhof would not attack that day because the girl who led Commando Meinhof had fallen violently ill. So the raid was postponed for twenty-four hours, and everybody knew that the attack would be that much more dangerous because of the delay.

What of Commando Badawi?

El Al's Flight 378 had taxied from pier 11 along finger A of the boxlike terminal buildings at Copenhagen's Kastrup international airport. This, after the most thorough baggage and body searches for all passengers.

The plane was soon flying at 25,000 feet at 470 knots. The aircraft was in clear, cold skies north-west of Auerbach, West Germany.

A beet farmer, whose name was Konrad Axelmann, later described what he saw.

He had been standing in a beet field, less than three kilometres from Auerbach, when his attention was drawn skywards by the Boeing 707's gathering roar. He thought he saw and heard a small, onboard explosion. He described the first explosion as small, because the next boom was much bigger, echoing down from the sky and across his farmlands. In that second blast the Boeing 707 also lost its right wing, and Axelmann saw bodies and luggage spew out of the fuselage.

What the farmer did not see was the actual crash. The stricken aircraft hurtled down into a field beyond an obscuring row of trees. But under his heavy leather boots Axelmann felt the ground shake, and when the thundering roar died down he did see rising into the sky a thick, coiling pall of black smoke.

Not fifty metres from Axelmann, something crashed into the freshly ploughed field. He ran to investigate, picked up a human hand, stuffed it into the largest pocket of his blue overall, and ran for his motorcycle.

In the little town of Auerbach, which is south-east of Bayreuth, he showed the policemen his proof. "It looked like a haystack on fire in the sky," he told them.

Within thirty minutes of Axelmann's report the Refusal Front also had the details and Hassan Jabril sent this news in code from Aden to Obama Okan.

Neither Okan nor Jabril were sure of how to consider the El Al hijack and crash: was it more of a success than a failure?

Whatever it was, the news of the El Al disaster had not reached Johannesburg, South Africa, when shortly after 1800 hours the motorcade of the secretary of state glided around the last of the turnings of the Carlton Hotel.

A door to the big car opened and a young man emerged. Speculatively, he ran his well-trained eyes over the thick crowd which gathered around the Carlton's main doorway.

This young man had strapped to his belt a Tactec personal communications system, a kind of walkie-talkie. Clipped to his ear was an earphone, which trailed a thin flex of wire to the transceiver. It was obvious from the Secret Service man's expression that he was listening to a message.

Now he nodded to Joseph Fackman, who immediately

bounced lightly against the heavily padded leather and launched himself on to the concrete paving.

Even as Fackman was in the process of alighting, in mid-step, the Secret Service agent spoke loudly in his ear, above the cheering of the crowd, saying, "Alpha Two requests you not to shake hands with the crowd. He'd like you to move directly through to the main entrance. Shake hands with the hotel boss. Then go straight to the elevator banks, to the north-west. To your right, front."

Fackman hesitated, and then he headed straight for the awning, smiling broadly for the crowd and the press.

He was feeling good, in spite of the mass march by black students in nearby Soweto. Someone from the US Embassy had told him that among the banners was one reading: "Fackman is a killer." But talks with the South Africans had gone well, and the secretary of state felt that he would be closing his stewardship of the foreign affairs of the United States on a high note.

Already he had proposed to the South African and Rhodesian leaders that, provided he could go back to the black nationalists with certain undertakings, he might arrange a ceasefire. What Fackman wanted was a firm agreement from the Rhodesian prime minister that his country would go over to black majority rule within a definite time period.

Having completed his say in the morning's session of talks, Fackman had arrived at the Carlton to host a cocktial party. He had invited South Africa's leaders, important Opposition members, and front-ranking coloureds, blacks and Indians.

Ahead of Fackman flashlights popped as press photographers worked their cameras. The secretary of state stopped by a little boy holding a small flag of the United States. "Where are you from, son?" Fackman's hand tousled the boy's hair.

"Peoria, Illinois, sir," the young American broke into a pleased grin.

"Never been there, son. Thanks for coming."

The bespectacled man in charge of US foreign affairs turned and walked into the Carlton's big entrance.

"There's a rumour doing the rounds in financial circles

127

in New York, Chicago, London and Toronto that you've been shot, sir," a newsman with a clipped American accent caught the secretary's attention.

"I'd say those reports are grossly exaggerated," Fackman grinned. As he disappeared through the hotel doorway, the crowd cheered and laughed.

Inside the plush hotel, the secretary of state walked a few paces on a red-carpet runner to shake the hand of a Carlton manager. "It's good to be here," the American said quickly before dodging past the hotelier, who was about to say a few words.

"Glad to have you here, Mr. Secretary," the man got in a brief greeting.

When he saw the secretary of state moving towards the lifts, Alpha Two spoke into his Tactec radio microphone. "Zero Six, this is Alpha Two. Do you read me? Ice Age will get to your position inside two minutes." With the message done, the Secret Service man pressed a black button to the walkie-talkie.

"Alpha Two, this is Zero Six. I read you. Ice Age my position two minutes. Only thing to report is that Zero Four has not come in for ten minutes."

"Zero Six this is Alpha Two. Message heard and understood. What was Zero Four's last position?"

"Zero Four was checking out hotel rooms on the twenty-fifth floor. He had the twenty-fourth to the twenty-sixth. His last report was about a little trouble with the walkie-talkie."

"Zero Six, Alpha Two. I got that. If he doesn't show in, say, ten minutes, we'll go looking."

Alpha Two, who came from Columbus, Ohio, was not particularly worried. Earlier in the day, the hotel rooms had been checked by members of the South African security police. Plainclothes security men were dotted all over the hotel, stationed in public and private areas. The Carlton was surrounded by soldiers in battle dress and carrying highly efficient weapons.

From time to time, a Westland Wasp helicopter of the South African air force fluttered over the Top-of-the-Carlton.

All the lifts were manned by members of the South African police who were armed with heavy-calibre revolvers.

128

Alpha Two had been impressed with all the security arrangements made by Colonel Botha of the South Africans. Besides, Alpha Two also had half a dozen of his own men doing checks. And a week ago, the Carlton had stopped taking reservations for travellers and others who had not booked in prior to the public announcement of Fackman's cocktail party.

Still, if Zero Four did not walk in with his report inside ten minutes, he would have to act. Just say that something happened to Ice Age and it became known that he had disregarded Zero Six's tip-off. He would not last five minutes in the Service.

"Zero Six, Zero Six, do you read me? Your package is in the lift with Zero Five."

"Alpha Two, I read you."

"I'm giving Zero Four another six minutes. After that, I'm alerting all stations."

Alpha Two scratched an itch under his neatly tailored jacket and felt for the automatic pistol which he carried in a quick-draw holster.

Zero Four lay in the white bath of the expensively fitted bathroom of room 2401 on the twenty-fourth floor of the Carlton Hotel. His arms hung loosely from the shoulders, his hands rested in his lap. Zero Four was fully clothed, and he was dead. His head lolled on the back rim of the bath, and his eyes stared unseeingly up at the ceiling. A large, jagged hole wrecked the frontal bone of his skull. It was here that a steel-and-nickel 7.62 bullet had exited, after being fired through the back parietal from a Model 52 Czech pistol.

Of course, the M-52 had been fitted with a silencer. But the bullet had come out of the muzzle so fast that it had drilled clean through Zero Four's skull, sinking into a wall of the room.

Gabriella Garst had fired the weapon. She and another member of Commando Marighella had pounced on Zero Four without giving him a chance. Once they had disarmed him in the room, it was his life—or a whole lot of other lives. He had tried to save his own.

"Do exactly as I say. Exactly," Garst had ordered. "Speak into the radio. Tell them precisely this: 'Having trouble with the radio. Over and out.'" A few seconds later he died anyway, after he had taken in the contents of the room with great alarm.

What he had seen was an assault squad, eight strong, crowded into the apartment. Some men sat on the twin beds, others lounged against the wall of the room.

Stacked against another wall were Hungarian-made AMD assault rifles. With their curved, staggered-row, detachable boxes, the AMDs looked very much like the Russian AK-47s, upon which they were in fact modelled. The difference was that the AMDs were shorter, and with their shoulder-stocks folded, they could fit snugly in an airline bag, which was why Garst had chosen the AMD over the AK-47.

Each member of Commando Marighella had retrieved his weapon from the Hillbrow flat of the petite woman who had, until a few days previously, worked as a shop assistant in the Yellow Panther. It did not matter that she was now in Paris, for her job was done.

Garst's team had smuggled its weapons into the hotel in Pan American, SAA, and Adidas airline and sports bags.

Once Zero Four had been dispatched, Garst was grateful for the intrusion. She immediately grasped the importance of the captured Tactec radio. Using the radio she monitored what the US Secret Service—and the South Africans—were doing. Garst sat quietly on the bed, listening through the earphone.

It was through the Tactec walkie-talkie that she learned of concern for the missing Zero Four.

"They've finally missed him. We have to go soon." Garst announced her decision to Commando Marighella.

"I'm leaving now," she said simply. "You know what the drill is, if anything goes wrong."

Garst saw a few of the squad members nod.

"Good. Whatever happens, I want no panic."

The attack on the Top-of-the-Carlton started in the late, sunny afternoon of that December in Johannesburg, when Garst let herself out of room 2401. Her immediate task was to commandeer one of the lifts so that the rest of the group could be taken to the Top-of-the-Carlton, six floors higher. She would call one of the lifts by pressing a button, and when it stopped outside room 2401—this room was closest to the bank of lifts—she would kill the armed lift operator. . . .

Room 2401 had been chosen for another reason too: it was anticipated that most hotel guests would have left the lift prior to arriving on the twenty-fourth level.

Garst stepped silently across the short distance to the nearest lift call button. She pressed it, knowing that a member of Commando Marighella was watching closely through a peephole in the door to room 2401.

Even if Garst's heart was pounding, her expression was serenely calm. It was not easy waiting outside the bank of lifts, the M-52 pistol gripped in her right hand, the gun hidden from casual view under the woollen jersey over her arm.

At any moment a hotel guest could come out of one of the many rooms on the twenty-fourth level.

The lift seemed to take long in arriving. But Garst knew that at a time like this every moment dragged slowly to the next. She was also so stimulated by the free, heavy flow of adrenalin through her that she had an almost eerie awareness of sound and movement, making time lag all the more. Without straining to hear, she could hear the loud whish of the lift's mechanisms as the boxes moved quickly up and down the shafts all around her.

A gong, announcing the arrival of a lift, clanged resoundingly in her ears. She watched, fascinated, as the doors slid open.

A uniformed South African constable stood inside the lift. He wore a peaked cap, and a Tactec transceiver hung from his belt. He was slightly bored now that most of the guests, if not all of them, were safely up in the Top-of-the-Carlton. But the girl was about the prettiest he had seen all afternoon. As if to acknowledge this, he smiled happily.

Garst smiled, too, never letting her guard down even as she pressed the trigger of the M-52.

She fired three times. Long tongues of flame burst from the muzzle, burning the woollen jersey. Under her hand the silenced gun coughed and bounced.

Every bullet struck the young policeman, sweeping him into the back of the padded lift. He crumbled to the floor,

131

blood welling through his mouth, washing over his jaw and neck.

Then Garst was inside, her hands at the controls. She gave a hand signal, and seven other members of the assault squad poured into the box. Someone lifted the Tactec transceiver, making sure that it was not transmitting any signals.

The box rose upwards, toward the thirtieth floor. Clicks sounded in the rising steel cage as the small squad readied its weapons. Garst herself snapped a fresh clip of ammunition into her M-52, then tucked it into the top of her track suit and panty elastic. Someone handed her an AMD and a Pan Am flight bag.

The lift reached the Top-of-the-Carlton level. A muted gong echoed outside.

Commando Marighella was about to storm into the passage.

"Here we go. Good luck." Garst smiled confidently.

All around her, the others either nodded or smiled too. They had trained long and hard enough for the next few minutes, and especially for the initial thirty seconds of the assault.

The mood in the Top-of-the-Carlton was congenial, at least in the minutes immediately preceding the attack by Commando Marighella.

Fackman was in the cocktail lounge, mingling with his guests. He carried a very dry martini in his left hand and flitted from group to group, a big smile on his face, his right hand pushed forward in greeting. "Pleased you could make it. . . . Nice that you're here. . . . We've heard a lot about you back home. . . . It's good to meet you. . . ." As he moved about the large room with its low ceiling, he tried his best to make everyone feel at ease.

The South African leaders were gathered in a little knot, near the centre of the cocktail lounge. They were talking mostly among themselves.

And so it was with the other groups, too: the coloureds, Indians and blacks were all making polite conversation with their own kind, rather than with others. But some of the guests were already mixing across the colour and racial

132

barriers, and fresh introductions were being made all the time.

Waiters weaved between the guests, with their trays of *canapés* and drinks precariously balanced on the fingers of their opened hands as they held them above their heads.

Members of the South African security police were also present, along with US Secret Service agents. They all intermingled discreetly with Fackman's guests. All of the guards wore plain clothes and were indistinguishable from the crowd, although they could pick out their own. Anyone who kept looking about—or who sometimes did not follow the trend of the conversation—was a good bet for a security man. So the man standing close by the curtained opening to the Top-of-the-Carlton, a drink in hand, talking to nobody, was very probably a Secret Service agent. In fact, he was Zero Two.

From where Zero Two stood, he could hear the low, droning buzz of cocktail chatter, pierced intermittently by the clink of martini glasses or whisky tumblers, or a woman's high-pitched laugh.

Beyond Zero Two was the reception area, the banks of lifts, and still more guards. These guards were all armed South African policemen in full, light blue and grey uniform. It was their job to secure the area outside the six lifts, as well as the fire escapes and stairs which led up to the swimming-pool deck and down to the twenty-ninth floor.

While two constables guarded the fire escapes, another two covered the curtained entry to the Top-of-the-Carlton. The remaining sentries patrolled the carpeted aisle between the banks of lifts where Commando Marighella was soon to storm out of their box.

The South Africans were vaguely lackadaisical: the Top-of-the-Carlton was so well guarded that any attack was much too unlikely. After all, there were guards in the lounge, guards in the reception area, guards in the lifts. Four FN-armed guards were on the pool deck, another dozen secured the twenty-ninth floor. In other parts of the Carlton Hotel, still more security forces were on duty. And outside the building, in the streets below, army regulars stood at attention and armoured cars were parked on the corners.

So, if the six police constables were not fully prepared for a powerful, merciless assault, that was understandable.

The person who first appreciated the enormity of the surprise attack—in spite of the great, mind-numbing shock—was a young woman called Billie-Jean Landers.

Billie-Jean Landers sat at the desk by the curtained entry to the Top-of-the-Carlton. She had an excellent view of the lift banks, which was precisely why she sat there. On that day, Billie-Jean was employed to check the invitations of all Fackman's guests. She worked in the US Consulate at Johannesburg. For the occasion, she was elegantly dressed, and she had spent an hour under the hands of a hair stylist only that morning.

Since Fackman had already arrived, almost all the guests were inside the cocktail lounge. Billie-Jean Landers was herself a trifle bored. While she gazed absently at the lifts, she talked into a handset to a girl friend on the Carlton's ground-floor lobby far below.

She was impressed by the police guards and their FNs.

"Boy, do these guys look tough. With rifles and all. Kind of out of place. They had all the guests doing double takes when they got out of the elevators."

"Down here its like an armed . . ." Billie-Jean's girlfriend started to reply.

Then the lift gonged. Commando Marighella disgorged from the farthest one on to the expensive thick, blood-red carpet.

Billie-Jean Landers saw all this happen without it registering in her brain. Instead, a great shock rolled over her mind, paralysing her thoughts.

What her eyes recorded was how Commando Marighella broke with fast, precise movements into a pattern of action. Later, she described them as having moved "like college footballers, making a play. You know how everybody goes in different directions. . . ."

Two of Garst's men stormed the guards at the fire escape. Neither policeman stood a chance: both went down under long bursts that clattered out of the AMDs. One of the guards was jolted off his feet and hurled on to the mid-floor landing, where he crashed in a heap.

At the same time, a squad hit the sentries on the carpet between the lifts. Digging the muzzle of his AMD into the

South African's belly, a commando squeezed the trigger. His crackling fire pitched his victim against the lift door opposite.

A burst hacked waist high through yet another constable, the bullets crashing through to chip into plaster and brickwork behind.

All four guards were dead in seconds.

A fifth sentry was at the curtained entry point to the Top-of-the-Carlton, frantically trying to unlimber his FN rifle. He got as far as to slip the belt off his shoulder— with his rifle at a queer angle—when criss-crossing fire shattered him.

The last of the guards brought his FN around. His finger slipped on the trigger, and the rifle spewed a few rounds, tearing chunks out of the ceiling. He was still bringing down the muzzle of his gun when a burst slung him backwards, impaling him on to the splinters of a glass-and-wood frame-work which instantly collapsed under the weight.

All of the South African sentries were dead before Billie-Jean Landers reacted.

"God help us! They're killing us! Blood everywhere . . . !" She screamed into the handset.

"What?"

"Killing us! Terrorists!"

"Oh, my God!"

Even as Billie-Jean Landers heard the other girl she tore a Star of David from around her neck. A man in a black track suit loomed over her from nowhere. "Bitch!" he shouted. "Get away from that phone! I'll blow your head off!" He swept the handset out of Billie-Jean's hand with a vicious jab of the back of his AMD. Then he hit the girl's head with the return stroke. She fell across the desk, her ears ringing with gunfire, her brain spinning with the force of the blow.

The first real opposition would come from inside the Top-of-the-Carlton, which was what Garst had foreseen. Nobody would stop them in the reception area; the surprise would have been too great. But the Secret Service agents who mingled with the party goers would have more time to react. . . .

Zero Two was the Secret Service agent closest to the

reception area. Like a hundred other people, he turned to face the opening. Through it charged Garst and three other members of Marighella. They were breaking up into another formation, firing their AMDs into the low wooden ceiling, splintering wood. . . .

Zero Two had time to fling aside his glass of chilled champagne, making the liquid fly in a long, thin arc. It was Garst's assault rifle that he seized, taking it by the hot barrel. Though his fingers burned, Zero Two twisted the weapon free of the girl's grasp. He swung it around, readying to turn the gun on her.

Garst hardly broke her stride. Even as he clawed for the AMDs trigger she coolly slipped the M-52 from out of the top of her track suit. Then she half emptied the magazine. Bullets broke through Zero Two, spinning crazily into the crowd of guests behind him.

As the agent crumpled, Garst scooped away her AMD and joined the other members of Commando Marighella in their long, raking bursts into the wooden ceiling and across the vast stretch of the Top-of-the-Carlton's viewing windows.

Bullets ripped through wood, sending fragments flying. A section of the spotlighting suddenly flashed very brightly—and fused. As the bullets stitched an irregular pattern across them, the big windows cracked and shattered.

Fackman's guests hurled themselves on to the carpets. They screamed with terror. They flung themselves behind pillars and overturned tables. There were cries of pain.

"We'll kill a lot of people! Do you hear?" Garst screamed. "Do not resist! I repeat! Do not resist! Lie flat on the floor! Everybody, very flat on the floor!"

In the lift corridor the air was sharp with the smell of cordite and of burnt wool where the carpets had been seared by gunfire. A thin haze of powdered plaster drifted between the lift banks. There were splashes of blood on the walls, fragments of human bone and tissue on the carpets.

The dead policemen lay in strange, unnatural attitudes.

By this time the whole of the thirtieth floor of the Carlton was quite securely in Commando Marighella's hands.

But the twenty-ninth floor was not. Here were at least a

136

dozen well-armed, able-bodied security police. And from here the South African security detail tried to strike back, in the first minute of the assault.

Poking his head around the corner of the landing between the two floors, a pale-faced police constable blindly fired his FN. It rattled away, making a deafening noise. Bullets zinged up to the thirtieth floor. The muzzle of the FN spurted flames, lighting up the dimly illuminated staircase with bright flashes.

It was a counter attack born out of confusion and panic.

Two commandos had posted themselves at the head of the stairs to stop any assaults from either the pool deck level or below, from where the shooting came.

Their response was immediate.

One of them pulled out an AM-26 grenade, sprung it, then bounced the small, explosive shell off the cream-painted hotel wall. The grenade thudded heavily on the landing and rolled down three steps, blowing up with a great roar and a huge, momentary blaze. It shredded the constable and his uniform, even as he dived backwards in sudden alarm.

In this way the initial phase of the attack by Commando Marighella, directed at capturing the thirtieth floor of the Carlton, was successfully completed. Next, Garst would need to consolidate her hold, before she made her demands.

But so far, so good. Garst stayed in the cocktail lounge until she was satisfied that all was well, prior to starting her inspection in the lift passage. A quick look around the corner of the stairs told her about the grenade blast. She doubted whether anybody else would try to harass them from below.

Smiling broadly, she extended the middle and forefinger of her left hand in a big V for victory. The three men who now held the reception area all smiled back. One of them coughed softly as pungent, acidic fumes irritated the lining of his throat and nose. Garst gently patted him on the back.

At the first possible opportunity she needed to contact somebody in authority. Accordingly, she stepped over to where Billie-Jean Landers sat whimpering. The American

137

girl was pale and scared, and she had her hands pressed against her head to block out the ringing in her ears.

Without a word to Landers, Garst picked up the handset. "Anybody on the line?" she asked in the mouthpiece.

"Yes." The response was instant.

"Good," Garst was relieved. "Identify yourself."

"Botha. Colonel. In charge of security."

"Excellent. Are you listening carefully?"

"Go ahead."

"I am the leader of Commando Marighella of the Refusal Front of the PLO. You've got that?"

"Carry on."

"PLO. Palestine Liberation Organization. We completely control all access and exits here. You understand?"

"I think so, *ja*."

"Very well. We control everything. Secretary Fackman, his entire party. They are all our prisoners. You understand?"

"I hear what you are saying."

"I want you to know this. There are eight of us. We are all very heavily armed. We have automatic weapons, a big supply of grenades. We have enough ammunition to kill every hostage many times over. Understand?"

"Yes."

"And we will kill all of them, if we have to. Without mercy, I assure you. . . ."

"What is it that you want?"

"What I want is for you to understand that you must not try to rescue any prisoners. I repeat. Do not try any rescue. I assure you this will cause many, many deaths. We are not afraid to die. Any attack on us will produce a high mountain of corpses."

"Understood."

"I sincerely hope you do, Colonel Botha. The lives of many people are in your hands. Now I have a few preliminary demands."

"Go ahead."

"I want all the lifts sent to the thirtieth floor. Empty. Send their keys, too."

"I think that can be arranged, *ja*."

"You must not think, colonel. You must do."

"What else?"

138

"I want short lengths of rope. Suitable to tie up our hostages. Also rolls of adhesive tape, and four pairs of scissors. I also want two megaphones. Powerful megaphones. Loud enough for me to give you messages in the square below. Yes?"

"Agreed."

"You'll find that if you co-operate, all will be well. In fact, once you have sent all the lifts up—empty, of course—we'll release some prisoners. Will you like that?"

"That is welcomed, *ja*."

"I'm sure. But please know that all hostages are in grave danger. We will not hesitate to kill, if we have to."

"I'm sure that won't be necessary. What are your other demands?"

"All in good time. But right at this moment I want to prove that we are serious. I want you to see for yourself what can happen."

"What kind of proof? That won't be necessary. . . ."

"Colonel Botha, we will talk more soon. Good-bye."

Having finished her first contact with the South African security chief, Garst gently cradled the receiver.

The next thing she did was to deliver her "proof." A member of Marighella set to work, dragging each of the bodies of the dead constables across the carpet into the waiting lift. The corpses of the dead men left wet, broken trails on the carpet. Counting Zero Two and the slain lift operator, the box was filled with eight bodies. Because of lack of space, Zero Two, the last of the corpses, was laid cross-wise over the other dead. Garst pressed a button inside the lift and skipped out of the box, back on to the thirtieth level.

Probably, for the moment, Commando Marighella was safe from external counter attack; Garst had now to consolidate still further her internal command. With that in mind, she returned to the cocktail lounge.

Her first action was to call out, "Where is Secretary Fackman? Please show yourself."

Though she was reasonably certain that the secretary of state was present, there had previously been no time to make absolutely sure.

139

"I'm here," Fackman stood up. He brushed his jacket with his hands.

"Good. Please remain standing where you are."

All around Fackman the other hostages lay as ordered: on their stomachs, flat on the floor. Also as instructed, each hostage linked his hands with those of the two persons closest to him, forming an endless chain.

Commando Marighella had banned any talking, and the cocktail lounge was quiet save for the involuntary groans of a few unlucky ones who had been struck by ricochets or splinters of glass or wood.

Zero Three of the US Secret Service also lay on the carpet. He had hit the thick, woollen pile so hard at the sound of gunfire that he might have torn a ligament or broken a small bone in his knee. Anyway, the knee hurt like hell. His sunglasses had gone flying from his breast pocket. Zero Three did not think he would ever get them back again. It was a silly worry, given all that had happened and who he was. But there was little he could do anyway.

He was lucky to be alive. Upon hearing the first violent bursts of automatic weapons he had instinctively reached for his Service pistol. Moments later he knew there was no hope: had he fired his gun it would have lost a dozen lives, including his own. Instead, he had pocketed the pistol as quickly as he had drawn it.

It occurred to Zero Three that all the other security men had come to exactly the same decision in their separate ways. Apart from Zero Two, nobody else had resisted the assault squad.

To give the security men any chance at all, any action would have to be perfectly co-ordinated. There was no prospect of this happening; besides, many would still be killed.

Who were they, Zero Three wondered. A man in an Adidas track suit stood close to him. Zero Three stole an upward glance, then turned away equally abruptly when the gunman glared at him. He had seen enough, though.

The gunman stood spreadlegged, an AMD held loosely in his left hand, index finger curled into the trigger guard. He had a grenade in his right hand, the pin between his teeth.

140

"This is Commando Marighella of the Refusal Front," he heard the girl announce. "You are our prisoners."

Zero Three guessed what was coming.

"Stay exactly as you are. We know that among you are armed security men. We ask these men to stand up. They must identify themselves. No harm will come to them. I repeat, no harm will come of it if they do as we say."

Garst let the words sink in before continuing, "They will know that any attack on us will cost lives. Many lives. For every one of us killed, we will kill ten or twenty of you. Understood?"

Again Garst paused. Then she said, "So I want all security men to stand up. Also, anybody who possesses a weapon of any kind. Please slowly get up from where you are lying."

From positions scattered across the floor, four men carefully got to their feet. Without being prompted, they all placed their hands behind their heads. Zero Three also rose in surrender. Still others followed.

"Good. Thank you. But now a warning. We will shortly begin searches of all of you. I can assure you that such searches will be quite professional. Perhaps an armed person can escape detection of his weapon. I doubt it."

Still another hesitation preceded her warning: "Any person. I repeat. Any person who does not stand now, should he or she be discovered later with a weapon, will be shot out of hand."

Garst's threat got another three men to their feet. She looked at them, shaking her head. "You are very, very fortunate . . ." she said pitilessly.

By this time, all of those standing had their hands on or behind their heads. Garst had no wish to disarm them: all she wanted was to get rid of any trained opposition. It was easiest simply to shepherd them to the lifts and have them whisked away.

"As I promised, no harm will come to you. You are the first to be released."

Garst nodded at Zero Three.

"Step forward. One by one. Walk slowly to the lift bank. Keep your hands securely on your head. I repeat. Hands always on your head."

Zero Three started to walk, stepping lightly over the hostages in his way.

In slow succession, each of the security agents was forced into the lift. There they waited, in two rows, under the cover of automatic rifles.

"Please press the ground-floor button," Garst ordered the man who stood nearest the control panel of the lift.

The steel doors slid shut, and the box sank to street level.

It was going well. Very well, Garst thought to herself. She had drastically lessened the chances of a successful attack by the hostages. In the following phase, for the sake of better crowd control, she would reduce the number of captives. With hostages galore, she could give many away. It would also allow her to make a little propaganda.

Back in the cocktail lounge, she addressed the prone guests: "We have no fight with the coloured peoples here. You are the rightful owners of the Republic of Azania." Garst used the name which some black nationalists gave South Africa.

"Your being here speaks of collaboration and treachery to your own cause. But perhaps you will learn from today. When I tap you with the muzzle of this rifle, you may slowly rise. Walk with your hands upon your head to the lifts. You may go free."

Thereafter, in groups of ten, the black, coloured and Indian hostages were all allowed to leave. Slowly, they threaded a way to the lifts—and freedom.

All was proceeding in terms of the Front's detailed plan. By giving up the blacks, coloureds and Indians the Front proved its solidarity with the enemies of the whites in South Africa. In the course of appearing to be generous, Garst had also eased substantially Marighella's task of watching over its captives.

It was time to release the wounded. The injured and sick were always a burden, and they were not fully subject to discipline and control because of their condition.

"I want the wounded. Those injured. Please sit up . . . or identify yourselves by raising your hands." Garst's voice had the same confident ring of authority.

Her call brought the wounded to their feet, or to sitting positions. Some dragged their feet, others held their sides,

142

a few supported one another. Eventually the wounded, after a brief inspection by Garst to satisfy herself that nobody was shamming, also struggled to the lifts.

By now Commando Marighella had concentrated its haul of hostages into the whites, among whom were the American foreign servicemen, South Africa's most prominent Cabinet ministers, leaders of the parliamentary Opposition, and a few important captains of industry and mining. This too had been approved in advance.

Soon Garst would be ready for another phase in the complex operation. Perhaps this was the trickiest aspect. She would control the hostages, whom she would use to bargain her way to an aircraft at Jan Smuts; Colonel Botha would have the overwhelming military and police power of South Africa at his disposal to try and stop her.

To begin the new stage of the mission, Garst needed a messenger. In order to find someone suitable she inspected the hostages. Finally, she came across a mini-skirted blonde young woman who lay flat on her belly, her arms extended, hands linked, nose dug into the carpet. Her fear had been such that she had plainly wet a pair of white panties, causing her skirt to cling.

Garst tapped the girl with the muzzle of her AMD, prodding her buttocks. "Get up, please. No harm will come to you." Garst's request was more of an order.

The girl got to her feet, her face red with shame. Confused, she dropped her hands over her lap.

"Go to the lift and wait. You will go free, but I have a message for you to take."

As the blonde walked stiffly away, Garst gave fresh orders to the members of Marighella who guarded the cocktail lounge. When she left to give the girl her message, the searches and bindings began.

The very first thing that the girl with the message did when she got to the ground floor lobby was to borrow a long overcoat. Ambulance men were still pushing stretchers into the spaces between the banks of lifts, and a couple of the wounded were being carried out. "Oh, God, it's beautiful to be alive!" the young blonde wept. Then she repeatedly demanded to see whoever was in charge, because she had brought something in writing from the terrorists.

"Here it comes." Colonel Botha's brow puckered in a frown as he moved away from Alpha Two and walked towards her.

Alpha Two watched Botha talk quietly to the girl. He saw the South African take something from her hand.

Colonel Botha, the US Secret Service agent told himself, was handling it all by the book. This was good news. Everything that Colonel Botha had said so far made sense. He could have been trained by the Secret Service itself, at the National Academy in Quantico, Virginia. For, unlike the Israelis who believed in storming terrorists quickly, the sooner the better, the US authorities tried to keep talking. They maintained calm and preferred to wait out the men with guns. Time always worked against terrorists.

On the other hand, any sudden attack on the terrorists would provoke slaughter: a single man with an AMD could cover the whole lift area, two or three other armed men could handle the hostages; Commando Marighella had men to spare. And Alpha Two was deeply conscious of the secretary of state's political importance, as Colonel Botha was doubtless keenly aware of the fact that his own prime minister was a prisoner. Apart from these major figures, Commando Marighella held many other notables and innocents.

"I guess you'll start gaining their confidence with a few concessions. Ropes and megaphones. That kind of start," Alpha Two had cautiously tested Colonel Botha's attitude. "Give them some food, coffee, cigarettes. Get them into a waiting game."

"I think that's the idea, *ja*." Alpha Two had been relieved at Botha's response. "All I want is to keep talking. If we talk long enough, we win. I don't want panic."

It was exactly how Alpha Two would have dealt with Commando Marighella.

After sympathetically patting the blonde girl on the shoulder, Botha walked back to where Alpha Two waited. "What I thought, *ja*," he said. "She wants us out in the square. Outside the hotel. She'll use the megaphone to shout the real demands. All for maximum effect. And I'll

144

tell you what: she'll demand a broadcast from the SABC."

"What's with the document?" Alpha Two pointed to the thin, typewritten paper which Colonel Botha held in his hand.

"The usual nonsense. Read it for yourself." Colonel Botha smiled grimly. "This she'll want broadcast."

Alpha Two read the document in silence:

The Refusal Front reaffirms basics of the pan-Arab and pan-African freedom struggles. No treaty, no talks with, no recognition of the aggressor Zionist, Rhodesian and South African states. The Refusal Front treats with contempt all attempts to mislead Arab and African freedom fighters to so-called negotiating tables and sell-outs in Geneva, or anywhere else.

The Front declares itself fully behind total nationalization of Arab oil and African gold and financial wealth, and a Third World economic policy so that oppressed peoples can use their resources for their own development. . . .

Having finished reading the message, Alpha Two thought that the SABC would not enjoy relaying the broadcast. But that would be one of the easiest of the demands for Colonel Botha to carry out.

"Come on. Let's get on with it." Colonel Botha led the way to the square.

The square was an expanse of concrete, broken occasionally by small beds of plants and trees. The tallest structure in South Africa, a huge office building, stood east of the hotel, and both were two major components of a vast office, underground shopping and hotel complex known as the Carlton Centre.

Colonel Botha positioned himself in the square, just north of the hotel's northern façade. He looked up at an impressive concrete and glass edifice. From about the tenth level, the hotel building swept down sharply to the square like a ski-ramp. Though the late African afternoon was drawing to a close, the sky high above Botha's head was still bright blue.

The megaphone clicked and hissed as Colonel Botha fiddled with it. Satisfied, he put it to his mouth. "I am

Colonel Botha," he began, his voice booming up towards the Top-of-the-Carlton. "I am in complete charge of security operations. Can you hear me?"

"Go on, colonel," a distorted, but unmistakably female, voice floated down to the square.

"I am addressing myself to the young lady who is the leader of the group holding sixty-five people in the lounge on the thirtieth floor."

"Carry on."

"You are totally surrounded. Look through the windows down into the streets and see for yourself. Hundreds of regular troops in the streets. We have Saracen armoured cars. Snipers are posted on all strategic points, as well as in the offices of that big building to your right. Please give yourselves up. You cannot escape. Do not harm your hostages. This will be held in your favour. Repeat, do not harm any of your hostages. Give up your weapons. Come peacefully out of the hotel. Do this, and I guarantee your physical safety."

"Is that all, colonel?"

"You gain nothing by holding your hostages," Colonel Botha tried again. "No benefit. You have made your point to the world. More bloodshed can only disgust . . . *ja,* disgust all civilized peoples. Surrender now and you will not be harmed. Do not harm the hostages."

Botha had offered nothing. Instead, he closed his opening gambit with the timeworn, well-known phrases. It was the start of a long, deadly, drawn-out war of nerves, in which the first moves always followed a pattern. Already the South African felt a strain in his throat. Of course, he knew that the girl would not even consider surrendering, not yet: surrender was a long way off. All he wanted was to manipulate her into carrying on long, time-consuming negotiations.

He was not to know that Garst was totally aware of how time worked against her. She had to keep the initiative . . . or lose.

"Is that all, colonel?"

"For now."

"Now pay attention. Listen carefully to our demands. One, the Refusal Front's manifesto in your possession

146

must be broadcast within thirty minutes over all the services of the South African Broadcasting Corporation.

"Two, we require helicopters to land on the swimming pool deck of this hotel to lift my people, together with some hostages, to Jan Smuts airport.

"Three, we require Secretary Fackman's Boeing 707 to be fuelled and serviced sufficiently for this aircraft to fly to anywhere in Africa, as far as Algeria. Am I understood?" The voice echoing in the square was firm and authoritative.

"Understood, but I cannot give orders to the SABC. It is physically impossible for helicopters to land on the pool deck. Also, I must contact the Government of the United States, for permission to prepare and refuel the aircraft, its property. All of this will take time."

"Four, I must have your agreement in precisely five minutes from now, 1834 hours. Failing this Commando Marighella will execute a hostage every five minutes until you capitulate. Immediately the Front's manifesto is broadcast as requested we shall release twenty hostages. Immediately the helicopters land, more hostages will go free. Once we arrive safely at Jan Smuts and board the aircraft unharmed, all South African hostages will be released, including your prime minister and his ministers."

"It is impossible for helicopters to land as requested," Botha parried again.

"My experts have had plans of the hotel with them for some time. Not only is it possible, but simple, to land Westland Wasp helicopters, singly, on the pool deck, which can carry much greater weights. We require four Westland helicopters. They can and must land as ordered. You have four minutes and fifteen seconds."

"If you have the plans, you must know there is no space in the pool deck's roof through which a helicopter can drop. It is technically not possible."

"The roof can be rolled back further along its runners."

"The helicopter cannot land on the pool itself. A wooden pergola—a trellis, *ja*—covers much of the other area. It's impossible, I tell you," Botha tried again.

"The pergola is supported by eleven six-inch-square, laminated timber columns. Two carpenters can remove

147

this simple construction in fifteen minutes. Not even carpenters. You may send up two men for this purpose."

"We have no saws, no equipment."

"From where you stand, colonel, 394 paces to the corner of Pritchard and Smal Streets, is a hardware shop which sells Black and Decker electric chain saws. A three-prong, 220-volt power point is available behind the pool deck bar."

"The area is too small," Botha's voice wavered slightly.

"The pool deck area is that of half a soccer field. I walked it yesterday. It was about thirty paces wide by sixty paces long. I know of no changes." Her voice filled with sarcasm.

"Can't be done."

"You have two minutes and twenty-five seconds, colonel. And I want your men on the pool deck down at the lifts, too. Unarmed."

"Can't contact them."

"Use your Tactec walkie-talkie. I have one too. So be careful what you say."

"I need more time."

"You have one minute and eighty-five seconds."

"What do we do now, colonel?" It was Alpha Two.

"Damned if I'll take my men down. We'll need them later. I need time to think."

"You've got a minute, twenty-five seconds."

"Need more time, damn her."

"Let's say 'yes' for now. Maybe we can stall later. Technical problems . . . can be created."

"Maybe she'll come back with a new deadline. The usual treatment. They always extend the first deadlines, *ja*. She's trying to shock us," Botha tried to convince himself. "What's Marighella anyway?"

"In the sixties Marighella ran a terror group in Brazil, wrote a handbook of urban guerrilla warfare. He was killed in 1969, but the book is standard."

"Damn him, too, in hell." Botha fidgeted nervously with the Sony megaphone, and it made scratching noises. He half lifted it to his mouth, then dropped it.

"Forty seconds, colonel. I say you tell her 'yes', we'll work something out later. Right now that'll buy time."

148

Botha came from a heritage that did not yield to terrorist demands. Maybe he had so far handled it like the American would, but his heart was with the Israelis.

Like many other modern, international hotels, the Carlton Hotel uses its highest covered level as a cocktail lounge. In the early afternoon, lunch—including an excellent *smörgåsbord*—is served in the Top-of-the-Carlton; after the cocktail hours it becomes a smart nightclub.

Apart from the food, expensive decor and entertainment, the Top-of-the-Carlton offers views of Johannesburg through the large windows which extend over long stretches along the north and south façades. To look south is to see the old gold-mining areas, with their exhausted, yellow-gold mine dumps. The view north is of the city's buildings and, beyond that, of still more buildings—the high-rise apartment blocks of Hillbrow and Berea.

From the Top-of-the-Carlton to the square below is a drop of 370 feet, so the views are fine. It is also a long way for a man to fall. And a man was precariously perched on the ledges of one of the northern picture windows. He had his back to the city and to Colonel Botha, far below in the square.

This man was tall, middle aged and well built, even if he was running slightly to fat. He had the palms of his hands pressed flat against the glass. And he was having trouble keeping his balance, because the soles of his shoes overlapped the ledge.

He faced the muzzles of the two AMDs with intense, silent alarm. Garst had used the same guns to force him from the carpet on to a chair, then from a glass-topped table on to the ledge.

The muzzles were six feet away from his midriff, pointing slightly upwards at a shallow angle from the horizontal. If the gunmen pulled the triggers, there would be a rattling, crashing burst of gunfire. The two streams of 7.62-mm bullets—coming at the rate of ten every second from each muzzle—would batter him through the thick, double panes of shattering glass.

Garst had her eyes on the dial of her digital watch. She had her head bent, her right forearm she held level and steady as she concentrated. She watched the digital numbers constantly changing shape on the liquid crystal: they seemed almost to be tumbling about. At exactly 1839 hours she said, without looking up, "Fire!"

The submachine guns rattled furiously.

When she did raise her head, all she saw was a big, irregular hole through the shattered windows and drifting wisps of blue smoke.

Far below in the square, Colonel Botha waited for the girl's echoing ultimatum. What he fully expected was that she would come back to seek a face-saving delay of her intended execution.

Instead, from the thirtieth floor of the five-star hotel came the chatter of rapid fire. Almost instantly Botha heard the tinkling crash of breaking glass. Virtually dead centre on the northern side was a form, tumbling through the air. A split second before it bounced off the waist of the hotel at the fifth level, the South African made out a human shape.

The falling shape scattered a small knot of security and press men before the body crashed with a sickening thud, shaking the concrete five paces away from where Botha stood.

Only with difficulty did Colonel Botha recognize the man who in life had been South Africa's ambassador to the United Nations.

"No more killing is necessary," Botha boomed through the megaphone, much more calmly than he thought possible. "We agree."

"Message understood." Garst's flat and unemotional voice trailed into the square below.

Botha wanted no more bloodshed. Later, he would try to escape the full blast of criticism about his handling of Commando Marighella. Probably he would be sacked anyway. But as long as the Front held important hostages whom they were prepared to kill ruthlessly, was his position not impossible?

In the Top-of-the-Carlton the lingering whiff of cordite constantly reminded the hostages of their ever-present dangers. Now they numbered sixty-four. Their hands and

150

feet were expertly bound. They lay on the carpet, face down, silent, fearful.

Garst did not expect any trouble from them, but neither had the South African constables imagined they were to be mown down in the initial moments of an assault which already seemed so long ago. "You must not relax. Not for a moment," Garst repeatedly told Commando Marighella. "Stay on guard."

And jubilant as they were, every member of the Commando remained alert. Had Garst not told them often enough in training that this was a time of great danger, when all seemed won?

Four men kept vigilant watch on the hostages inside the cocktail lounge. In the reception area, three other men covered the stairs. Here all six of the lift boxes hung stationary in the shafts.

But it was true: the most difficult parts of the attack were over. Waiting for the Wasps, getting aboard, the trip to Jan Smuts, all this was going to be much easier. The attack itself had been ruthlessly efficient. And Garst had totally smashed Colonel Botha's strategy. With such success already achieved, most leaders would be euphoric; Garst carried on like a computer, calmly and precisely.

While they waited for the helicopters, she rearranged the hostages yet again, splitting them into groups of Americans, South Africans, and others. Her plan was to take twenty-four of the most important hostages to Jan Smuts airport, four groups of six. As she had promised, the remaining prisoners would go free.

Even as the new groupings were being sorted out, Garst practised her well-learned psychology. "Be calm, be patient," she told the hostages soothingly. "Most of you will soon be free. The worst is over. We know what we are doing. All our demands are being met. There is no need for alarm. . . ."

The party of Americans was top heavy with VIPs: the secretary of state, the ambassador to South Africa as well as the consul general, the under secretary of state for African affairs, another high-level diplomat, and two of Fackman's top aides. If anything, the South African party was more important, relatively speaking, consisting as it did of the prime minister and five Cabinet members. The other

151

groups were made up of Opposition and business leaders, including the head of South Africa's major multi-national corporation.

During this period of reshuffling, Garst divided her time between reordering and comforting the prisoners and whispering encouragement and commands to her commando—so linking her forces inside and outside the cocktail lounge.

She also tuned in to SABC news bulletins. At precisely 1851 hours she was gratified to hear an English-language announcer. In a modulated, unruffled tone, he broadcast the Refusal Front's manifesto over all the SABC's services, both internal and foreign.

But there was no news yet of the Athens skyjacking, nor of the El Al attack.

At 1904 hours, the first of the Westland Wasps arrived. In the bright, long summer's day, it hovered over the opening to the Carlton's sun-and-swimming-pool deck. Twenty-four hours earlier, guests had been relaxing around the area directly below the helicopter, drinking cocktails and sitting in the last of the warm twilight.

Now, as the ungainly, insectlike machine landed, gusts of wind beaten from the air by the Wasp's turbojet-powered blades fanned the sparkling blue swimming pool water into a rough spray.

Garst's plan for travelling to Jan Smuts airport was foolproof. She had demanded four Wasps. Into each Wasp would go six hostages and two members of Marighella. Garst would be part of the two-man squad which would escort Fackman's group; her deputy would take the main South African party. Each of the helicopters would land and rise separately from the pool deck.

At all times, all Marighella's squads would be in constant radio communication. If anything untoward happened to any squad, all the hostages would be instantly imperilled. This was obvious. None the less, she would warn Colonel Botha very explicitly. Garst was sure that he would take her threat seriously.

In the meantime, she needed to check the pool deck area. To do that, the girl climbed a short flight of carpeted stairs on to the roof garden. As instructed, the small contingent of South African security forces had already quit the area. Prior to leaving, they had obeyed Botha's orders and piled the garden furniture and other obstacles into a corner of the big, flat pool deck.

Apart from the Wasp, the next thing she noticed were the carpenters who had dismantled the pergola. They stood quietly, raising their hands to their heads when the girl emerged on to the roof.

Holding her AMD in an efficient, businesslike manner, Garst walked briskly over to the Westland Wasp. All the way to the Wasp she guessed she was in the sights of a sniper, probably somebody on the roof or in one of the offices of the neighboring building. In fact, she was in the sights of half a dozen sniperscopes. They were all using Winchester 52s, and 10 X 15 telescopic sights. Any one of them could have crashed a bullet through her cerebrum. Unfortunately, any such thing would signal a general massacre. So all they could do was to track the girl through their sights, impotently.

Garst completed a brief search of the Wasp. She was pleased to find only the pilot inside. To make room for eight passengers, the helicopter's interior had been stripped down, and therefore Garst's quick inspection was good enough. "Just do your job. That means do as I say," she said curtly to the pilot, who nodded his submission.

A minute later she proceeded back down the stairs to the thirtieth level, with the carpenters marching ahead of her. Rather than have them use the lift, and risk even the slight possibility of an attack from the steel box on its return, she had the carpenters walk down the stairs.

Wherever she was able to do so, Garst minimized the hazards. She did so constantly. Thus when she climbed back on to the pool deck, it was with an evenly mixed party of South Africans and lower-ranking Americans. Doing it that way she guarded against a whispered plot that any of the old groupings might have hatched among themselves. Then, on the deck, she exposed only three of her number including herself, at any particular moment. Yet inside the Top-of-the-Carlton and anywhere else her men more than adequately covered all the prisoners.

While the selected hostages climbed slowly into the stationary Wasp, those who were to remain behind were steadily set free. They made their way down the stairs, and by the twenty-eighth floor they were able to untie the short lengths of rope around their ankles. The ropes had prevented any run, and though the freed hostages could rid themselves of the binding, the prisoners who boarded the Wasps could not.

This delicate release of prisoners was itself a clever stratagem. It was designed to show Colonel Botha that Garst could be trusted to keep her word; the constant freeing of the captives down the stairs, in bands of four, inhibited any counter attack by Botha; and as the number of hostages steadily diminished, so did Commando Marighella's control tighten on those who remained behind.

By now the first of the Westland Wasps was ready to lift off the pool deck. Two hostages shared the co-pilot's seat. Four others sat cramped in the back. They were warned by one of the gunmen to look for handholds and grip tightly.

As the Wasp's door slid shut, the Marighella men braced themselves against the sides of the Wasp's interior in the manner in which they had been taught. The gunman nearest the pilot held the muzzle of his AMD three inches from the back of the flier's head. "Go now," he called out to the pilot. "Gently. Up a thousand feet. Then circle the deck."

The pilot acknowledged the order.

When the rotor blades started to spin with a clattering roar the gunman was making last minute adjustments to the spare set of earphones. The mechanical dragonfly's four wheels rose smoothly off the pool deck. In a fine exhibition of skilful flying, the pilot lifted the ungraceful craft very carefully through the yawning gap above him, into a sky of deepening blue.

The fourth Westland Wasp got off the deck, carrying the secretary of state and Gabriella Garst with the remaining passengers, into the last of the twilight. In a loose formation with the other three helicopters, it thudded on to Jan Smuts airport.

Below them, in the hotel building, at last the South African security forces cautiously made their way up the stairs—and found nobody at all.

The trip to Jan Smuts airport lasted less than fifteen minutes. All the helicopters settled down safely within three minutes of one another, close by Air Force 720, the Boeing 707 that had brought Fackman to Johannesburg.

Garst waited for the Wasp's turbojets to splutter into silence, then she got the door open and hopped on to the concrete apron. Diagonally ahead of her, Air Force 720 was bathed in floodlights; an orange and blue painted gangway was in place up against the port side entrance.

Now she needed to examine the interior of the aircraft. On this occasion she would take more time, because the Boeing 707 was much bigger than the Wasp. It was not impossible that weapons were hidden on board, to be used later by Air Force 720's crew.

Although she knew that she was again under the guns of sharpshooters, the girl walked unhesitatingly to the big jet-liner. Not that Garst was unafraid. She felt a feathery, ticklish sensation over her exposed back, an unpleasant fear of a bullet suddenly crunching into her spine.

For whatever his orders, a sharpshooter, somewhere up on the roof of one of the terminal buildings, could decide otherwise. Or Colonel Botha, for whom time was quickly running out, might do something. . . . All the transfers were occasions of great danger. Colonel Botha might have taken it into his head to launch a multiple, co-ordinated sniper attack. It could start with a bullet in her back.

All that restrained Colonel Botha was the knowledge that a single grenade blast in one of the Wasps, or a long burst from an AMD, would land him with more dead.

It was a complicated battle of wits and psychology. Commando Marighella had the hostages, some of whom would soon be forced to board Air Force 720. Once the plane was in the air, Colonel Botha would lose any advantage his massively superior forces might have given him. In desperation, he could gamble that if he did launch a quick, efficient assault, he might possibly rescue the prisoners without too many casualties. With their own lives suddenly endangered—and with no hope of surviving a fight—the skyjackers might capitulate. . . .

Garst had considered all these possibilities long ago. Thus the murderous attack on the Top-of-the-Carlton had a message for Colonel Botha: Commando Marighella was totally ruthless. While an attack by Colonel Botha might succeed, it would probably be calamitous. Besides, Garst had promised to release still more prisoners, once she and her men reached Jan Smuts safely. Had she not undertaken to free the South African prime minister? Accordingly, Botha faced awesome dilemmas, with little time available for clear thinking.

Under such conditions, Garst gambled that Colonel Botha would most likely do nothing. His own confusions and uncertainties would encourage inaction.

Still, Garst felt the itch on her back.

It was only after the last of the twenty-four hostages were safely on board Air Force 720, and all the members of Commando Marighella, too, that she experienced a lifting of her anxieties. In their place came mounting exhilaration. Euphoria gradually swelled in her chest.

They had almost pulled it off. Almost. Instantly, the girl warned herself not to relax. And as she went about her business in Air Force 720, Garst whispered her warnings to the others. She asked each of her men in turn how he felt. Anyone who was fatigued or drained by the mixed tensions and elations of the preceding few hours was ordered to chase down a couple of amphetamines with cold water.

Having checked on her men, Garst made her way to the aircraft's cockpit. She found Captain Popjack busying himself with pre-flight procedures. His face was rigid with worry, and most of his responses to the girl's queries and instructions were monosyllabic. "I just want you to do your job, captain," Garst tried to be reassuring. "Your job is to fly the aircraft wherever I tell you. We'll all be fine, you'll see. Are you married?"

Popjack said he was.

"Kids?"

"Three."

"I'm happy to hear it, captain. You'll see them all again. Just do as I ask."

"I will, ma'am."

"Don't blame yourself, captain," Garst went on. "I'd like you to set a course for Cairo. I'll want to touch down for refuelling at Entebbe, Uganda. I understand this aircraft does not have the range to get to Cairo without a stop. That right?"

"That's right, ma'am."

"Well, then we'll land at Entebbe."

Garst did not want to alarm Captain Popjack unnecessarily. She was sure he would prefer to think their final destination was Cairo. In the event, this time her deceit failed. Popjack was certain that Air Force 720 would stay at Entebbe.

Outside the silver and blue Boeing 707, the air was heavy with diesel fumes discharged by a compressor truck. Through thick, black rubber pipes, refrigerated air was being pumped from the compressor into the aircraft. Ground crew of the South African Airways were carrying out last-minute inspections. It occurred to Garst that among the men in white overalls were security plants. This did not concern her overmuch because her hostages were well guarded, and two of her men were covering the entrances at all times.

During this interval she and another two-man squad completed a further, thorough search of the aircraft, checking the lavatories, peering under seats, inspecting the overhead racks. As the examination continued, Garst released a pair of hostages every ten minutes, freeing the prisoners of the least importance.

Each pair stumbled down the gangway, legs still secured by the short lengths of rope, crossing over the starkly floodlit no man's land between Air Force 720 and Colonel Botha's post in the glass-fronted departure lounge, which was on a level with the apron outside. Bedraggled but relieved, they were immediately taken away to be debriefed on conditions inside Air Force 720, the intentions of the hijackers, how the other prisoners were being guarded, any weaknesses in the gang's procedures—and other things Colonel Botha considered relevant.

Later, beyond the area of the departure lounge roped off by Botha's order, they faced a barrage of press camera flashes, SABC and VisiNews microphones, TV and movie cameras.

As the released hostages came down the gangway, Colonel Botha tried in vain to pick up through his binoculars a sight of a South African Cabinet minister. The girl had promised to release the South Africans. Finally, to his great relief and joy, he did identify a pair of Cabinet ministers. But his delight was shortlived. Promptly after they stepped on to the concrete apron, Botha noticed that the gangway was being swung clear. The port doorway to Air Force 720 was sealed. Soon thereafter, the big jet proceeded to taxi towards the main runway, its engines whining fiercely.

When it lifted off the tarmac into the night skies above Jan Smuts the jetliner carried Fackman, the ambassador, the consul general, two aides and the South African prime minister, as well as three senior Cabinet members.

It was with a heavy, sick feeling in his stomach that the Colonel watched the twinkling red lights of the Boeing grow smaller and smaller, then disappear from his view.

"All that, and she lied, too," Botha told Alpha Two sadly.

"We could both use a drink." Alpha Two hung a comforting arm about Colonel Botha's sagging shoulders. "Bet you could use one. I can."

But all Botha could think of was whether to scramble a squadron of Mirage fighters from Waterkloof airbase, thirty miles away. He supposed he should. Let the Mirages trail Air Force 720 to the border. Whatever happened next was not for him to decide. Let whoever now constituted the Government of the Republic of South Africa decide whether Air Force 720 was to be shot out of the skies before it crossed out of South African air space. He had done all that was possible.

"Come on, colonel, you played your part. Now it's over to somebody else." Alpha Two told him what he already knew.

14

By about midnight East African Time, Air Force 720 was cruising at 32,000 feet, high above the vast Tanzanian plains of Serengeti, which are north-west of the Ngorongoro crater.

A vintage USAF Boeing, the aircraft derived part of its

name from the last three digits of its registration number of 8720. It was by coincidence the very aircraft in which President Lyndon Baines Johnson had been sworn into office on 22 November 1963 by Judge Sarah Hughes.

Since it had previously served as a presidential aircraft, the jetliner was well fitted with expensive and tasteful furnishings. Much of the decor was hand made, and all the seats in the aircraft were of the type found in the first-class area of commercial flights.

Air Force 720 was also equipped with a kitchenette: ovens, a multi-plated electric stove, and a large refrigerator-freezer with double doors. Garst had no objection to her hostages being made comfortable. With the equipment and supplies available, it was no trouble to cook crisp bacon, scrambled eggs and coffee—poured into blue and white china cups which bore the seal of the secretary of state. A steward served the meal to the kidnapped South African leaders and two of Fackman's aides, all of whom sat around a kidney-shaped, green conference table in the forward cabin. Two of Garst's men watched over them. And while the prisoners were hungry enough to manage the food and coffee, they were also quiet, despondent—and very worried.

Garst herself was with Fackman in his private quarters. She allowed the secretary of state the privilege of relaxing in his chair, an even more luxurious seat than any found elsewhere on 720. Fackman leaned back in it, with his stockinged feet on a heavy, curved table.

Garst sat across the table from him on a bunk. She held her M-52 pistol loosely. She still wore her green tracksuit.

"What will your president do?" she asked matter-of-factly.

Fackman had no way of knowing, but he saw no harm in making intelligent guesses, if that would satisfy the girl. There was no point in provoking her. He might even gain her sympathy.

Hoping to establish some kind of rapport with the girl Fackman said: "He must have got a long, detailed message from our consulate in Johannesburg. He'll be kept advised every half hour of what's happening. Pretty soon he'll be hearing a CIA assessment that this aircraft is heading for Entebbe."

"From an analysis by your ground stations and satellites that are even now tracking us?" Garst suggested.

"That's it."

"But how did you guess? About Entebbe? You had no way of knowing."

Clever girl, Fackman thought to himself. Of course, he had guessed because he knew now that this was the operation Okan had planned. They never had all the details, but it had to be something big, like this. Fackman hoped the CIA were on track with their assassination. . . .

"You don't have to be a genius. Where else can you be assured of a haven . . . ?"

"Yes . . . where else? Please go on. What sort of action will the White House take?"

"Pretty obvious stuff. He knows who you are, thanks to that manifesto broadcast, among other things. He'll have to deal with Okan. I can see the lines hotting up between Washington, Bonn and the West German embassy in Kampala. The West Germans have handled our interests in Kampala, as you know, I'm sure. . . ."

"Since 1973."

"I'm sure you're right."

"I suppose your president will consult other African and Arab leaders?"

"I'd say so, yes. He might get the Libyan president into the act."

"That's what I'd do," the girl smiled. "Get on to Libya. What will the US do if none of this works, and a crisis starts developing?"

"You mean, like it's developed?" Fackman quipped, and they both laughed.

"A whole lot will be happening. Emergency operations. The Pentagon will have ordered warships into the Indian Ocean, to sail off East Africa, including an aircraft carrier. I'd guess that fighter-bombers from such a carrier could strike Kampala. If Kenya permitted it, you can expect troops to be airlifted from Nairobi."

"A very fair summary, Mr. Secretary," said Garst. "But what about the CIA? You've left out the CIA."

Fackman looked levelly at the girl. He hoped his face was expressionless. "I imagine that the CIA will also be

160

busy working on something. Don't you think so?" he asked coolly.

"Yes, I think so, Mr. Secretary. It's really the CIA I'm worried about."

"Anyway," Fackman smiled sardonically, "you seem to have done all right. . . ."

"Thank you, Mr. Secretary . . . for the flattery. We'll be trying much harder tomorrow. But get a good night's sleep. I'll see that you're not bothered."

With that Garst rose from the bunk. She pressed a plastic button to draw a heavy curtain across the opening, sealing off Fackman's private compartment. Then she walked to the cockpit. Garst was sure that Hassan Jabril had picked up her earlier radio signals from Air Force 720. He would be proud of her.

Air Force 720 landed at Entebbe airport. The time was 2405 hours, East African Time.

As ordered by the control tower, Captain Popjack taxied around the southern curve of the main commercial runway, past the tower itself, and on the apron in front of the new terminal buildings. A squadron of armoured cars escorted the jetliner all the way, from the moment it turned off the main runway.

Okan would not take any chances, this time.

More proof of that fact came even before Air Force 720 shuddered to a standstill. Four huge T-55 tanks rumbled on to the apron and into position around the aircraft. Mounted with heavy-calibre machine guns, jeeps and armoured personnel carriers patrolled the airport's perimeter wire. Troops armed with rifles also surrounded Air Force 720.

Next, the ground crew trundled a gangway into place. While they did so, an Arab put down his rifle and hurried across to the aircraft carrying a pail of white paint, which sloshed on to the apron. Using a thick paint brush, he daubed the Front's name on to the fuselage in large, crude Arabic letters. Then he darted back to his rifle, in time to join a force of Front commandos as they ran up the gangway steps. These men would relieve Garst's team. But the first thing they did was to wire up satchel explosives in the flight deck and three toilets.

161

All in good time, Obama Okan arrived. As soon as he appeared, the Ugandan troops began clapping, something which did not stop until Okan disappeared into the plane. The cheering and applause rose to a climax when he stopped at the forward door. Before going through the entrance he stood at attention and saluted.

Throughout, press bulbs flashed and an entourage of local reporters followed Okan into the cabin.

Okan's smile froze when he saw the South Africans. "You are my prisoners. Africa's prisoners," he told them brusquely. "It may definitely be necessary to put you on trial for war crimes. But we will see."

As he was talking, he glimpsed the secretary of state. Instantly, Okan's black face beamed. He made his way over to where Fackman was standing and clapped him on the shoulder. "But you are welcome to Uganda, Mr. Secretary," Okan said expansively. "I love your president. He is a very great leader. I love Americans very much. I have many American friends."

Before addressing Fackman again, the Ugandan waved a greeting to the two Marighella gunmen who were guarding Fackman.

"You'll be comfortable here," Okan said to the still silent Fackman. "We'll do all we can."

"I'm sure."

"You can be, Mr. Secretary. Definitely. But negotiating your release will be very, very difficult. You understand." Here Okan paused to wave a hand at the members of Garst's team again. "These men want all kinds of impossible things. They want their friends—heroes of their own movement—released from prisons in Israel, France, Switzerland, West Germany, even Kenya. I don't know how we can start. Your government is powerful. It must try to get these other regimes to co-operate. Africa itself will want freedom fighters to be released from prisons in Azania, Namibia, Zimbabwe."

"Yes, I understand. But I don't know how I can help. I'm a prisoner here myself."

"You can help, Mr. Secretary. Truly. I have already agreed with these Front people that you be allowed to contact your government from this very aircraft."

"I appreciate that very much," Fackman responded.

"You see, you must tell your president that you are well. Tell him I love him."

"I'll pass that on to the president," Fackman smiled.

"But also tell him that I hear bad news from Nairobi. There are American warships in Mombasa. I hear American Marines want to attack Uganda. I have these reports from many reliable persons. Tell your president this. Any invasion force must be destroyed by Uganda."

"I'll give him your message."

"Tell him I know CIA wants to kill all strong leaders like me."

Fackman said nothing.

"I am very, very unhappy about lies told about me and Uganda." The Ugandan dictator's eyes narrowed and the edges of his mouth turned down. "Your president must ask UN to investigate his own crimes, instead of Ugandan business. Redskin matters."

"Very good, Mr. President. I'll convey that, too."

"Anyway," Okan brightened unexpectedly, "now I must go. When this is all over, you must stay in Uganda. We will tour together. Shoot crocs. I want you to go back to Washington only with good reports, my friend."

"I look forward to staying in your country, Mr. President."

"You know, I am glad you are here," Okan said slyly. "You'll be able to see the truth for yourself. People are happy in Uganda. Free." Okan pounded the secretary of state on the back. "Okay, my friend. I'll see you. You tell your government what you like, on the radio."

Then the Ugandan faced the Marighella gunman nearest to him. "Now who is your leader?" he feigned ignorance. "Take me to him."

A short while later, he and Garst were walking down the gangway. Even before they got to the floodlit airport building, he broke the news of the two missions.

The hijacking of the El Al Boeing had succeeded—or failed, depending how it was viewed. The president of Libya was delighted.

In Athens, the leader of the hijacking squad had been taken seriously ill. But a message from Jabril was that the attack was not cancelled, merely postponed.

Garst received all the news impassively. She had always

163

believed that the El Al hijack would be the most dangerous. It had not come as a surprise to hear of the crash. Knowing the dedication of Commando Badawi, and the tough, uncompromising Israelis, something like this was to be expected.

"But you have definitely done well," Okan told her as they stepped on to the green carpet of Uganda's hall for international arrivals.

Thereafter, far on in the night but before daybreak, Garst and Okan listened carefully to the tapes of Fackman's radioed report and guarded discussion with the president of the United States. Fackman was concerned not to claim that Okan was in league with Commando Marighella, and this pleased them both. For in such circumstances, Okan could maintain the fiction that he was some kind of innocent, thrust into the role of mediator.

15

So that he could be on hand for the landing of Air Force 720, Obama Okan had driven from Kampala to Entebbe late at night. Thanks to the darkness no attack was possible, and thus he travelled to the airport safe from Yazov and Kruger. In fact, during this period, both these men were in their separate rooms on the eleventh floor of the Hotel International. Yazov was fast asleep. Arnie Kruger lay awake, smouldering. He had suggested to Yazov that—for safety's sake—they ought to share the same room. Yazov had not agreed. The rejection had rankled with Kruger, who had never wanted a man more.

Early in the morning, soon after daybreak, their weapons were delivered. The arms came in two large, strong leather cases, carried by a couple of black Ugandans. After stacking them in the clothes closet, Kruger knocked on the door to Yazov's room. "It's all happening. The hardware is here. Let's check the stuff out," he told the Bulgarian.

Kruger went back to his quarters. Both men cleaned up: Kruger bathed, Yazov showered. The American called room service and ordered breakfast. After they had eaten, Yazov began to check the weapons.

Meanwhile, Leonid Bevz had at last managed to arrange a meeting with Obama Okan, for Major Wakholi finally returned his call. It was decided that Bevz would spend part of the morning with Wakholi, at the bureau's headquarters; shortly after lunch, Obama Okan himself would grant the Russian security expert an audience.

By now, the Russian embassy was buzzing with news of the Refusal Front's coup. It was also much clearer to Bevz why the KGB had so urgently sent him to Kampala: the following days could be very perilous in the life of Obama Okan.

Already Bevz was somewhat disillusioned. He had wasted much time in trying to get hold of Major Wakholi and Colonel Oyok would not see him at all. It occurred to Bevz that Colonel Oyok was piqued at the fact that Okan had sought a KGB review of Uganda's security procedures, something which fell squarely within Oyok's jurisdiction. He would have to get Okan to have a word with Oyok.

At Command Post, Obama Okan was still slumbering by mid-morning. It had been a long day and night, and he did not want to start any serious parleying with Fackman until his and the Front's hands were considerably reinforced. This would happen when the Athens hijacking was a fact, and the ICA aircraft was brought to Entebbe.

It was a little past 11 a.m. when Okan awoke. Earlier in the morning, Jabril had radioed a coded message, and immediately Okan got up he was told that Commando Meinhof was due to hijack Inter-Continental Airways Flight 881, scheduled to leave Athens airport at 1300 hours. The Ugandan president decided he would immerse himself in a long, hot bath. Afterwards he would lunch with Garst, and if there was time, he would have a talk with the Russian.

An hour later, Okan still lay in the bath in Kampala, when Captain William Charles Funston walked through the departure lounge at Athens airport. Funston was the man who would be in charge of ICA's Flight 881, which was due to fly non-stop from Athens to New York.

The ICA captain was badly out of sorts. He was brooding, prickly and depressed. In short, he was in no mood to have his Boeing 747 hijacked. The man who captained the same flight twenty-four hours earlier would surely have been easier to deal with than Funston.

For one thing Funston had got to bed late. Until the early hours, he had roamed through the narrow, winding streets and lanes of Athens' nightclub and taverna district. For nothing. The closest he had come was a prostitute who wanted $150. The price was way over the going rate and Funston had gone to bed at the Athens Hilton in a frustrated, scratchy frame of mind.

Just as he fell into a deeper sleep, shortly after sunrise, an urgent rap on the door roused him. It was a terse cable from his attorney in White Plains, New York. The message was that his wife had finally cracked under the rigours of being married to an airline pilot. The communication told him that no reconciliation was possible, and that she was that day proceeding further with litigation to break up a marriage of twenty-two years. She wanted custody of their three minor children and a large alimony. She required immediate instructions as to what Funston wanted her to do with his tanks of rare, tropical fish.

After unsuccessfully trying to sleep again, Funston lay worrying whether his wife would pour his fish down the drain or starve them of oxygen by switching off the pump.

The airline captain's mood was increasingly morbid and ratty. His poor humour continued all the while he showered, pulled on his ICA uniform and drove to Latakia airport. To relieve his tensions, Funston tried a little deep breathing. He felt so wretched that at one stage he even contemplated scrubbing his trip to New York. But he needed to get back home as soon as possible: if she had tampered with the oxygen supply. . . . Besides, he did not want any trouble with the airline.

Ahead of Funston, on the concrete apron, two mobile staircases were already in position outside the doors of the ICA jumbo's port side. Two highlift loaders were packing cargo into the big jet's holds. The baggage and other containers were being loaded with care, according to a diagram, so that the combined masses of passengers, fuel and

166

cargo would not critically alter the aircraft's centre of gravity.

A constant flow of blankets, pillows, magazines, newspapers, food and drink, even flowers, was going aboard the Boeing 747 from tall catering hoists.

A fuel dispenser was parked under each of the plane's wingtips, pumping scores of tons of kerosene into vast tanks—enough fuel to drive a fleet of a hundred medium-sized cars for more than a year.

It was the usual pre-flight activity around a big jetliner, and Funston was hardly aware of it. He clumped up the gangway, and when he got to the top he abruptly touched the rim of his peaked cap to a pretty air hostess. Climbing a spiral staircase, he went through the first-class section to the jumbo's upper deck and cockpit.

The co-pilot and third pilot were already on board. Despite himself, Funston tried to smile. "Hi, Jim, sorry I'm late," Funston said, easing himself into the captain's seat on the left.

"Hello, 'Wild Bill.' Pleased you made it. We were getting . . ." Jim Chase started to reply.

"Wild Bill" was a nickname, a hangover from Funston's exploits over Viet Nam in a B-52 bomber based at Guam. But Funston did not want to hear it that day.

"Look, Jim, cool this 'Wild Bill' stuff, huh? Call me skipper, because that's who I am. I earned it." Funston tried not to sound too cantankerous as he pointed to the five black and four gold bars that alternated on the cuff of his left sleeve.

"Sorry, skipper," Chase apologized instantly.

"So far all systems are go." Third pilot Joe Mantoni quickly changed the subject, as he packed into place a blue leather satchel which contained Jeppersen Flight Guides. These were updated references to all the world's major airports. In any emergency, ICA Flight 881 could be directed to any one of the world's airstrips within fuel range.

"Weather reports are good. No trouble there." Jim Chase gave Funston the information.

"Okay. Start the checks," Funston said tersely.

While the aircrew carried on with their pre-flight checks, the cabin staff went about their own tasks. Hostesses sorted out magazines and newspapers, checked the toilets for cleanliness, stewards in the jumbo's galleys stowed food and bar supplies.

Now and again, an air hostess tested the sound systems to randomly chosen seats. The movie selected to be shown during the long flight over the Atlantic was *Murder by Death*.

In due time, ICA Flight 881 was technically ready for take-off. Funston gave the necessary signal to the ICA man who was in charge of handling the passengers. "ICA 881, ready for passengers," the handler in turn spoke into a walkie-talkie.

Less than a minute later, a female voice boomed over the public address system in the departure lounge: "Passengers for Inter-Continental Airways Flight 881 to New York are now boarding through gate number four." She spoke in Greek and English.

Commando Meinhof had planned to hijack the previous day's flight. Owing to a twist of fate, hundreds of different travellers who would otherwise have been perfectly unharmed were Meinhof's unexpected victims.

Tittering and posing for a couple of Polaroid instant photographs, three beauty queens from New York State prepared to board the airport bus and start the return leg of a fully paid holiday on Rhodes.

James Thomas and his wife got up from their seats in the departure hall. They had completed a ten-day holiday, including a cruise around the Greek Islands.

The beauty queens from New York State had won their trips to Greece as prizes. Marcia Williams and Peta Baker were also prizewinners: they were the two leading sellers of Tupperware in the state of New Jersey, rewarded with a trip to anywhere in west Europe. Greece was their choice.

Martin Shady was a middle-level executive in a multinational corporation. He had come to Athens to close a big deal for his company.

But it was because of Charles Koenig that the hijacking went wrong.

Koenig was a botanist at a college in the Middle West. He also edited a magazine called *Plant Weekly*. He and

168

his wife, Lilian, had come to Rhodes for a two-week holiday.

These people, and hundreds of others, now began to move out of the departure hall, with its gay Christmas decorations, to the Mercedes buses parked outside on the tarmac.

If Charles Koenig specially interested himself in a tall, sallow-skinned man of heavy build, he could hardly help it. Koenig stepped on to the bus and the much bigger man barged into him, almost knocking the botanist down. Koenig was doubly upset: he had lost his place in the line, and his ribs hurt.

"Mean sonofabitch," Koenig thought to himself.

The sixty-two-year-old, slightly built botanist was also a chronic worrier. Among other anxieties, he fretted that every aircraft he ever boarded was likely to be hijacked. Having been knocked about by the big man, Koenig looked him over carefully: he was unhappy that the mean bastard could easily pass as an Arab.

Koenig started to worry.

In fact, the man was an Arab. His name was Muhamad Mukarbal, and he was leading Commando Meinhof. What was more, the hijack had already started—with the heavy shove which Mukarbal had given Koenig.

Mukarbal wanted to board the bus ahead of anybody else, so that he could be sure of a place alongside the bus driver. This was the driver who had smuggled on to his bus two ICA flight bags, both of which were crammed with arms, ammunition and hand grenades.

The idea was for Mukarbal, who had no hand luggage, to get to the front of the bus and stand by the bags. Later, upon disembarking from the bus, he would casually take a bag. His companion, another member of Commando Meinhof, would remove the remaining weapons.

Hence Mukarbal's determination to board quickly. None the less, his actions were not strictly essential; he could have been second, third, fourth or even fifth on to the bus, without harm. Besides, what he did betrayed a certain edginess.

It was true. Mukarbal was nervous. Fortunately for him, Commando Meinhof had not been compelled to bring in the arms through Latakia's security systems. Owing to the

El Al tragedy and Commando Marighella's success in Johannesburg, even the easier going inspections at Athens had sharpened.

Thus Mukarbal was grateful to the bus driver, and even more thankful when he saw the two ICA grips alongside where the man sat, leaning over the steering wheel, staring vacantly ahead of the bus.

When the girl had suddenly become ill, he had recommended abandoning the mission. He had passed on his suggestion to a courier. Later, a different messenger had brought him the Front's decision: Commando Meinhof was to hijack the following day's flight and Mukarbal was to be in command. Now he had to make all the decisions. Mukarbal had felt jittery even with the girl in charge.

Other passengers got into the bus. Charles Koenig stepped right forward and was stopped by Mukarbal. He promptly noticed the two ICA bags. Koenig could not recall whether the Arab had carried a bag or not; two bags he definitely had not carried.

But for the jostling which happened earlier, the botanist might not have been so attentive. Now he was alive to anything and everything about Mukarbal. So he was also quick to note that the Arab was standing. Why should he stand in an empty bus, unless he wanted to be by those ICA cases?

While these thoughts churned over in Koenig's mind, Mukarbal was joined by another member of Commando Meinhof. This man brushed against Koenig, who immediately was aware of two things: he stood right alongside the Arab, and he carried no hand luggage.

The new arrival was a youth in his mid-twenties. He had long hair, and he was dressed in tight, faded Levis. He was obviously not Arabic.

Though he watched as carefully—and as unobtrusively—as he could, Koenig detected nothing that passed between the two men.

Was it a coincidence? Koenig fretted.

The botanist pretended to write notes on a copy of *Plant Weekly*. After letting his pencil slip to the floor of the bus, he had a good look at the bags as he retrieved it.

If there were any weapons inside, they could only be a

few pistols, clips of ammunition, grenades. But that was enough.

Although he was not an arms expert, Koenig would have been surprised to know that each bag contained two submachine guns, six clips of 7.65 ammunition, as well as four hand grenades. The grenades were of a new kind, the shrapnel bursts of which were the most devastating known to Jabril; each clip of ammunition was of the detachable, staggered row type, taking twenty rounds.

It was hardly credible that there were two submachine guns, too. However, Garst's choice of a Czech Model 61 was perfect. With its stock folded, the Model 61 had an overall length of less than eleven inches. A true machine gun, it had a cyclic rate of fire of 750 rounds a minute. Though the gun fired cartridges of relatively low power, the weapon was easily controlled in full automatic fire. It was fast and accurate, allowing multiple hits on target.

At last, the driver got the bus started. And if Koenig had not seen everything from the start, all would have looked normal: bags of various sizes, shapes and colours littered the floor space of the entire bus. Those by the feet of the Arab and the other man could easily be taken to be theirs.

As the bus lurched off, the botanist could not resist a quick look up into the face of the Arab. Momentarily, their eyes locked. Koenig turned abruptly away. He glanced at his wife Lilian. She was oblivious of any danger. Lilian sat looking out of the window.

When Koenig averted his glance, he made Muhamad Mukarbal more troubled than ever. It seemed to Mukarbal that the American—he was so palpably an American—was on to something, from the way he watched the two of them, using his peripheral vision. The American had also studied the weapons bags.

Sooner rather than later Mukarbal might have to act. But what could he do? For the umpteenth time he cursed the girl and her illness. If only she were present, she could have decided. Admittedly, he had been trained as deputy leader of Commando Meinhof. He had even been flattered by it. But Mukarbal knew he was much better at taking than giving orders.

171

Yet again Mukarbal caught the American's gaze as it strayed on to him momentarily. Once more, the American quickly looked away.

Now Mukarbal's stomach was twisted into a knot. Manifestly, the American suspected something. Raging briefly through Mukarbal's mental blockage was the mad thought of taking the thin little man by his bony neck and shaking him to death. Just two, at the most three, violent shakes.

Instead, Mukarbal felt his companion dig him lightly in the ribs with an elbow. His accomplice must have sensed Mukarbal's tension. He wanted to know what was wrong.

"The American behind us," Mukarbal had to twist his mouth slightly, speaking into the other man's ear. "Could be trouble."

His companion nodded. "What are we going to do?"

"I have an idea . . ." Mukarbal lied miserably.

Koenig saw them whispering. It jolted him into near panic. The secret contact almost confirmed everything. The two men were in cahoots. The botany professor's heart beat wildly.

Could he whisper a warning to Lilian without being seen?

At that moment the Mercedes bus slowed and squealed to a gentle halt. It stopped about twenty paces from the ICA Boeing 747. The pneumatic doors hissed open and passengers began to file out, straggling in an uneven line to the aircraft.

When Koenig got off his seat, he noted that the Arab and his friend were not moving. But neither had they picked up the flight bags. Perhaps he was imagining things, the botanist told himself. The bags could belong to the driver. He needed to get a grip on himself.

Koenig joined the tail of the queue out of the bus. Lilian walked ahead of him. Halfway to the doorway, trying to look casual, he allowed himself a glance over his shoulder. He was in time to see Mukarbal and his friend pick up the ICA bags.

It was too much.

With that, Koenig gripped his wife's upper left arm, painfully, propelling her vigorously forward. She squealed with the hurt. "Honey, we've got bad trouble," Koenig whispered urgently in her ear. "There's hijackers back

172

there. Nobody and nothing is getting us on to that plane."

Lilian Koenig felt the hot, moist blast of her husband's breath in her ear. She shot a glance to the front of the bus. There was a startled look in Mukarbal's eyes. The Arab was unzipping an ICA flight bag. . . .

Now Charles Koenig felt a jolt from his wife as she suddenly dragged him forward to get ahead in the queue.

Martin Shady had heard her painful squeal. He turned to see what was wrong with the frail American woman. "Please excuse us. We have to get off fast," he heard her low, insistent voice.

The corporate executive gave way, not without some resentment.

To squeeze by Marcia Williams and Peta Baker, Lilian Koenig was blunt. "Get out damned quick. We've got hijack trouble."

As a result of the El Al hijack and the events in Johannesburg, most of the travellers on ICA Flight 881 were jittery. Peta Baker and Marcia Williams were jumpy about Athens's unhappy record. So when they heard Lilian Koenig's warning, they shot forward, almost knocking down the man ahead of them.

This man was himself rushing to get out fast, having heard Lilian Koenig's urgent warning.

"Christ, hijackers!" he cried, stumbling forward.

Martin Shady whipped around and saw Mukarbal drag an ugly-looking weapon from a ICA bag. The Arab was trying to snap into place a fat, lethal magazine.

"Run! Run for your lives!" Shady screamed.

He charged into the people ahead of him like a footballer into a scrimmage, hurling the other passengers down the narrow passage.

"Sit down!" Mukarbal shouted. "Sit down!"

Here Marcia Williams shot back a terrified peep, even as she scrambled forward. She saw both men with guns. They stood side by side. And the guns were up.

"God help us! They'll kill us!" she screeched.

Mukarbal opened fire, and his accomplice fired a fraction later. The stubby machine guns crackled and rattled. Bullets smacked heavily into the panic-stricken travellers. From the crowded doorway came screams of pain.

If things went wrong on the bus, the pre-arranged plan

was for Commando Meinhof to take hostages. They would use them to force a safe passage from the Greek authorities.

But for a few moments Mukarbal panicked, driving the passengers out of the bus with his killing blasts.

Shady, Marcia Williams, Peta Baker and the Koenigs all went down in the first spray of gunfire.

It was for Koenig that Mukarbal reserved a vicious revenge. The Arab leapt forward and found the hapless botanist on the floor, dying of multiple bullet wounds. Stepping up to him, Mukarbal held the Model 61 over Koenig, and flayed the little man with a long, implacable burst. Koenig's body rattled on the floor under the impact.

This wasted time for the Arab.

Already the other passengers had stampeded out of the bus. They scattered all over the tarmac like a drop of quicksilver bursting on a table.

Mukarbal and his companion rushed out in hot pursuit.

The Arab pressed a button, slipping out the empty magazine. Pulling back a bolt, he slapped in a fresh clip. The two men stood spreadlegged, crouched, their feet riveted to the tarmac, wire-like stocks digging into their shoulders. Then they raked the runways and apron, firing at the wildly fleeing men, women and children.

Heavy bullets kicked up spurts from the concrete and tarmac, like hailstones beating on placid water.

Mukarbal lobbed a grenade. It bounced high, exploding with a roar—uselessly.

Another press on the button, again the magazine slid free.

By now, twenty-six seconds after Mukarbal had opened fire in the bus, two other commandos had joined them. But they had not panicked. Seizing their weapons, these two commandos jumped up the target aircraft's staircases, blocking the exits for passengers already on board.

This was fortunate for Commando Meinhof, because the second busload of passengers escaped without harm.

The other Mercedes was driven by a middle-aged Greek woman who had some presence of mind. She had followed the first Mercedes and was slowing down when she heard the gunfire. In her ears the shooting had sounded like a string of Chinese fireworks.

She saw passengers spilling crazily out of the forward compartment of the reticulated bus ahead of her. Without hesitating, she drove a wide, roaring circle around the plane, accelerating until she was well out of range.

The bus which had carried Mukarbal also got away—with the driver as the only live person aboard. As soon as the Arab and his partner had charged off, the bus driver crashed his engine into gear. With the big diesel throbbing powerfully, he got the bus off on a lurching run, throwing about the corpses of those killed at the start.

James Thomas's body was hurled across the doorway. When the driver closed the pneumatic door, the dead man's right foot got trapped in the rubber piping. As the bus thundered down the tarmac and concrete, Thomas's body trailed macabrely behind. Seeing this, his wife kicked off her shoes and ran after the rear of the bus, choking in the thick, oily smoke of its exhaust. A hundred yards later she collapsed into a sobbing, hysterical pile.

Around her were groups of other passengers, some in couples, other survivors alone. Some were wounded. Most were still jogging to the safety of Latakia's terminal buildings. All were stunned.

Behind them, abandoned flight bags lay scattered on the ground. Grenade blasts had dug shallow holes into the concrete and tarmac.

"It did not go too badly, comrades," Mukarbal told two of his men. "We've got enough here." He was talking about the fifty-seven hostages and all but two of the crew who were aboard the Boeing 747. But the Front had set out to capture hundreds of hostages. Whatever face Mukarbal tried to put on it, the mission had gone awry.

The Arab knew as much himself.

Therefore, he would have certainly preferred not to deal with someone like Captain Funston, who was in even less of a mood than ever to be bullied. At the best of times, Mukarbal would have wanted a docile, even-tempered captain on the 747.

This was the worst of times.

Feeling that somehow he was going to be blamed for everything, Mukarbal strode to the flight deck. He had his Model 61 in his left hand and his right hand was wrapped around a grenade.

175

Captain "Wild Bill" Funston and the others on the flight deck had heard the dull, chattering pops. They had a grandstand view of the short, furious attack.

Later, Funston had been contacted by the tower: he was told of the massacre that had taken place in the bus. The Greek authorities wanted him to be fully aware of whom he was going to have to deal with.

"The lousy motherfuckers," Captain Funston cursed.

"How's that, skipper?" asked Jim Chase.

"These schmucks aren't going to have it all their way, Jim," said Funston.

Funston had been in a tough, uncompromising, sour temper all morning. Given the least opportunity, he could have snapped at anyone for relief. Suddenly, he had the terrorists on to whom he could fasten his slow, burning anger.

"You know the drill, skipper." Jim Chase reminded Funston of the careful training and sound instruction given by ICA on the handling of hijack situations.

"All I'm saying, Jim," Funston retreated a little, "is that we don't have to lick their fucking boots."

Funston had not bothered locking the cockpit door. It was at this point that Mukarbal walked through the opening. After glaring briefly at all of them, he asked, "Who is your captain?"

Funston lifted up his sleeve, pointed with his left index finger at the bars of black and gold.

"Good. I'm El Kudesi, leader of Commando Meinhof of the Refusal Front." Mukarbal paused. "I'm your new captain." He raised his right hand with the hand grenade, pointing with the muzzle of his Model 61 at the little bomb.

Nobody said anything.

"Do as I say and no harm will come to you." Then Mukarbal asked, "How do I operate the intercom?" He had operated the system before, but without great interest, during the training. After all, the girl was going to do all the talking.

"You're the captain. That's what you said," Funston smiled grimly. "The captain ought to know every little thing. . . ."

176

"Already I don't like you, captain," Mukarbal flared.

"Bad vibes, eh?"

"What do you mean?"

"Bad vibrations, brother. We're not hitting it off. Personality clash, that kind of thing."

From the Arab's expression, Funston could see that he did not understand completely.

"You no like me. I no like you," the ICA captain said.

"I understand, I assure you," Mukarbal spoke his stiff, correct English. "That's what I said . . . already I don't like you."

"Right on, brother."

"You know, captain, we're going to have to get something clear." Mukarbal turned the Model 61 on to Funston. "Just do as you're told. If you don't . . ."

"Yes, sir. What if I don't?"

"Take it easy, skipper." Jim Chase could not stop himself.

"Then, captain," Mukarbal's voice was rising steadily, "I'll take one of your little bitches and fuck her with this!" The Arab shouted, shaking the muzzle of his machine gun. "I'll take one of them on to the tarmac right now!" Mukarbal still spoke fiercely. "Have you ever seen a woman fucked by a burst of machine gun fire, captain? Would you like to? I have, captain! In my village!"

Even Funston was taken aback by the outburst.

Jim Chase squeezed the captain's shoulder, pleading, "Please get it under control, skipper. Keep it cool."

"Sure, Jim. It's all under ice." Funston's eyes took on a faraway, glazed look.

"That's right, skipper. Keep it cool," Mukarbal mimicked. The Arab was also calmer, his voice was back to normal, and he merely nodded at the muzzle of his weapon.

"Give him a hand with the intercom, Jim." Funston had collected himself.

"Sure, skipper."

"Thank you for your co-operation, captain." Mukarbal relaxed. Earlier, for a moment or two, he had been unrestrained. He had felt the same kind of rage wash over him in the bus. What was wrong? During training he had experienced none of this; he had been controlled. Perhaps it

177

had something to do with the stress of being in command.

Jim Chase handed over the intercom microphone, and Mukarbal began speaking to Commando Meinhof's hostages: "Ladies and gentlemen, kindly fasten your seat belts. This is your new captain speaking. My name is El Kudesi, and I am the leader of Commando Ulrike Meinhof of the Refusal Front. We have taken over full control of this aircraft. Remain seated, do as we ask, and nobody will be hurt."

While he spoke into the microphone, Mukarbal covered the crew with his machine gun. In the same hand which held the microphone, he also clutched the grenade.

"You must relax. Soon all will be well. Unfortunately a certain amount of bloodshed became unavoidable. I assure you, no more will be necessary, provided that we all co-operate with each other."

It was all coming back to Mukarbal, what he had to say, how he had to act. As he spoke, he became a little more confident. Using the back of his hand, he wiped the perspiration off his forehead, making the microphone rasp while he did so.

"We are revolutionaries for peace. Flight 881 was taken to remind the world of injustices. . . ."

In all, the Arab spoke for about six minutes. Among other things, he informed the hostages that the United States was an enemy of the Palestinian nation, and a collaborator with the illegal regimes in southern Africa. It was a very bad and evil thing that the United States had done to supply Israel with weapons, even the atomic bomb. America was the mainstay of all imperialist, colonialist, oppressive regimes. . . .

Mukarbal concluded by saying, "We bear you passengers no ill will. You are in no danger. But you must obey all our orders, promptly and without question. Soon we will take off for our final destination. We want this trip to be safe and comfortable. Meantime, I repeat, obey all orders. Thank you."

Mukarbal slotted the microphone back into place. He was about to say something to Funston when the ICA captain spoke to Jim Chase. "Get out the Jeppersen for Entebbe, Jim. That's in Uganda. Never been there myself."

Indignation began to well inside the Arab. He managed

to bottle it before he said, "You are a clever man, captain. Clairvoyant."

"You speak English well. That's a big word."

"I learned English well, at the American University in Beirut."

Captain Funston said nothing.

"In future, I give the orders. Understand? I'll tell you where we're going."

"Sure."

"You may set a course for Entebbe. . . ."

At 1321 hours Captain Funston pointed the nose of the Boeing 747 into the wind of the main runway.

"ICA 881. Clear for take-off," the message came from the Latakia tower.

"I am moving for take-off," Funston told the controllers.

The big aircraft rolled down the runway at an ever increasing rush and finally lifted off into a clear blue sky, climbing steeply over the azure Gulf of Corinth. It soon left behind the airport and the jetty close by, where scores of small sailing boats were anchored.

"ICA 881, good day and good luck." Latakia control crackled a parting.

After the big aircraft levelled off, Mukarbal called one of the other commandos on to the flight deck. "Keep the door open at all times," Mukarbal told him. Thereupon he proceeded to the cabin to check that everything was secure—and to make it still more safe.

To crush in advance any opposition to what he wanted done, the Arab spoke firmly into a microphone in the middle cabin: "Your seating has been rearranged to make everything simpler for all of us. Now obey this order very carefully. I assure you that anybody who resists will suffer badly. Commencing with cabin crew, every person must remove all garments, except underthings."

Mukarbal waited a few seconds, then explained: "The reason for this is simple. It is an additional safety precaution. You will appreciate that your embarrassment will help keep you in your places."

A pretty, blonde air hostess was the first to carry out the instruction. While Mukarbal looked on dispassionately, she slipped off a blouse, skirt, brown shoes and light

179

brown pantyhose. Having stripped down to her bra and panties, she sat quietly in her seat, legs crossed. Her face was flushed.

"We have been humiliated for twenty-seven years," Mukarbal said unfeelingly. "A few hours won't hurt you."

Once everyone had stripped as ordered, the Arab spoke into the microphone again: "Thank you for your help. Now my men will collect all travel documents. Please have your passport available."

With these tasks completed, Mukarbal returned up the spiral staircase to the flight deck. Now he wanted Captain Funston to contact the tower at Ben Gurion airport, Tel Aviv. Funston quickly raised the Ben Gurion tower, and Mukarbal recited into the radio transmitter a long, rambling attack on Israel, the United States and white South Africa.

The Arab concluded his diatribe with the demand that his speech be published in seven major newspapers: *The New York Times, Washington Post, International Herald Tribune, Le Monde, The Times* of London, *Jerusalem Post* and *Rand Daily Mail* of Johannesburg.

Mukarbal did not say what would happen if his demand was not fulfilled.

Having attended to all these matters, which completed his preliminary assignments, Mukarbal was in a more expansive state of mind. He was altogether happier, and sufficiently relaxed to decide on a small gesture of goodwill to his prisoners. He instructed Commando Meinhof to hand out copies of the day's edition of the *Herald Tribune*.

It was cold in the aircraft, and most of the hostages covered themselves with the newspapers rather than read them.

16

In the course of the flight to Entebbe, Mukarbal mellowed still further: he allowed the ICA hostesses and stewards to dress, so that they could serve the hostages hot coffee and biscuits. He felt even more generous when the aircraft reached the hot skies over the dry, reddish-brown desert of the south Sudan, so much so that he toyed with the idea of serving a full-course, in-flight meal. However, the prospect of the hostages using the cutlery as weapons made him decide against it.

The Arab spoke no more than a few sentences to Captain Funston, and though the atmosphere was strained, the two men had little time to provoke one another. In fact, Mukarbal only returned to the flight deck once—for the purpose of radioing a coded message to the Refusal Front, on the frequency selected in advance from Commando Meinhof.

The Boeing 747 flew at 600 m.p.h., slightly faster than its ordinary cruising speed. This was by Mukarbal's order for he wanted to reach Entebbe as soon as possible. By 1600 hours East African Time the aircraft was about an hour from its destination.

At this time, the US Secretary of State's Boeing 707 was still parked on the apron, where it had stood in the hot sun all day long. Inside, the heat was making the cabin uncomfortable. Otherwise the hostages were safe but filled with foreboding.

Fackman was puzzled that Obama Okan and the girl had not returned to Air Force 720. He had not been allowed to contact Washington again, nor to listen to any news reports on the aircraft's receiver. Thus he waited in ignorance of what was taking place outside the cabin of the plane.

Meanwhile, in Kampala, Kruger and Yazov also marked time. They were both in Kruger's room, no. 1102,

181

of the International Hotel. The CIA man's quarters were adequate: it was the impersonal, relatively clean kind of room available in thousands of medium-grade hotels all over the world.

Kruger lay on one of the beds, his head resting on a pillow. He had not bothered to remove the bedspread. For at least three hours he had lain awake, waiting for the call. Most of that time he watched a shadow move across the ceiling. It made slow progress. Kruger would close his eyes, drowse, open his eyes again. He would measure how much the shadow had moved in relation to a dirty mark on the ceiling.

Later, he observed a spider crawl up the wall, making a patient, erratic tour. When it reached the corner where ceiling and wall were joined, Kruger wondered if the insect would cross over the join. The spider did, tracing a hesitant, irregular path across the ceiling. Kruger speculated on whether the thing would move into the shadow or keep to the sunlit part of the ceiling. After wavering for a long spell, the spider crawled into shadow.

Kruger closed his eyes briefly and guessed how far the spider would move in the meantime. When he looked again the spider was gone. One minute it was up on the ceiling, the next it seemed to have passed from existence.

Just like Yazov would soon pass from existence, Kruger caught himself thinking.

The Bulgarian was sitting up on the other bed with his back to the wall, reading the Russian military magazine, *Polar Bear*. He was alive. If the call came soon, they would assassinate Okan. Yazov would return to the room, and Kruger would kill him. Yazov would pass out of Kruger's ken, like the spider.

Thoughts constantly mulled through Kruger's mind. He ruminated about what went wrong at the Taft, about what a scheming sonofabitch Mike Tarrant was. He recalled his mother's face on a Christmas long ago. He remembered how he once won a geography prize at school. He examined his love life and how Yazov had spurned him.

As he lay on the bed, Kruger had given up the chase. Short of taking down his pants—or reaching for Yazov's crotch—Kruger had tried everything.

He would have bet money that the Bulgarian was gay.

There had been nothing in Yazov's record about a wife or girlfriend. Yazov had not been turned on by a whole chorus line of naked, bouncing fannies. He had also declined the massage parlour routine. And the polygraph readings had jumped. . . .

The polygraph had misled him most, Kruger thought. When it jumped, he had got excited. And he had been strongly attracted to a man with so many kills.

Anyway, all that was in the past.

Now everything the Bulgarian did irritated Kruger, which was good. He would enjoy putting a bullet in his back.

The cold, unfeeling sonofabitch had simply lain about the bed all day, Kruger reminded himself. No tension in him, he seemed indifferent to everything—except the inanimate, unfriendly weapons.

Yazov had got to them as soon as he could, once breakfast was over. Kruger had locked and chained the door to his room and drawn the curtains tightly. Yazov had opened the leather cases to remove the weapons from the mouldings of the polystyrene boxes, where they fitted so snugly. The parts of the Sagger anti-tank missiles, as well as the Dragunov rifle, had been packed like the components of a complicated game.

Yazov built the Dragunov in less than five minutes. It had aggravated Kruger to watch how the Bulgarian moved his fingers lightly, almost caressingly, over the cold steel parts. He forced nothing. Yazov's sequences were smooth and exact. Kruger had been reminded of foreplay between a man and his passive lover.

It had all slightly disgusted Kruger.

The missiles had come in their containers, ready to fire. To get to the plastic packs with the carrying handles Yazov had removed the outer polystyrene boxes. He completed a pre-launch check with an electrical testing device, which confirmed that the missiles would fire. Having finished his inspection, Yazov had repacked the weapons, keeping the Dragunov intact. Later, he had ordered a lunch consisting of cheese and wine.

This also had annoyed Kruger. Yazov had found listed among the wines a strong, red cabernet from Bulgaria. The discovery had delighted him, and since noon he had drained glass after glass with obvious relish. His only contact with Kruger during this time had been to point proudly to the bottle's rich red and gold label, which proclaimed that the wine had won 108 gold medals during its history.

In the first place, Kruger resented the fact that Yazov had found the wine on the list. And secondly, for some mixed reason, he was galled by the obvious enjoyment that the wine afforded Yazov.

The Bulgarian contentedly read *Polar Bear*, washing down chunks of goat's milk cheese with a succession of wine-filled glasses.

"Better lay off that stuff, Crystal. We don't want your aim dented, buddy. All those buildings out there could start swaying for you." Kruger could not stand it any longer.

"Good stuff. From the old country, Butterfly."

Even the use by Yazov of the code-name irked Kruger.

"You don't care a damn, do you?" Kruger snapped.

"I do. About this." Yazov held up a glass of wine in one hand, a chunk of cheese in the other.

What had he ever seen in this bum, Kruger asked himself.

"Relax, Butterfly. You have lain there like your foot was in a bear trap all afternoon."

"I'm all right, fella. I don't have to do any shooting. . . ." Arnie Kruger replied, going on to think to himself: except for the slug I'll be putting in your back, sucker.

The American went back to watching the ceiling, listening for the pips that could sound at any time from the little bleeper by his head. An electronic pageing device, the bleeper was housed in a small, black box about the size of a cigarette pack. The tiny radio receiver would bleep when Colonel Oyok pushed a button on a similar transmitter.

The code was simple enough: three bleeps meant that Obama Okan was preparing to leave Command Post; two bleeps, and the dictator's black Mercedes was starting down the driveway.

If he wanted to scrap the mission—because of some danger or sudden emergency—Colonel Oyok would bleep ten times.

184

This was the easiest system the CIA could devise for Oyok.

At 1621 Kruger heard three urgent pips.

The high-pitched sounds broke a tense silence in the room.

"Killing time. Weapons handling time," Kruger called across to Yazov, raising himself on to his elbows. "You'll love it."

Yazov drained his glass quickly. After sweeping a few crumbs of cheese off the palm of his hand, he dry washed his hands.

Colonel Oyok was at Command Post when he sounded the bleeps. He had just learned that Obama Okan had decided to drive to the airport at Entebbe, and the woman from Commando Marighella would go with him.

Okan and Garst had lunched pleasantly at Command Post. During the course of a long meal, they had discussed the successes and failures of the combined operations.

Garst's mission was, of course, a total success. Okan had again commended the girl. Indeed, in his clumsy way—because he did not easily admit error—he sheepishly apologized about his earlier baulkiness over Garst's key role.

"If you had been at Copenhagen it definitely would have worked," Okan flattered her.

Still, by terrorist standards, the El Al crash was not a defeat. The Israelis had lost more than the Front, and the president of Libya was overjoyed, Okan repeated. It was almost as if the Libyan preferred it that way. The Athens affair had not gone smoothly, but, again, the killings would have their impact. Commando Meinhof had managed to secure some seventy hostages and a valuable aircraft. Although the Front had wanted hundreds of Americans, the Athens attack had panned out adequately.

"A pity that the woman got sick," Okan said. "This fellow lost his head. Your man, Kudesi."

Garst conceded to herself that her choice of Muhamad Mukarbal had probably been wrong. Later, she and Jabril would analyse their shortcomings, including the mistakes in Athens.

Whatever the failings, the whole spectacular mission

185

was so far a major defeat for Israel, the United States and the regimes of white southern Africa. The blowing up of the El Al Boeing, the killings in Johannesburg and Athens—these would make the bargaining that much easier.

Okan and the Front had some stiff demands. Already Garst had been in coded radio communication with Hassan Jabril in Aden. He had congratulated her, said he longed for her—and he approved her preliminary negotiating tactics. These were along the lines she and Jabril had long ago discussed in detail.

To begin with, the Front would bargain with Fackman, who would relay their demands to Washington, so that the exchanges and transactions would be speeded up. Besides, Fackman could be their best advocate.

It was in Fackman's interest to have their demands met. In principle the Front would call for the release of all freedom fighters held in Israel, Azania, Namibia, Zimbabwe, West Germany, Kenya, even in Egypt; the president of Libya wished to have freed a number of Libyans behind bars in Cairo. That was the broad basis: all prisoners had to be liberated. The bottom line consisted of seventy-three freedom fighters who were listed in a document. If the hostages were to be traded, these seventy-three men and women had to be part of the bargain. . . .

ICA would fly all the revolutionaries to Entebbe and the airline would fly out the hostages, too.

The United States and South Africa would also have to agree to a large Refusal Front "tax," and Okan, through the Front, would make certain other demands on the Pretoria regime.

The negotiating strategies, where the hostages would be held, what was to be said at the press conferences, how to deal with requests from local embassies—all of this, and more, occupied Okan and Garst for much of the early afternoon. The Leader of Commando Marighella and the president of Uganda talked in his study for hours.

While Obama Okan was so preoccupied, Leonid Bevz waited in the large ante-room. The Russian had been growing increasingly restive until, at long last, Okan granted him an audience. After Okan and Garst had concluded their lengthy discussions, and the girl had left to shower and change her clothes, the Ugandan's private secretary reminded Okan of Bevz's appointment.

"Come in, my friend. Come in," Okan beamed as his private secretary presented Bevz.

"Comrade Leonid Bevz. I am at your service, Mr. President." Bevz leaned over Okan's desk and presented his credentials. "I am here at your request, Mr. President. . . . A security liaison officer between our two peace-loving governments."

"Yes, definitely, my good friend." Okan made a pretence of studying the document which had been handed to him. "This seems to be perfectly in order. Perfect." He passed the credentials back to Bevz, who knew that Okan was, for all practical purposes, illiterate, but let his face betray nothing of this knowledge.

"I must apologize, my friend. You know, I have been busy with affairs of state. These hijacker fellows. I'm trying to do my best with them. . . . I'm going to be very busy for days. Trying to help everybody out of their troubles." Even with Bevz, Okan clung to his role as honest broker.

"Yes, Mr. President. I understand."

"So how are things in Moscow, eh?"

"Very well, thank you, Mr. President. The people are happy and . . ."

"You are happy, my friend, to get away from the cold." Okan was not listening. "Moscow is very cold. Especially in winter times. Now it is cold there, eh?"

"December is cold, of course, Mr. President. But the people. . . ."

"Uganda has a wonderful climate, my friend. Believe me." Okan was still not taking any notice of what Bevz was saying. But since the Ugandan considered that the introductory small talk was over, he came down to the nub of Bevz's presence. "I hear from my men that you arrived in Uganda two days ago. Can you report anything?"

"I can see how we can straight away improve entry and exit checks, Mr. President. Especially at the airport."

"Have you spoken to anyone? Major Wakholi . . . Colonel Oyok?"

"I did speak with Major Wakholi, briefly. This morn-

187

ing. I have not been able to see Colonel Oyok. I was going to speak to you . . ."

Yet again Okan would not allow him to finish. It was obvious that the dictator was in a hurry.

"Yes, my friend. I would not worry my head a very good deal about Oyok," Okan said mysteriously.

"I'm sorry, Mr. President," Bevz was alert, seeking clarification.

"I may send Oyok on a very long and dangerous journey. This man may not return."

"I think I'm starting to . . ."

"Believe me, my friend. Oyok is a good man. He has served me well, very well. But he has been chief of security for too long."

"I see, Mr. President." That was why Okan had called for the KGB's help. When Oyok went, Okan would need an expert to reorganize everything. He could not trust his own men.

"I do not like to keep people too long on the same job," Okan continued. "You know, they get stale. Then one day they are not happy in the job. They lose interest. They start to think of bad things. Believe me, I know. . . ."

Naturally, he knew, Bevz thought to himself: when Okan had tired of commanding Uganda's army, he had taken over the presidency in a lightning coup.

"Yes, Mr. President."

"Come to think of it, my friend. I don't see much of Oyok these days. You see? That is definitely a sign. A year ago, he was accompanying me all the time. This man is definitely not one hundred per cent keen on the job. Yes, Oyok is stale."

"Or worse, Mr. President. Perhaps."

Suddenly, Okan's tribal scars stood out again. His eyes narrowed with suspicion. "You know, my friend, Allah may have sent you. Believe me, I am well looked after in mysterious ways," Okan said very seriously. "It is not impossible that Oyok is up to something. Nothing is impossible. Perhaps you can check this for me, eh?"

"I will, Mr. President."

"You are a good man, my friend. Of course, Oyok must not know what I am thinking. If he hears that I want him

188

to go on a trip, he will very definitely have a depression. And a man having a big depression is dangerous."

"I will be careful about what I discuss with him, Mr. President. Are you thinking of replacing Oyok with Major Wakholi, if I may ask, because . . ." Bevz wanted to tell Okan that he had not been impressed with Wakholi, who had been uneasy throughout their short discussion.

"Wakholi is a good fellow. Nothing wrong with Wakholi. But he is Oyok's fellow. These people like to put their own under them. Wakholi may also have to go on some kind of trip. . . . No, my friend, I want a total shake-up when the time comes. Definitely."

At this point, Okan's private secretary interrupted the meeting. He gave the Ugandan president a message from Colonel Oyok, who had been in the communications room when Entebbe tower had radioed that the ICA Boeing 747 was about half an hour's flying time from the airport.

"I must go, my friend." Okan instantly raised himself from the chair. "Please, remember what we spoke here. We will talk again, soon."

When Bevz next saw Obama Okan the Ugandan was with the girl whom Bevz took to be the leader of Commando Marighella. They passed through the open doorway on to the portico outside the main entrance to Command Post where half a dozen members of Okan's guard raggedly presented their AK-47 assault rifles. Okan returned a far smarter, crisp salute.

His right hand snapping up to a kepi of the kind once used by President de Gaulle, Okan was undeniably impressive in his dress. He wore a uniform of light blue, with gold braid, piping and epaulettes. A long row of seventeen medals stretched from the centre of his chest to under his left armpit. Under the medals were pinned three rows of large, circular medallions, all of which glinted brightly.

Simultaneously with Okan's appearance on the portico, two cars and a group of six motorbike-mounted outriders drew up in the driveway below the steps to Command Post.

Okan walked down the steps to the waiting Mercedes, medals banging and jangling. The big black car was Okan's favourite. It could cruise at 105 m.p.h., and had a maximum speed of 140. On the front of the bonnet was mounted the familiar, three-pointed star which Okan found pleasing: it reminded him of a gun sight.

There was a light breeze in the air, and the flags of Uganda and the PLO flapped from two short holders which were fitted into holes on the front sides of the Mercedes.

Before Okan climbed into the lead car, he nodded curtly in the direction of a black Lincoln Continental, waiting stationary behind the German car. If Oyok had seen to it, as he always had done in the past, there would be five SRB men sitting in the Lincoln. All would have Model 61 machine guns across their knees. And Okan's personal physician would be in the Lincoln, too, his emergency medical kit at his feet.

On impulse, Okan crossed over to the Lincoln to make an inspection. . . .

All was in order and the five armed men, as well as the doctor were in their usual places.

Okan climbed into the Mercedes, and Garst settled into the rear, alongside him. The outriders revved the motors of their Triumph motorbikes.

Provided that Oyok had planned with his ordinary efficiency, Okan knew that all traffic would be halted along the route to Entebbe airport. This would permit the Mercedes to travel at speeds which were too fast for accurate sniping. In the critical bend, which Oyok had once suggested be straightened, the security boss would have positioned a small detachment of troops. And all along the way, Oyok's men would keep a constant contact. For this purpose they were issued with powerful walkie-talkies.

Okan's Mercedes started to move. The wheels of the two-car and six-outrider motorcade crunched on the sand of the driveway.

As the motorcade approached the sentry boxes which guarded the exit from Command Post, Okan observed them get ready to present arms. He was always nervous when they did it and even the fact that the Mercedes's windows were bullet proof had never reassured him completely.

Then the motorcade sped by the sentries, on to the open road. The faster it travelled, the better Okan liked it.

190

Behind the motorcade, before it had quite reached the sentry boxes, Bevz had jumped into an embassy Zil. "Go like the devil's about to take you," he ordered the driver in Russian.

Bevz did not know precisely what was troubling him. Perhaps it was his instinct. Now that he knew of Okan's plan to replace Oyok, he was much unhappier about his dealings with Wakholi and his inability to contact Oyok. If Okan was thinking of removing his SRB chief, had this possibility not communicated itself, in some indefinable way, to Oyok? Something was not quite right. Anyway, perhaps he should study Okan's motorcade. Maybe there were obvious improvements which he could suggest. The route, the speed of the motorcade, the distance between the lead and following cars. . . .

Bevz worried whether the Zil could catch the motorcade. "Get a move on, comrade," he leaned forward and ordered the driver.

17

Oyok had been avoiding Okan as much as possible, without needlessly arousing the president's suspicions, and he did not want to meet Bevz at all.

Oyok's motives were simple: he was afraid. He was scared that Okan might pick up in Oyok's demeanour the treachery absorbing the SRB colonel. For that same reason he could scarcely see Bevz, who was trained to spot security risks.

Colonel Oyok hoped, though, that he was not as jittery as Major Wakholi. He had seen Wakholi the previous afternoon, and the man had been in a patent state of funk. Wakholi was persuaded that Okan's help from the KGB—ostensibly to improve the SRB's security procedures—was a big warning of a probable purging of the SRB.

As Colonel Oyok put it, "We'll be joining the club, Wakholi. Make no mistake."

Oyok referred to the "Club of the Dead," to which so many civil servants and military men for whom Okan had no further use had been "retired."

After Wakholi had left him—with instructions to see Bevz briefly, and to baulk him as long as possible—Colonel Oyok had himself lapsed into nervous uncertainty. The whole damn coup was going to be touch and go. Everything was based on the momentum created by Okan's assassination. The president's death would create an instant power vacuum. Colonel Oyok, being forewarned and prepared, would rush into the vacuum, seemingly to restore and maintain order. Troops loyal to Okan would simply be taking new orders from an apparently natural successor.

This was why Colonel Oyok would not move openly against Okan. Should he do so, Oyok could provoke a bloody civil war. It would have to appear that he had perforce taken over from the dead leader. After all, somebody would have to assume power, and the prize would go to whoever acted the fastest.

Oyok had bossed the SRB for a long time; eighteen months was a lifetime, often literally, in Okan's service. Okan definitely preferred short-term appointments. Colonel Oyok remembered a graphic illustration of Okan's philosophy when he had accompanied him and the Cuban ambassador through the gardens of Command Post six months earlier. Though Oyok had kept a respectful distance, he had heard the Cuban distinctly ask how Okan managed to keep safely in power, despite all the obvious rivalries in Uganda. "My friend . . ." was all that Okan said, before lopping off the heads of the tallest flowers with a swagger stick. The message had not been lost on Colonel Oyok.

Another occurrence was indelibly imprinted on Oyok's mind a month later. Okan had lain restlessly in his bedroom, shortly after the Entebbe rescue by Israelis. Oyok was called to his bedroom. "Oyok, the heavens are too bright tonight," Okan had complained. Under Okan's personal orders he had machine-gunned the moon.

The episode badly jolted Oyok's confidence in Okan—and in his own ability always to please the Uganda president, something which Oyok considered quite essential.

Therefore, when Colonel Oyok was approached deviously by a black agent of the CIA, not long after these incidents, he was ready to listen. Working subtly on Oyok's appetite for power, something which the CIA had exposed in its personality analysis of the SRB colonel, the American intelligence service recruited him within a month.

As he watched Okan's motorcade start down the driveway, wheels kicking up dust from the gravel surface, Oyok was standing in an upstairs room, behind a curtain.

Probably Okan would wonder where his SRB chief was. No matter. On condition that the men in the International did their job properly, he might never have to explain anything to the president again.

Unbuttoning the pocket of his khaki shirt, Oyok withdrew a unique radio transmitter shaped like a cigarette pack. It had three buttons, above each of which was a picture etched into the plastic, for Oyok could not read: a picture in white, of a man heading for the door; another of a Mercedes, its wheels spinning; the last was of a yellow snake, in the act of spitting.

As the motorcade roared past the sentry boxes which guarded the exit to Command Post, Oyok pressed the button under the drawing of the red Mercedes.

From where he stood, the colonel noticed a man rush to the Zil—the KGB security expert, Colonel Oyok guessed. He also observed how the Zil pulled off down the driveway, wheels skidding, grit flying.

The KGB man was in a great hurry, Oyok thought to himself with some discomfort. Then he slipped away from the curtain and headed for the communications room. He had much to do in the next hour.

Had Colonel Oyok followed the Zil for a mile and a half past the gates to Command Post, he might well have pressed the snake button. It was about this distance from Command Post that Bevz forced the motorcade to stop, by catching up with it and playing a long, hard tattoo with the powerful Zil horn.

Bevz got out of the Zil.

He walked past the Lincoln, the doors of which were open. Two of the SRB men were lounging against the car's

193

sides, holding their Model 61s ready. They wore bored expressions.

Beyond the Mercedes, the outriders had stopped in an untidy group. Their Triumph motorbikes were all askew, at different angles to the tarmac road, as they balanced on either their left or right feet.

They all looked back, watching Bevz with curiosity.

As he got closer to the Mercedes, Bevz considered whether he was doing the right thing. He wanted as soon as possible to establish some authority with Okan. But perhaps this was ridiculous . . . stopping the whole motorcade. Still, it was a good time to start work. Unless he got the president to knuckle under to his security fiats, he could go back home to Moscow.

The rear door window, on President Okan's side, rolled down. As it steadily descended, Bevz felt rising uncertainty within himself.

"Yes, my friend. What is it?" Okan poked his head out of the window and spoke impatiently. "We are all in a hurry here."

"Mr. President, I need your backing."

"Yes?" Okan sounded suspicious.

"It is a time of maximum danger. You must make frequent changes in your travel plans. Break patterns. Make last minute alterations. This can vitally affect the timing of any attempt to kill you."

"Of course, my friend," Okan smiled indulgently. "We know about all that here. Believe me. But you are unnecessarily . . ."

It was Bevz who cut Okan short, saying, "Sudden change is the best guarantee of your life. I recommend that you change cars, Mr. President. From this Mercedes into here." Bevz pointed at the Lincoln.

"You are unnecessarily worried today, my friend," Okan tried to keep a happy face. Moreover, it had been reported to the Ugandan president that the air-conditioning in the Lincoln had broken down. And Okan was not in the mood to sweat all the way to Entebbe in his heavy uniform, with all its furniture and, under all that, a bullet-proof vest. Otherwise, the luxury American car was also equipped with a siren, fire extinguisher, bullet-proof tires and windows, armour plating. The chassis could take the blast of a small bomb. The Lincoln contained radio transmitting and receiving equipment, too.

"I must insist, Mr. President. In my country, our highest leaders obey the security officers responsible for their safety. This is the case too with the president of the United States. All great leaders . . ."

"My friend, please, we are in a hurry over here. I am not used to taking orders in my own country. Now you are making me gloomy." Okan meant that the Russian was angering him, and Bevz understood as much.

It was a battle of wills. If Bevz could not impose some authority, he could give up.

"Mr. President, please, I . . ."

"My friend, are you deaf? I mean, are you definitely deaf?" Okan bawled.

Bevz would try one more time. He did not hold out much hope. And he was aware of his own rising temper.

18

Arnie Kruger had a fine view of Kampala. He was on top of the East African Airways building, and from where he crouched he could see the hairpin bend which Entebbe Road made with South Street.

Wearing his EAA coveralls, he had simply walked into the lift and taken a ride up as far as it would travel. Thereafter he had walked up the last flight of stairs, which led on to the roof.

The CIA agent sat on his haunches, eyes level with a three-foot-high wall, exposing himself as little as possible. Once, he had tried to kneel. He quickly got back on to his haunches, for the heat of the roof was too painful.

It would all happen soon enough.

There were no helicopters up in the sky. Kruger had expected one or two, high over the buildings, fluttering over the route, checking the roof tops. If that happened, he would have to risk it. Unlike Yazov, he could not move

195

under a water tank, because his job was to signal the arrival of the motorcade.

Kruger credited the absence of helicopters to Colonel Oyok. It was Oyok's job to decide whether to put up choppers, and on this occasion he had dispensed with them. He could do it this once, and nobody would ask questions later: Okan would be dead.

Well, here they came.

A flash of sunlight, reflecting off a windscreen. This was the first sign Arnie Kruger picked up. Then, through a shimmering haze, the outriders materialized. Behind the motorbikes came the black Mercedes. Soon they were all clearly in view, the second car, too.

Kruger had to wait a few seconds. The Mercedes had to get in line with the tree by the roadside.

When it did, Kruger pressed a button on the same device with which he had picked up Colonel Oyok's signal. The small transmitter was good over at least a mile, and from where he was sitting to the top of the International was much less than that.

That was it. Kruger had done his bit. Now it was up to Yazov.

The signal from Kruger—nine high-pitched bleeps which came in groups of three—jolted Yazov. He was sitting under a large, round corrugated-iron water tower, concealed from the view of any helicopter which might have whirred overhead.

A thin flex of wire connected a pocket-sized receiver with a plug stuffed into his ear. To be sure of hearing the signal, Yazov had turned up the volume control so the strident bleeps made him yank the plug out of his ear hole.

Before settling down under the water tower to await Kruger's signal, the Bulgarian had completed two simple tasks. After getting on to the International's flat, silver-painted roof up stairs leading to a wooden door, he had locked the door with a strong Bulldog padlock and strung the key round his neck. Next he had walked quickly to the wall which ran around the perimeter of the International's roof to check that four marks were scratched on to the concrete topping. Between these marks the Sagger missile cases would be locked into position.

He had found the marks. The CIA was good at this kind of thing, and it would be like firing from the gantry at Camp Peary all over again.

When the pips sounded in his ear, Yazov knew he had less than thirty seconds in which to carry the missiles to the wall set them up, and fire.

Getting quickly to his feet, he moved into precise, mechanical action. Taking the missile cases by their handles, Yazov crossed the six paces to the edge of the International's roof in less than four seconds.

Even as he walked, he pressed a button to the underside of each carrying handle to release the spring-loaded tubular supports beneath each pack. Because the distance between the front and rear supports on either of the packs was slightly over eight inches—the width of the wall enclosing the roof area—Yazov simply slotted the tubular supports over the top of the wall, in place between the scratch marks.

He tested how firmly they were locked in place by trying to rock the cases by their handles. In spite of the Bulgarian's exertions, the cases held fast, not budging at all.

While he jammed the cases on to the wall, Yazov had also snatched a glance down Sikh Street, between the EAA and National Insurance Corporation buildings. There were troops guarding the hairpin bend, but the motorcade had not entered the turning yet.

Now Yazov pressed two other plastic buttons at the front of the cases, which leaned over the edge of the four-foot-high wall. At the press of each catch, a square front cover-plate popped free of either missile case. The cover-plates—plastic flaps—swung down on their hinges.

The motorcade had still not reached the bend.

Using his thumbs, Yazov pushed yet two more buttons, this time at the back of the packs. Two things happened. The missiles moved slightly forward in their moorings and the buttons also popped the rear flaps, allowing him to get at the control boxes. After removing them, Yazov retreated a few paces to the sides of the missiles case, paying out electric cable as he stepped clear.

Was he clear of the blast of the rocket motor? Yazov wanted to be as close to the rear of the missile as he could

197

get, without risking injury from the searing gases that would explode from the rocket's nozzle.

After briefly considering the matter, Yazov shifted position.

He was ready.

He had a few seconds to spare. First he spotted the troops stiffening to attention in the bend. The second thing he saw was the start of the motorcade. The outriders swept into view, and Yazov could hear their sirens.

Next came the black Mercedes. It braked, swung into the bend, slowing for the shot for which he had trained. If anybody looked up at the hotel roof, it was much too late.

Yazov thumbed the button on his joystick, instantly plunging a battery-driven current from the control box, along the cable, into the missile motor's circuit.

Simultaneously, the missile's solid fuel propellant flamed and smoked. A split second later, the rocket sprang into the air. The Sagger's partially folded wings snapped open and the flying bomb zoomed away, weaving erratically, trailing a spiral of smoke and fire.

It rushed with a roar into the gap between two buildings, hair-thin wires uncoiling from the spool to the back of the rocketing missile. Yazov moved smartly. His first two swings of the joystick were crude before he gathered the Mercedes into his line of sight.

The missile started a long, smooth arc, Yazov's sensitive hand movements keeping it framed on to the oncoming Mercedes.

The outriders broke formation.

It was much too late for the driver of the Mercedes.

The missile crashed into the bullet-proofed, front windscreen. The warhead's flat nipple of a fuse detonated. A flash dissolved into a much bigger flash.

Within the warhead, the hollow-charge—a cylindrical block of high explosive into the front end of which had been pressed a smooth, conical space—blew up with a smashing, concentrated burst.

Inside the Mercedes the air was thick with shrapnel as the bomb fragmented into a shower of metal splinters.

Out of control, the Mercedes mounted a grass verge and broke through a roadside barrier. Its front suspension ripped free, with wheels intact. The two wheels and suspension coasted a short way along the road.

As the wheels rolled on the runaway suspension, a man broke headlong through the roof of the Mercedes. He travelled up in the air, taking a path of a rough, parabolic curve, slowly somersaulted three times and crashed into the tarmac.

The Mercedes was a twisted, torn wreck. Each and every window was shattered. Its wheel-less front end had cleaved deep slashes in the tar before grinding to a halt. Then the fuel tank blew. Flames boiled through all the openings. A rear door buckled in the fresh blast, gave way and bounced on its hinges, yawning open.

Obama Okan's physician hung through the shattered glass window of the door. The bodies of the SRB men inside were strewn like burning jackstraws around the hulk of a compartment shell.

The driver cradled a V-8 engine on his lap.

From the top of the International, Yazov looked through the Dragunov's fourpower sniperscope. He confirmed that the Mercedes was a mangled, smashed and burning wreck. It was not necessary to fire the reserve Sagger.

Yazov turned the scope on to the outriders. They were scrambling their motorcycles round. The men who guarded the bend picked themselves up off the grassy verge, or stopped running, and edged back to where the Mercedes had ground to a halt.

In quick succession, the Bulgarian pulled the Dragunov's operating handle fully to the back, releasing a cartridge into the chamber, then flipped down the safety lever. He got set to shoot everybody in sight, systematically, for as long as they would stand it.

19

In the seconds just before and after Yazov's missile exploded in the Mercedes, a hundred things happened.

Leonid Bevz was looking ahead of him. Yes, some kind of projectile was flying. He shouted a Russian oath. His eyes retraced the Sagger's smoky trail and briefly registered the figure—head and shoulders—of a man on top of a tall building. This was all he had time to see before the explosion.

Okan was in the Lincoln. He and Garst saw nothing until it was over. But Okan's driver had a glimpse of it, enough to make him spin the steering wheel crazily, bouncing the front wheels on to the curb. With the Lincoln well clear of it, the Mercedes gushed flames with a roar.

Continuing the Lincoln along a terrified circular swerve, the driver jolted the car back on to the tarmac to face the opposite direction.

"Get down!" yelled the SRB man in the seat in front of Okan. He whipped about, pushed Okan on to the floorboards wedging the president in the space between the front and back seats.

Garst sat without moving. She was impassive.

"What happened?" Okan's cry was muffled.

"A missile of some kind," Garst replied calmly. "Probably an anti-tank missile."

"Where did it come from?" The president sounded more controlled.

"I think the International's roof, excellency," the driver answered this time.

"We're out of sight. Behind cover," Garst spoke reassuringly.

From somewhere, not far away, came the stuttering rattle of heavy machine-gun fire. "Ours?" Okan was extricating himself from the floorboards.

"I don't think anybody can say," Garst said.

"Can't be sure, excellency," the SRB bodyguard confirmed. "But here's the Russian man. He's stopped close by."

"Yes, I see." Okan was dusting his kepi. "Okay, driver. Move our car behind the Russian motor. I want extra cover. Definitely. And call the motorbike men back." Okan was much calmer.

"Yes, excellency." The SRB man grabbed the radio telephone and called to the outriders, ordering them to circle back to the Lincoln.

Okan looked back to the bend and the burning Mercedes. He was in time to see a trooper clutch abruptly at his throat with both hands. Yazov's bullet hit near the top of the man's neck, slightly left of the spine, ploughed a little downward, ripped his windpipe and sliced out of the front of his neck, nicking an elephant-hair amulet which its owner had worn against evil.

The shot caused the rest of the guards in the hairpin bend to drop to the ground. Unlimbering their AK-47s on the grass, they scanned the Kampala skyline. An AK-47 belched flame from its muzzle. Then all the others let fly, a few guns rattling on automatic fire.

"Kill him! Kill them!" Okan clamoured helplessly.

Bevz got out of the Zil and hurried to where Okan sat in the back of the Lincoln. He kept an eye on the men in the hairpin bend.

A man bounced from the grass up into the air. Bevz watched fragments of something—he knew they were pieces of flesh and bone—erupt from his back. "What a shot!" the Russian marvelled through his angry dismay.

Sounds of skirmishing drifted across to the Lincoln: the crump of heavy mortars; the familiar blasts of grenades; a steady chatter of automatic weapons. It was obvious to Okan that much more was underway than an assassination attempt.

"Get Command Post," he ordered.

"Immediately, excellency."

A heavy-set trooper got up from the tarmac in the bend. He threw away his AK-47 and began a weaving run, tripping after five paces. Scrambling to his feet, he lumbered

201

on. As he got into full tilt, a bullet slammed into his shoulder spinning him like a child's toy top.

"Serious trouble, Mr. President," Bevz came to the window. "A well-planned coup. Enemy forces will head for all main points. The radio station, airport, State House, Command Post. Act quickly, or all is lost." The Russian ended with something that was self-evident.

"No contact with Command Post, excellency," the SRB man reported.

"Try State House," Okan instructed calmly.

"Yes, excellency."

Yazov's fourth shot exploded in an outrider's head, sending the motorcycle crashing on to the grass verge, to ride over men who lay there. With that, every man got up and broke into a wild, erratic run across the bend, discarding his weapon. A few had kicked off their boots, too.

Three of the runners collided with a couple of motorcycle escorts. All fell in a tangled heap on the tarmac.

"Sniper. Up on the building," Bevz merely stated it as a fact.

"The International Hotel, my friend," said Okan.

As he spoke, he watched an outrider frantically trying to drag his overturned machine clear. A bullet in the back crashed him over the handlebars.

"The damn fool chaps! Why don't they get away faster?" Okan raged in frustration.

"They're trying hard enough, I assure you." It was Garst.

"He's a cool fellow, our sniper friend, Mr. President," said Bevz. "An expert. . . ."

"You know him?" Okan demanded.

"I think so, yes, Mr. President."

"I can't get through to State House, excellency," the SRB man broke in with his report.

"Get Colonel Oyok," Okan gave a fresh order.

"I don't think that will help, Mr. President," Bevz stopped Okan. "I believe that Oyok is your traitor. . . ."

Another of the outriders was struggling desperately to free his bike from the tangle. At last, he wrenched it free. Sitting on the saddle, he stamped his right foot viciously on the starter pedal. The Triumph's engine spluttered and died. Again he stamped viciously. As the engine took, the

202

motorcyclist revved wildly. He was about to spring the clutch when a bullet splashed low down into his left side, kicking up a tiny fountain of red. The outrider jerked both his hands high, suddenly letting out the clutch. The Triumph bounded forward, bucking its rider off.

Okan cursed foully. "What can we do?" he asked.

"Nothing . . . yet," Bevz shrugged. It seemed that they could not make radio contact with any units. The SRB contingent had been slaughtered in the Mercedes. And those of the outriders and troopers who had not been killed or wounded had run away in panic—or were trying to do so.

"What do you advise, my friend?" Okan had respect for this amazingly unperturbed KGB agent. This was how to be in a crisis. Besides, had the Russian not saved his life? Garst and the Russian, actually. Breaking the earlier deadlock between himself and the Russian, the girl had simply got out of the Mercedes and walked over to the Lincoln. Her action had unsettled Okan, who, despite his anger, suddenly felt unsafe in the Mercedes. He had changed cars, sulking all the way until they reached the bend. . . .

"Your enemies think you are dead. We must keep the fact that you are alive from them for the moment, Mr. President."

"I think . . ."

Bevz dismissed Okan's thinking in advance. "If they know you are alive, here, they will send a unit to finish the work. You are unprotected, easy meat here."

"I see. Definitely, my friend."

"You must get among your most loyal troops. Then broadcast the fact that you are alive. When you are safe, the news must immediately go out. It will win half the battle. The undecided will join you. The committed will become undecided."

"Then I must get to Entebbe airport. Definitely."

It was at Entebbe airport that Okan's most powerful forces manned a strong detachment of T-54 tanks, armoured cars, and other tactical weapons. The best of Uganda's arms were under their control. This small but heavily armoured column—with supporting infantry from the barracks at the airport—could put down the rebellion.

Okan's small, Russian-equipped air force was also at Entebbe. He had only to get there in time.

"You cannot go by road," said Bevz. "Use a helicopter, if possible." The Russian was considering how to get around the inevitable roadblocks.

"Contact with State House, excellency!" The SRB's excited call sent relief pounding through Okan. "They are under siege there!"

"Give me that!" Okan grabbed the microphone. He kept a helicopter on standby at State House at all times. He dictated orders into the instrument, commanding the helicopter to land in the car park north-west of South and Burton Streets. Thinking ahead, Okan ordered the landing for the extreme south of the car park, where the chopper would be safe from anyone on the roof of the International.

"Very good, Mr. President." Bevz had been impressed by Okan's firm, barking injunctions.

"What do you think?" Okan turned to Garst.

"I agree. We must get to Entebbe. This can save everything," the girl said shortly.

Once Garst got to Entebbe airport, she would have to reconsider everything. If Okan failed to put down the coup in short order, she would have to save herself and Commando Marighella. The secretary of state's jet would still have some reserve fuel on board, enough to reach Aden or, if Jabril did not want to embarrass his hosts, Somalia. At any rate, she could get to Nairobi.

She would prefer Mogadishu in Somalia, but it all depended on the 707's present range. The Kenyans would be hostile, no doubt about it. There were probably US Marines at Embakasi airport, and they might try to storm the aircraft.

Still, she held a few trumps herself. Garst smiled at the thought. To increase her leverage, she would transfer everybody to the ICA 747, if it landed in time.

Everything rested on whether Okan regained control fast.

"Good. Then we are all definitely agreed," Okan said. "What about you, my friend?"

"I suspect that our comrade sniper is a professional assassin, Mr. President. A traitorous madman. He once worked for us, so you will understand very well that I have some business with this man."

"If you wait, my friend, I will send a detachment of loyal fellows."

Bevz shook his head. "No time, Mr. President. This man will try and escape now, in the confusion."

"I think that is definitely the case," Okan agreed.

Okan pushed his hand through the window and shook that of the KGB man's warmly.

"Excellency! The helicopter!" The driver and SRB bodyguard had been anxiously searching the skies in the general direction of State House.

Bevz could feel Okan's grip suddenly tighten, and the big man beamed.

It was true. Looking to where the driver pointed, the Russian observed a fat speck in the sky, growing steadily larger.

"You must go, Mr. President."

Okan nodded, and the Lincoln pulled away, heading for the nearby car park.

Bevz hastened his steps to the Zil. He gave quick instructions, and, as soon as he was finished, he heard the harsh clatter of the helicopter's rotors. It was, Bevz knew, a Kamov—a gift from the Soviet Union to Okan.

The Zil began to crawl forward.

Was it really Yazov up on the International? Bevz deliberated with himself. His instinct told him that he had tumbled on to the Bulgarian. Supposing it was so, that was good. Bevz could finish the task which had miscarried in Spencer and outside the Taft in New York.

For the job he would use his favourite pistol, the same kind of gun that Garst had wielded in the Carlton Hotel. This was the Czech M-52, with its exceptionally high muzzle velocity of 1,600 feet a second.

In the back of the Zil, Bevz checked that the pistol was fully loaded with a magazine of eight 7.62-calibre bullets. It was, of course. After making the check, all he had to do was pull the slide back smartly, and release.

Yazov was going to be on his guard. But Bevz doubted that the Bulgarian was expecting a killer quite in their class. So he held a small advantage. In this sort of affair, the man who held that edge usually won.

20

Arnie Kruger had his own reasons for killing Yazov. Apart from anything else, he had his feelings and his pride.

The shot from the International had been something to see. He would savour describing it to Tarrant when he got back to Washington. The series of shots which followed had also been glorious. Kruger had only watched the start, but that was enough.

It was going to be a waste of a good man.

He was thinking along these lines when the lift in the EAA building got to the ground level. Swinging his EAA bag in his left hand, Kruger ambled through the lobby. There was a small knot of employees present, their faces betraying confusion and worry.

Kruger mumbled something unintelligible, stepped out of the lobby, walked down the steps and started for the International, which was only a couple of blocks away.

Burton Street was empty. But when Kruger got to the corner with Buxton Street, he had to wait for a couple of jeeps to pass. The army vehicles were crammed with soldiers who had their rifles unslung, at the ready.

One of them shot an angry look at him. Next thing, he fired his rifle. Kruger had no time even to react. All he heard was the harsh bang, a chipping sound, and a ping where the bullet bit into the masonry work above him.

The CIA agent was suddenly more careful. He stepped up his pace.

As he got to Market Street he could hear the rising volume of chattering machine-gun fire, as well as a higher frequency of mortar blasts.

Like a fire that had been slow to start, the coup was taking its hold.

Kruger walked even faster. But in Market Street he was overtaken by a dozen students. They were laughing, shout-

206

ing carrying rocks. "Death to tryanny, death to slavery," they chanted.

Bevz came across the same group of students. They danced in the street, and a few of them swarmed on to the bonnet of the slowly moving Zil. Clambering over the windscreen, they chanted: "One, two, three, four, we want civil war!"

A bottle smashed into the street from one of the buildings. Instantly, the mood of the students changed. Seeing this, Bevz ordered the driver to step on it. As the driver accelerated, two of the students fell off the bonnet; others jumped clear to save themselves.

Bevz heard shouted curses and felt a big thump on the back of the Zil: he was too late to see, but a rock the size of a tennis ball bounced off the Zil's boot, leaving a big dent. Bevz saw other rocks carom erratically off the tarmac.

Once the coup was crushed, all in good time, Bevz reckoned, it would be the turn of Makerere University. As if to confirm the Russian in his thinking, the students kicked over a couple of dustbins, then hurled them at a heavily barred storefront window.

The KGB man would have worried had he known the state of the Makerere campus at that moment: six thousand students were meeting in the square in front of the main building. They demanded Okan's overthrow.

Some students were tearing down pictures of Okan, for the purpose of burning them and "burying" the ashes in "graves." Other students—the vast majority of the crowds—were preparing to march in their red gowns from the campus to the streets of central Kampala, two miles to the south-east.

Meantime, the Zil turned east into Market Street. And as it did so, Bevz leaned forward to shake the driver by the shoulder, ordering him to stop.

The reason was that he had spotted Arnie Kruger, who was on the point of ducking into the driveway of the International Hotel.

Bevz had last seen Kruger only days ago, outside the Taft in New York. The Russian had a good memory for faces, particularly when he took the trouble. He was

207

trained to do it, too, and with Arnie Kruger he had tried hard to remember.

For the first time that day, Bevz was not sure what to do. Yazov was the main target, and Kruger confirmed Yazov's presence.

While sitting in the Zil's back seat, Bevz had tried to work out how to finish Yazov. He had thought of taking the Bulgarian on the roof, circling around him from the back.

Seeing Kruger, he had a flashing inspiration. Kill Kruger in his room, and wait for Yazov. Why not? No obvious objection sprang to mind. That way, he could do the KGB a double service.

How was he going to get into Kruger's room? That problem he would solve on his way there. . . .

Bevz gave instructions to the Zil's driver, got out of the car, and took big, rapid steps to the driveway where Kruger had turned and disappeared. He strode into the lobby, to the deserted reception desk.

Flicking through the hotel register, Bevz found the rooms of the two EAA mechanics. An obvious cover, he grimaced.

At the bank of the two lifts Bevz noted that one indicator board registered a lift stationary on the eleventh floor, which confirmed what he had picked up in the hotel book.

Bevz pulled open the door to the remaining lift and pressed a black button to take him to the tenth floor. From there he would take the stairs so that he could peer around the corner before stepping on to the target level.

He had still not quite hit on a ruse for getting into Kruger's room. In fact, he was not even sure which of the two rooms was occupied by whom.

What he did have was a good deal of confidence in the high-velocity M-52 pistol and his ability to use it. The pistol was a real comfort to his right hand.

Arnie Kruger was in room 1102, making his own preparations, which consisted mainly of checking his Smith & Wesson double-action revolver. It had a short, 3½" barrel, but Kruger was using Magnum shells. He knew the Magnum bullet could drill clean through an automobile

208

body because he had tried it. This was a good enough piece for the job in hand.

Kruger was thumbing the last of the .357 Magnums into a chamber of the revolver when he thought he heard a rap on the door to room 1101. However, he was not sure, above the noise of the battles going on outside. The moment he spun the cylinder in a final check, though, the rapping sounded again. This time he was certain about the rapid knocking.

Kruger made ready to investigate, carefully.

As he got halfway across the room, a loud thunking on the door to 1102 stopped him in his stride.

Given the time, the knocking was out of place. Or was the management checking to see that the International's guests were safe? Kruger thought not. The manager was more likely to be in the cellar, if one existed.

"Okay. Who is it?" Kruger asked very loudly. Already he was moving to the side of the door, re-examining it. He had looked at it during the previous evening, for agents on a hazardous mission had to know how much protection they got from the doors to their bedrooms. Kruger's fresh assessment did not change his opinion: the door did not offer much of a safeguard.

"Room service." The voice was a little unclear.

"I don't recall ordering any room service." Kruger spoke loudly again, making sure his voice carried through the door.

Already a plan had formed in his mind. The door was standard: a little over six feet high, a little under three feet wide. And the wood was not solid. Unless he was mistaken, the door was made of plywood.

A Magnum, which tore through an automobile body, would slice through plywood.

"Maybe it was the other man, sir?"

Other man? What other man? This could only mean Yazov. The man outside knew about Yazov, but Yazov was up on the roof, and he was hardly going to call for room service.

It also niggled Kruger that the man's voice was not overlaid by that thick Ugandan accent with which he was now familiar. It was more like . . . a thickish, Slavic accent. Yazov did not speak like that any more.

209

Kruger held his Smith & Wesson ready. He was not going to take chances. If it was not Yazov, a hostile was out in the passage. If it was Yazov, he would kill him anyway. Something was up. At times like this, Kruger shot first and pieced everything together later.

"Room service. Please open up."

To Kruger, the sounds seemed to come from the front of the door, where he would place a series of shots. Standing just left of the closed door, he aimed at a spot about nine inches from the door's edge, holding the revolver at the shallow angle of about 20° for the starting shot.

Then he fired, rapidly. As he blasted away, Kruger changed the angle, fanning swiftly through to 50°. In quick succession, four Magnums punched ragged holes through the thin wood. Cement powdered on the corridor wall opposite.

To a man standing in Bevz's position, which was clear of the door and flat against the wall by the doorway, it became obvious from where the CIA agent was firing.

Bevz noted the heavy marks gashed into the plaster opposite, and the holes pierced through the door. From this he quickly computed their trajectory. All he had to do was open fire quickly too. If he was fast, the Russian knew he could do it.

It was a very old trick, this.

He had learned it well, baiting Kruger as he did, getting Kruger to bang away.

The CIA agent had not stopped to think. Unfortunately, there had been no time for quiet, deliberate reflection. Kruger was in a strange city, at a tricky moment, right after a mission, with fighting going on all around.

Bevz got off his first booming shot a split second after Kruger fired his fourth. He kept going, counting until the magazine was almost empty. When he got to seven, he held his fire, keeping a bullet in reserve.

Under the impact of his successive discharges the door splintered badly. Noise rang in Bevz's ears, each boom temporarily deafening him. The passage filled with smoke.

The last six of Bevz's shots crashed harmlessly all around Kruger. It was the first that hit him, just as he was ducking for the wall. Kruger felt his guts flame. Still, out of reflex action, he got off another Magnum, drilling yet another hole through the plywood.

That panicked Bevz.

Instinctively, the Russian charged backwards. Adrenalin pumping much harder, he smashed his shoulder against the door to Yazov's room. The door hung crazily on its hinges before Bevz crashed it shut again.

The KGB killer was puzzled. He ought to have got the man inside 1102. Provided that it was done fast enough and the timing was good, the action rarely failed. And Bevz had been very fast, nothing wrong with his timing either. At least one bullet should have hit.

As the Russian's heartbeat slowed, his mind filled with thoughts of escape. Take it easy, comrade. Get a grip on it, he had to tell himself forcefully. But he had to admit that suddenly it was all a mess. Why had he let this distract him from the main job of killing Yazov? Damn his impulse. He should have known better when he had not worked out a foolproof way to get into the room.

The whole idea had been to kill the accomplice and wait for Yazov in the room. But the Bulgarian was hardly likely to open a door shattered with gaping bullet holes.

Bevz rapidly considered that he was well armed—already he had reloaded—unhurt, could cover the passage, and escape was available through the window. On condition that he prepared for his getaway, he could stay a while.

What was the risk like? Bevz could not say, because he was still not thinking too clearly. Since this was so, his instinct was to run for it. Only then he might never have another shot at Yazov.

Not in a long time.

If he waited, with some luck he could pick the Bulgarian off as he came down the passage.

Bevz had his mind partly on escape, partly on killing Yazov.

Seconds later, he pulled a sheet off the bed. Using his teeth, he ripped a hole in the white cotton fabric. While he kept watch on the passage, through a crack between door and jamb, his fingers tore the cloth into strips.

He wanted a makeshift rope, long enough for a swing

211

through a window on the ninth floor after slipping a knot around the steel window frame.

His fingers working on the strips, eyes on the passage, it struck Bevz that he had not reckoned with the man in the next room.

Fortunately, Bevz had the corner apartment. He would escape around the corner, out of view from anybody in room 1102.

Otherwise, the Russian did not know what to think. His brain pounded more than he would have liked.

Of all the stupid things that he had done—and he had done some—this had to be the stupidest. Or so Arnie Kruger reflected, through all the pain. To have fallen for the crude gimmick, as he had, was unpardonable—not to say possibly fatal.

Most of the bullets had holed cupboards, the bed and a table-top, or had sunk into the wooden floor blocks after ripping through the carpet.

His own bullet had carved right through him.

In very detailed fact, this bullet had come out of Bevz's pistol at hundreds of feet per second. It struck the plywood and deflected, which was Kruger's bad luck, because with the chance shift in direction, he collected it.

Kruger took the slug in the abdominal area, on the right side. Here the bullet punched a wound of entry shaped like an old-fashioned keyhole. As the bullet plunged forward, it also drove ahead of it hundreds of particles of tissue as secondary missiles.

In the brief time that it took the round to crash through him, Kruger suffered ruptures of his spleen, part of his stomach on the right, and his intestines.

The projectile wobbled out of Kruger's left side, at the back, causing a large exit wound of irregular shape and everted edges. Fragments of metal were strewn all along the erratic track of the bullet.

Altogether a bad wound, and Arnie Kruger knew it. Kruger had qualified as an MD, and he knew that primary shock and haemorrhage had set in, even as he sat against the bed.

The whole disaster area was rich with blood vessels. He could die of shock, loss of blood, tissue poisoning. . . .

Unless he got help soon, he was done for. It occurred to him that this was going to be a dumb way to die: a big bullet through the gut, in a forgotten room halfway across the world, with nobody around to grip his hand. Only with much effort had he dragged himself to the bed, propping himself up. Now he tried to reload the Smith & Wesson.

From where he sat, he had a good view through the door, which hung in strips. The smell of burnt cordite was drifting in the air. It was a heavy, loathsome stench, and Kruger knew he had to be careful. If he retched, he could easily die. He did not want to do that, not before he got Yazov. . . .

21

Yazov had seen the Kamov duck down out of sight, some-where to the south-west, not far from where he was. Since there was a car park in that area, a flat, open piece of ground—something which he recalled from the maps he had studied of Kampala—Yazov guessed that was where the helicopter had put down. Shortly afterwards, it had risen high over the buildings, veering sharply to the west, well clear of the International, and with rotors slapping through the air it had swung towards Entebbe.

None of this meant anything to Yazov. He did not sus-pect that Okan was aboard the Kamov: nobody could have survived the direct hit on the Mercedes. He conjec-tured that the helicopter was part of the confusion which had overtaken the streets of Kampala.

So far, Yazov had been safe and unharmed on the roof. The troopers firing from the grass in the bend had not come close to hitting him. Their shots had all gone wild, as far as he could tell. Probably, most of the guards had not seen him on the roof, and they had simply popped away in panic. The worst that anyone had done was to chip the International's south wall, about two o'clock high.

Once a jeep had stopped briefly under the hotel. It was mounted with a heavy machine gun, which somebody used to pepper the wall yards below where Yazov had crouched. The attacker fired a short, three- or four-second burst, and, before he could retaliate, the jeep had made off.

The troopers and the jeep constituted the net counterattack on Yazov's position. Otherwise, he had gone about his sniping unhindered.

However, having spent two of the Dragunov's magazines, the Bulgarian found that he was running out of targets. The troopers had disappeared into the surrounding streets and behind buildings; the surviving outriders rode out of range, fast.

It was time to get out. Yazov felt a heavy raindrop spatter on his shoulder. He looked up at the heavy skies and decided that at any moment it would start to pour.

Before quitting the roof, the Bulgarian moved quickly around the parapet to see for himself how rapidly the fighting had spread. He had already observed three trucks, filled with troops, on the Kampala Road. Of more significance were a few French-made, medium tanks, lumbering in the direction of the Jinja cross-roads.

It had surprised Yazov how soon fighting had broken out. He was not sure whether Arnie Kruger would be pleased or not. From what Kruger had said, the coupmakers had wanted a relatively bloodless takeover. Well, that was not going to be.

Within minutes of the Mercedes exploding, light mortars had given way to heavier explosions, 120-mm rounds, if the sounds were anything to go by. Yazov had even seen rockets, Katyushas, whooshing like express trains as they trailed long flames. Now he heard the crash of a howitzer shell, then another, probably fired from robust 152-mm guns made in Russia.

There was no doubt whatever that a coup, disorganized and ragged and bloody was under way. Under these conditions escape was going to be much easier.

As he slipped the key into the padlock to the heavy wooden door, rain began pattering on the roof. Yazov hurried. A few seconds later, he had the door open and was padding down the stairs.

214

He got to the eleventh floor and stopped at the foot of the stairs, halted by the sharp, familiar smell of cordite. The fumes were a warning.

Although he had abandoned the rifle, several magazines and the missile gear on the roof, Yazov was not unarmed. He had a Luger pistol shoved into the waistband of the Levis he wore under the EAA coverall. Before going any further, he unzipped the front of his coverall to the waist and worked the Luger free with his right hand.

Next, Yazov peered very cautiously around the corner, exposing only an eye and small areas of his cheek and head. What he saw were traces of blue haze still clinging to the air in the corridor. This had to be gunsmoke. Yazov looked down on to the carpet, searching. He thought it was the glint of two spent cartridge shells he saw under the light in the ceiling by room 1102. There was also some kind of litter outside Kruger's room. Probably Kruger had been involved in a gunfight. How, or with whom, Yazov could not expect to know—not yet.

Then he noticed the way the door to his own room hung slightly awry. The entranceway was directly opposite him, down the passage. Was Kruger dead? Yazov decided to find out.

"Butterfly, are you damaged?" Yazov shouted down the corridor. "Can you give me your status?"

The Bulgarian's voice carried down the passage, over the thirty paces to room 1102.

Arnie Kruger heard it.

He was sitting against the side of the bed, on a dull orange tufted carpet. Kruger's legs were fully extended. The tip of the Smith & Wesson's bright blue muzzle rested on the orange carpeting.

The CIA case officer's side was aflame with pain which radiated throughout his trunk. Where he sat, the carpet was soaked with blood. Kruger's face was pale, his skin was cold and clammy, and a rapid, thready pulse beat inside his wrist.

Yazov's shout suddenly dispelled his steadily mounting apathy.

Kruger was alert again, hatching. . . .

"Butterfly, do you hear me! What's your status?"

Kruger was weak and drained. He had three options.

He could muster his strength and shout a warning. He could spare himself and say nothing. Or he could try and trap Yazov into being killed, if not by him, then by the man who had shot him.

Occasional tremors gently racked Kruger's system. He was worried that when the good time came, he would be too weak to squeeze off the shot.

"Got myself . . . a few scratches," he croaked as loud as he was able. "Need a hand here, Crystal. Need help."

Kruger slumped back against the side of the bed.

Yazov never heard him.

Though he could not make out what the CIA agent was saying, Bevz heard the rattling, croaking sounds coming from the room alongside his.

He had got in a shot, after all. The anguish in the tortured voice told the Russian that the man was badly wounded, even dying.

It pleased Bevz that he had not miscalculated. Less satisfying was that Yazov had not walked down the passage, allowing Bevz his chance. Perhaps he should have waited by the stairs, Bevz chided himself. Yazov must have picked up the smell of burnt cordite. Bevz had expected him to walk the passage cautiously to investigate, but the Bulgarian was even more guarded than he had foreseen.

In dealing with Yazov's accomplice, Bevz had surrendered his element of surprise. Butterfly's laboured, croaking reply—Butterfly was obviously some kind of code name—made matters worse. If Yazov had heard it, which Bevz doubted, he would be even more careful.

Another warning to Yazov was the crooked door. Bevz had tried to hang the thing straight, but in breaking it open he had done something irreparable and it stood that telltale bit skew.

Yazov would probably conclude that someone was in the room, waiting. If he got safely on to the tenth floor, maybe he could still get behind the Bulgarian, whose attentions would be concentrated on the room in which Butterfly was badly wounded or the one where Bevz hid.

So . . . bait another trap! Bevz was brilliantly inspired. He would draw the Bulgarian's fire to the corner apartment, escape to the tenth floor and circle round. . . .

Promptly Bevz raised the Model 52 pistol, before even dragging the broken door open a trifle. Taking careful aim, he banged four shots down the passage to the corner of the stairs where he had observed Yazov peeping.

The big bullets zinged down the long corridor. They skipped off the cream-coloured wall, their pitches changing to whines after the ricochets. All the shots were fired with no hope of hitting Yazov. Their purpose was to signal that Bevz was still in the room, and also to keep Yazov at bay while the Russian escaped out of the window.

Bevz crashed four more bullets down the corridor. After forcing back the pistol's magazine catch, he stuffed home a fresh magazine.

Another glance down through the crack between the door and doorway satisfied Bevz that he had at least fifteen seconds in which to act.

Earlier, he had given up tearing the sheets into strips—it took much too long. Instead, he had knotted together two sheets and two blankets, which he reckoned would stretch long enough for what he wanted. Bevz had already fastened the sheet over the steel frame. Accordingly, when he got to the window, all that remained was to throw out the improvised line. Then he tugged heavily at the knot over the frame yet again, ensuring that it would indeed support him. The knot held.

Bevz noticed that outside a very brief tropical downpour had almost let up. Looking down, he rechecked that his rope of sheets and blankets was long enough to get him to the tenth floor. It was. In fact, the rope would enable him to reach a window on the ninth floor, if he wanted.

The Russian was ready. He would inspect the corridor to see that it was still clear, and fire a couple of warning rounds to gain the extra time needed for escape down his makeshift line.

Pistol in hand, Bevz hurried back to the door. Halfway across the carpet he was in midstride when Yazov's reserve AT-3 missile knocked the door down with its flattish nipple of a fuse.

The muzzle of Bevz's pistol flashed, purely in some inexplicable reflex action.

Simultaneously, a little less than three kilograms of high explosive detonated with a great, thundering roll in the confined space of the room.

Had anybody been present with a slow-motion camera, standing on the pavement below looking up at the correct perspective, he would have recorded how the wall and window bulged for part of a second, then burst into pieces.

Bowled over by the hot, instantly expanding gases, Bevz was hurled into the air above Market Street—along with mortar, bricks, glass fragments and a steel frame.

The KGB agent was suffering from mild concussion and felt no pain. It was apparent to him that he could float forever—he wore an expression of benign content, a shaft of sunlight crossed his face—until he hit the tarmac eleven floors down.

22

The sudden rainstorm striking Kampala, ceasing as abruptly as it had started, was too localized to extend more than a few miles out of the capital. Apart from the few drops splattering on the windscreen and viewing windows of the Kamov, it had hardly been noticed by the passengers or crew.

Seven persons were being carried in the Russian aircraft. A pilot and co-pilot sat on the flight deck. Three SRB bodyguards took up that number of the Kamov's twelve folding seats. Okan and Garst completed the tally.

The girl sat quietly. She had asked Okan for permission to radio a report to her commandos on the airfield, but he had declined her request. Garst was not aware of the reason for the refusal. All she could guess was that Okan felt he was too vulnerable in the helicopter. There was an armoured column of troops moving on Entebbe airport, and among the weapons in the formation were mobile anti-aircraft guns. He would wait until they were close enough

218

to the airfield, rather than risk being shot down by disclosing his presence aboard the Kamov.

During the flight Garst was making plans for all eventualities. In the event of Okan crushing the revolt, no problem would arise. However, should he not do so—or not manage it quickly enough—she would have to make certain decisions.

Troubling her even more was how to make the transfer of hostages to the bigger Boeing 747—should it land on time—or whether she ought to order Commando Meinhof not to stop at Entebbe at all. Once the jumbo landed, it might not get off again. Possibly it would have to come down anyway, because of lack of fuel. Therefore she might have to transfer everyone to the secretary of state's aircraft. . . .

These problems, and others of a like kind, kept Garst preoccupied.

Obama Okan was plagued by his own uncertainties. It became clear five minutes out of Kampala that Colonel Oyok had mounted a surprisingly large-scale takeover but was meeting resistance from others who wished to sntach the governing authority for themselves. None the less Oyok had seized Command Post, Radio Uganda and other strategic points. State House was likely to fall soon.

Radio Uganda had consistently reported Okan's own death—by accident, of course—in a motor collision. It seemed that even Oyok was still unaware of the truth, and that he was engrossed in the battle with his rivals for power.

Let them fight and smash one another, Okan was glad of it. He would join the fray soon enough, fresh and with strong backing. The announcement that he was not dead at all, but very much alive—broadcast at the best psychological moment—would be a further, crushing retaliation against Oyok.

Below the helicopter, as it flew towards the marshy areas surrounding Entebbe airport, Okan could make out a ragged strike force of armour and troops. These would be Colonel Oyok's men, on their way to challenge the troops at the airport.

Okan's arrival promised to be timely. Without firm leadership, the airport garrison could easily surrender or

219

join the new regime. They were confused, down at the airport. They were loyalists, who probably thought Okan was dead.

But were they loyalists?

This was precisely why Okan was in two minds—should the Kamov land, or fly on to north-west Uganda? Here he held in reserve durable, southern Sudanese allies, men of his own tribe and kind. These well-equipped troops, backed by armour, were kept in hand for just such occasions as the present.

If he was tempted to go on to his northern stronghold, other considerations were against it. From the north he would wage a long, uncertain civil war. But with the backing of the Entebbe troops, Oyok would be short work, as would be anybody else who tried to oppose him.

The very best arms and soldiers were at Entebbe, or in the barracks nearby. Here Okan had brought up the bulk of Uganda's armour—T-55 battle tanks, two dozen BTR armoured personnel carriers, a few BRNM reconnaissance cars, all Russian-made, all heavily armed. With their 100-mm high-velocity guns that fired up to five rounds a minute the T-55s outclassed completely the medium tanks moving towards Entebbe. Let loose on Kampala, they would crash roadblocks and other strongpoints in minutes.

Moreover, the troops were Uganda's elite, equipped with the country's finest light weapons: light and heavy mortars, RPG-7 grenade launchers, Bren and RPD light machine guns. And parked in specially constructed protective bays was Uganda's air force: a small, powerful force of MiG and Mirage jet fighters and fighter bombers.

Now Okan could clearly see the runways, taxiways, apron, old and new airport buildings of the airport, as well as the secretary of state's Boeing 707. Soon he would contact the Entebbe control tower, and thereafter the commander of the Entebbe garrison. He hoped that the co-pilot was ready with the microphone on the correct frequency, as instructed.

As if he had read Okan's mind—so it seemed to Okan—the co-pilot turned about. But it was not to do with raising the tower. Shouting, trying to make himself understood above the scream of the two Glushenkov turboshaft engines, he waggled and pointed a finger vigorously at Okan's window. At the same time, the pilot banked the Kamov.

Through the plexiglass Okan saw the long-awaited Boeing 747. It was high in the sky, circling Entebbe airport.

Okan in his turn looked around at Garst, beaming. The girl already had her face up against the plexiglass. Still beaming, Okan grabbed the co-pilot on the shoulder and nodded at the microphone in the co-pilot's hand.

Yes, the co-pilot understood. All was in order, he grinned, and Okan could carry on with the transmission. As he passed the small microphone to Okan, the coils of the insulated connecting wire stretched to accommodate the longer distance to where the Ugandan sat.

"This is the President of the Republic of Uganda speaking." Okan began the broadcast which he had rehearsed in his mind. "I emphasize very much that this is President Obama Okan. Definitely. At about seventeen thirty-one hours local time, an attempt was made by SRB traitor Oyok to assassinate me in Kampala. . . . This evil attempt to kill me has failed. I repeat. This try has very definitely failed. It is clear to me that imperialist racists in the pay of CIA have tried to crush the Ugandan people. Their attempt is doomed. This is very definitely the case. I will save Uganda without mercy. . . ."

At that moment a 75-mm shell from a breech-loaded, recoilless gun burst about a hundred yards south of the main airport runway. Oyok's column had opened fire. To those in the army camp alongside the airfield, the blast sounded like a huge dustbin falling from a great height on to concrete.

Elevating its gun and traversing its turret to face the Entebbe–Kampala Road, a T-55 tank's muzzle spewed smoke and a long flame in a random response.

Meanwhile, having won over the control tower, Okan got ready to call the commander of the Entebbe armour. Already the tower had promised to repeat Okan's broadcast to units of the airport's detachments with which it was in contact.

Okan was optimistic. The response from the tower had been, quick, clear—and overwhelmingly in support of

221

himself. If he was persuaded of the armour commander's allegiance, he would instruct the pilot to land immediately. For some time the air controller at Entebbe international airport had tracked the ICA Boeing 747—renamed Charlie Bravo for identification purposes—on his green radar screen. Flying at 35,000 feet, high up over the many veins of the greasy brown rivers meandering through the brown hills of north Uganda, Charlie Bravo was constantly monitored. As the data flowed in, it promptly materialized on the radar screen at Entebbe tower as a tiny box which progressed across the circular glass in a series of little hops.

With the hijacked aircraft still some way from Entebbe, the traffic controller instructed: "Charlie Bravo, descend to 3,000 feet. Stand by for visual landing clearance on to main north–south runway."

"Roger, Entebbe approach control," Captain "Wild Bill" Funston replied.

A little later, the airfield came into view. Without any warning, a geyser of tarmac and earth rose off the ground near the main runway. It was the shell which had been lobbed by the recoilless gun. Funston also saw the smoke which boiled out of the T-55's muzzle.

"Charlie Bravo, you are not yet cleared for landing." It was the controller again. "Repeat, you are not yet cleared for landing."

Seeing that the airfield was under attack, the call came as no surprise to Funston.

"Roger, Entebbe control."

"A Kamov helicopter carrying President Obama Okan is in your air corridor. It will land soon," said Entebbe control. "You must circle until then."

"Roger, Entebbe control."

Funston adjusted the green sun visor ahead of him. He turned to Muhamad Mukarbal, who stood between himself and Jim Chase, the gun ever ready.

"Hold tight, brother," Funston said laconically, "we're going to make a wide turn." Mukarbal nodded and braced himself with his feet jammed tightly against the bottoms of the two seats occupied by Funston and Chase, spreading his legs wide in the space between pilot and co-pilot.

The ICA captain rolled the aircraft's port wing, banking the big jet in a vast, gentle circle. Fat Albert—that was pilot's jargon for the Boeing 747—belied its nickname. It was a splendid, frisky aircraft which gave no trouble. Maybe it was the best that Captain Funston had ever flown, and he had sat behind the controls of enough aircraft to give an opinion that mattered.

Looking through the front window, Funston saw the Kamov in the distance. Through the port window of the circling aircraft he watched fresh explosions splash debris from the surface of Entebbe airport. The stuff was coming from the thin column of armour advancing on the airfield. A couple of small geysers of earth spouted from the ground 3,000 feet under him. Funston had seen all of it before, over Viet Nam.

Quite obviously, the battle for control of the airport had commenced.

Funston glanced up at Mukarbal, who wore a worried, agitated expression, and then jerked his left thumb in the direction of the explosions below. "They've got some real trouble down there, brother."

Mukarbal glowered. But it was a fact. He could see it for himself.

"We're not landing there. Not now, or later. Get the Jeppersen's out for Embakasi, Jim. We're too low on fuel for anywhere else." It was a lie, of course. The aircraft had been fuelled for the long trip from Athens to New York without a stop. And it did little good for the tension between Funston and Mukarbal—a strain which had never slackened.

What did the man take him for, Mukarbal asked himself: a big idiot? The Nairobi airport of Embakasi was a hostile place for Commando Meinhof. It was probably jam-packed with US Marines. Why had he lied about the fuel? Did the captain think that he, Mukarbal, was so feeble-minded? Above all, why did this man presume that the aircraft was not going to land at Entebbe?

Mukarbal had tried to keep the peace all the way from Athens. He had been pleasant to the passengers, endeavouring to make them comfortable, on condition that Commando Meinhof's safety was not endangered. He had

223

even admonished the Venezuelan member of the squad for stalking up and down the aisles, brushing a hand grenade against passengers' heads.

But this captain was impossible.

Jim Chase was spreading out the Jepperson chart for Embakasi.

Mukarbal's inner rage took over. Though he tried to suppress it, anger welled up irresistibly to boil over like milk frothing out of a saucepan.

The Arab sideswiped Jim Chase viciously, bashing the muzzle of his pistol over the co-pilot's face. He smashed two of Chase's teeth and knocked him unconscious. Chase struck the side of his head against the starboard window and slumped back in his safety harness, lolling all askew.

"Land, you black sonofabitch! You take this plane down right now! This moment!" Mukarbal was uncontrolled. The gun in his hand shook violently with his fury.

"Wild Bill" Funston's spontaneous reaction was triggered by almost every calamity that had befallen him during his lifetime.

As a barefoot boy in Mississippi, he had seen his old man lynched. The uncle who had brought him up had been a stern disciplinarian, and he beat the Funston kids unmercifully. Funston had learned not to show resentment or to vent anger; instead, he buried all the pressures deep inside himself, at school, at college, and in the USAAF when he flew B-52s against Hanoi.

Being black was not easy. His marriage to a white beauty queen had cracked up. Even prior to his marriage, Funston had been a powderkeg of treacherous emotions; lately he had felt his resentment rising dangerously and had sought professional advice. The psychiatrist was aware of how desperately Funston was trying to bottle up his temper, but said that if he blew up, it might not be a bad thing—provided nobody was around.

That was ten days ago. At 1747 hours on 23 December, "Wild Bill" Funston finally snapped.

If he landed Fat Albert on the airfield, they were all likely to be killed anyway. If he and the passengers and crew had to die, so would Commando Meinhof, and any accomplices he could take with them.

Already there were so many ifs.

Leaving aside his personal life—and what a mess that was—if he had not been outraged by the El Al explosion over Germany; if he had not been revolted by the killings in Johannesburg; if he had not been sickened by the ruthless massacre at Latakia.

If it had not been for all of that, he might have held on this one more time.

If El Kudesi had been less of a mean sonofabitch, less of a bully, like his uncle in Chicago, he might not have broken down. If El Kudesi had not brought his colour into it or called his mother a bitch.

If Obama Okan was not so obviously an accomplice of the hijackers; if Funston did not think the Ugandan was regressing blacks hundreds of years by his misdeeds; if he did not identify Okan with his own desperate plight in Fat Albert. . . .

If the Kamov helicopter had not been about to land; if Okan had not been on board . . . then Funston would not have had the sudden revelation—and opportunity—to crash Fat Albert into the Kamov.

If Obama Okan had boarded the Kamov twenty minutes sooner, or later, nothing would have happened. Instead, all aboard Fat Albert and the Kamov had at last arrived at their fate in time and place, in the skies over Uganda.

Funston abruptly stood the plane on to its port wingtip. Under his hands, the Pratt and Whitney turbofans surged to full power, as reliably as always, with engines shaking in their pylon-mounted pods. Using all his magnificent skills, the captain slung Fat Albert at the target.

An onboard safety device, which warned against flying into obstructions, flashed a red light, whooped an alarm, and set off a pre-recorded order: "Pull up! Pull up!"

The forces in Funston's tight, banking dive tossed Muhamad Mukarbal on to the cockpit floor, amost blacking him out. His anger dissipated instantly, being replaced by a consuming fear, but it was too late to cut out his mad tongue or sever the hand which had whipped Jim Chase. . . .

In the Kamov, Okan had just finished talking to the commander on the ground at Entebbe. The pilot had orders to get down fast. An urgent, painful nip of his soft

225

upper arm made him gasp and whip about to confront his co-pilot.

He could hear the other man's howl above the racket of the Glushenkovs. His co-pilot's mouth was an empty hole, like a painting by Edvard Munch of a terrified scream. The pilot glanced up, and already the Kamov was in Fat Albert's shadow.

What he saw was incredible: a huge Boeing 747 jumbo was closing rapidly on to the Kamov, in a steep, banking dive.

"Get up! Get up!" screamed the Palestinian pilot. Frantically, he gunned the Glushenkov engines, trying to side-slip his eight tons of helicopter clear of Fat Albert, which swooped down at 473 m.p.h., tens of thousands of gallons of fuel splashing against its tanks.

Obama Okan was savouring the thought of getting on to the airfield and taking command. The officers on the ground were all with him. The armour commander had sounded truly relieved that Okan was alive and about to land. The whole affair was fast becoming exhilarating. How he would shatter and crush and mince Oyok. Oyok's head would be kept in a refrigerator and taken out on special occasions.

Okan also saw the co-pilot's open scream of a mouth. Then he was aware of a sudden, deep shadow, descending on the Kamov. He did not quite know what to think until he saw the Kamov's rotor slice into Fat Albert, below the flight deck window and the ICA insignia, painted red as blood.

In this last moment, Garst's calm disintegrated. She clutched her head with both hands and kicked against the side of the Kamov, to get away from Fat Albert's nose, mouthing a soundless cry for Hassan Jabril.

Inside the flight deck, Fat Albert was a jumble of dials, switches, and flashing lights. Already a wreck, the Kamov bounced into the jumbo's wing, smashing into the fuel tanks. Simultaneously hundreds of gallons of fuel spurted into the air to vaporize by the engines which ran 2,000° C. hot, mixing with the searing exhaust gases. Some of the volatile liquid splashed directly on to hot engine parts.

Fat Albert, with the broken Kamov still clinging to it,

exploded into a giant fireball. Within the mushrooming blast much of the aluminum and steel evaporated. A few seconds later, as parts broke off the flaming ball of destruction, the main wreckage plummeted into Lake Victoria, sending up a funnel of water more than 150 feet high.

From below the water came another, thumping explosion.

For hundreds of yards along the lake's shoreline, and over the water itself, thousands of birds flapped into the sky, screeching.

Echoing through the hills beyond Entebbe airport were the peals of three distinct booms.

23

The wall of room 1102 closest to the blast of the Sagger warhead was the east wall which separated the two bathrooms of rooms 1101 and 1102. Therefore, the detonation and concussion occurring in room 1101 had to penetrate three six-inch brick barriers before any effects were felt by Arnie Kruger, who sat propped up against the side of the bed.

In the event, the warhead's explosion largely demolished the wall between bathroom and bedroom in room 1101, blew a large hole in the common wall, and cracked the wall of the room occupied by Kruger.

If Kruger was spared direct injury from the blast—through flying debris or shrapnel—he was severely jolted and shaken. The concussion flung him to the carpeted floor, aggravating his acute agony, and dust stirred up by the blast made him gag.

He was on the floor when Yazov broke the door down. It was already badly splintered so that the Bulgarian simply needed a few well-aimed kicks to boot open a large, irregular entry through the plywood.

Yazov saw Kruger on the floor, how much blood the

American had lost, how his intestines hung out of his side, how his face was caked in dust.

"How are you, Butterfly?" he asked.

No response came from Kruger.

The first thing that Yazov did was to lift Kruger gently off the carpet and set him upright against the bed.

Both men noticed the Smith & Wesson. It had fallen from Kruger's grasp, and lay three feet away from him. The gun's bright blue barrel shone in the last of the daylight. Yazov left it in place.

Having settled Kruger against the bed, Yazov ruffled the CIA agent's hair, brushing away with his fingers the dust and powder from the ceiling. It was the only tender gesture he had ever made to his case officer.

"We're going to get you to a doctor, Butterfly. As soon as we can. Keep going until we do."

Yazov looked deep and hard into Kruger's eyes. The Bulgarian's eyes were opaque. And reflected in Yazov's eyes, Kruger saw his own. They were, in some peculiar way, slightly magnified. Kruger could even see his own eyelashes in the other man's eyes.

Who did this big, latent queer think he was kidding? Arnie Kruger asked himself. Both he and the Bulgarian knew he was dying on his arse on the carpet by the bed.

Kruger had a sharp, burning sensation in his side—as if his intestines were stripped of all protective tissue, and the wind was blowing hard against them, and against his guts and spleen too.

If the poor bastard had just let Kruger explain to him that he was gay too. Nothing wrong in it. They could have enjoyed one another. But, no, he was too proud.

Kruger tried to reach for his Smith & Wesson.

When he could not do it because the pain and effort were too much, he broke off to see what Yazov was doing.

Yazov was at the built-in clothes closet, throwing a few things into an EAA canvas bag. Just a few little things, like Kruger's favourite jacket, a well-worn suede, and a pair of Kruger's brown pants. The jacket was black and battered, and wherever Kruger had gone in the previous ten years, he had taken his black suede.

The jacket would not fit into the EAA bag, naturally.

So Yazov peeled off the coveralls, climbed into the brown trousers and pulled on the jacket. Then he carried on poking through Kruger's personal effects.

Of course, the explosion had probably blown Yazov's stuff to pieces. Or else his clothes were unwearable. But to Kruger he was a scavenger, ransacking the pockets of a dead man. Any second Yazov could reach with a hammer or the butt of his Luger for the gold in his teeth, Kruger told himself with biting, bitter facetiousness.

It was good to feel angry, because that got the adrenalin pumping again. Maybe he could make it across the three feet to the gun, and still have enough to pull the trigger.

As Kruger watched with disgusted fascination, Yazov stuffed a fake passport and other false documents into the suede jacket's pocket. Into another pocket went money, mostly dollars, and all the gold coins which had come packed with the supply of weapons. Yazov also took the reserve Smith & Wesson.

Before pocketing the gun, he spun the cylinder to see that all the chambers were loaded. After completing this check, Yazov broke open a box of .357 shells. He poured the cartridges loose into the last empty pocket, a hidden one sewn on the inside.

How did Yazov know about that? Kruger marvelled. He must have been snooping. . . .

The CIA agent felt nauseated, and the room smelt so badly that he knew he would soon retch.

Still, he could not tear his eyes off the Bulgarian, whose every movement was like that of a jungle cat: he was smooth and fluent, neither too quick nor too slow. The way Yazov handled the gun, he had almost stroked it into his pocket. Once again he was the lethal, deadly man that Kruger had seen for the first time so long ago, undergoing the polygraph at Langley.

At last, Yazov had everything he needed.

He walked over to where Kruger sat, breathing heavily, sweating with pain. "I'll have to go now, Butterfly . . . for the doctor."

Kruger looked into his eyes again, as he had done before. Yazov's eyes were as opaque as ever. Once more, Kruger saw his own eyelashes reflected.

"Here, Butterfly. Take this," Yazov reached for the Smith & Wesson. "Make you feel safer, while you wait." This was the last thing Yazov said. He put the gun in Kruger's right hand, and helped him to clasp the butt. Then he ruffled the dying man's hair again, got up and walked to the ragged opening in the broken door.

He had his back to Kruger. Again Kruger felt the force of the menace which marked Yazov as everybody's enemy.

With all the strength of his loathing, Kruger dragged up the Smith & Wesson, clasping it with both hands. His right index finger was over the trigger.

The gun wavered badly in his grasp, but Yazov's back loomed large. Kruger pulled on the trigger spring, as hard as he could.

A paralysis, an overwhelming weakness, washed over his arms and hands.

Kruger's face was an ugly mask of bursting effort and bitter hatred. A bead of sweat started down his nose, rolled, hung on the tip—and was shaken free by the tremor which overtook his twisted, unrecognizable features.

To overcome the trigger's resistance, Kruger jammed into the guard yet another finger—the index finger of his left hand.

Under the combined force of both fingers, the trigger finally gave way.

Kruger never knew it, but, by that time, Yazov was on the carpeted passage outside, stepping towards the lift. In spite of the crash of a fired gun, he never turned nor looked back.

Hours later, he was out on Lake Victoria in a small powerboat. By his reckoning, he would reach the shores of the Rwanda by the first light.

Later too, in the night sky, he heard the noise of a big jet. Looking up, he saw thousands of feet high the winking, red lights on a wingtip and under the fuselage. It was Air Force 720 on its long flight back to Johannesburg, but Yazov did not know that. He knew he was alive, and that when he got to Kigali, which is the capital of Rwanda, he would contact Tarrant from the US Embassy.

Tarrant would get a full report. Or maybe Tarrant would not get a full report, and perhaps Yazov would not contact him at all.

ABOUT THE AUTHOR

WILLIAM WINGATE, a resident of Johannesburg, South Africa, has turned from journalism to a career in patent and copyright law. His attention to detail and his grasp of the mechanics of weaponry may be attributed in part to the fact that he holds two degrees—one a B.Sc. in engineering and the second as Bachelor of Law. His first novel, *Fireplay*, was published in 1977.

MOSCOW 5000 by David Grant

July 1980—the 5000 meter race at the summer Olympics brings together the most spectacular and troubled field ever presented. And in the stands CIA agents use the games as a cover to rescue one of their men. The KGB is trying desperately to prevent disaster as a terrorist bomb threatens the entire stadium.

THE 65TH TAPE by Frank Ross

A deathbed confession forces our hero to find the whereabouts of one tape, made in Nixon's office, that proves a gigantic conspiracy by some top officials to run their own man for president and take over the country. Only two men can stop this—our hero and Richard M. Nixon. "Knife-edge suspense," says *Publishers Weekly*.

THE WATCHDOGS OF ABADDON by Ib Melchior

A page-turner about a retired Los Angeles cop and his son who stumble on a Nazi plot which, 33 years after Hitler's death, is within weeks of deadly fruition. Their investigations uncover a fiendish plan to set off a nuclear blast and start the Third Reich. By the author of *The Haigerloch Project*.

PARTY OF THE YEAR by John Crosby

Chosen by *The New York Times* as one of the best of the year, this fast-paced story centers on a wealthy international jet set in spite of terrorist warnings. An woman who decides to give an elegant party for the ex-CIA man tries to defuse the situation which could erupt in a shocking bloodbath.

THE LATEST BOOKS
IN THE BANTAM
BESTSELLING TRADITION

☐	13545	**SOPHIE'S CHOICE** William Styron	$3.50
☐	14200	**PRINCESS DAISY** Judith Krantz	$3.95
☐	20025	**THE FAR PAVILIONS** M. M. Kaye	$4.50
☐	13752	**SHADOW OF THE MOON** M. M. Kaye	$3.95
☐	14773	**INDEPENDENCE!** Dana Fuller Ross	$2.95
☐	14066	**NEBRASKA!** Dana Fuller Ross	$2.95
☐	14849	**WYOMING!** Dana Fuller Ross	$2.95
☐	14860	**OREGON!** Dana Fuller Ross	$2.95
☐	13980	**TEXAS!** Dana Fuller Ross	$2.75
☐	14982	**WHITE INDIAN** Donald Clayton Porter	$2.95
☐	14968	**THE RENEGADE** Donald Clayton Porter	$2.95
☐	20087	**THE HAWK AND THE DOVE** Leigh Franklin James	$2.95
☐	20179	**A WORLD FULL OF STRANGERS** Cynthia Freeman	$3.50
☐	13641	**PORTRAITS** Cynthia Freeman	$3.50
☐	20071	**DAYS OF WINTER** Cynthia Freeman	$3.50
☐	20070	**FAIRYTALES** Cynthia Freeman	$3.50
☐	14439	**THE EWINGS OF DALLAS** Burt Hirschfeld	$2.75
☐	13992	**CHANTAL** Claire Lorrimer	$2.95

Buy them at your local bookstore or use this handy coupon:

Bantam Book Catalog

Here's your up-to-the-minute listing of over 1,400 titles by your favorite authors.

This illustrated, large format catalog gives a description of each title. For your convenience, it is divided into categories in fiction and non-fiction—gothics, science fiction, westerns, mysteries, cookbooks, mysticism and occult, biographies, history, family living, health, psychology, art.

So don't delay—take advantage of this special opportunity to increase your reading pleasure.

Just send us your name and address and 50¢ (to help defray postage and handling costs).